From the note left at Cedar Cabin, Six Rivers,
Pacific Northwest . . .

I take an innocent of your people to sacrifice for
all of the innocents you have murdered. Thus will
sky and earth balance.

I am Katsuk who does this to you. Think of me
only as Katsuk, not as Charles Hobuhet. I look
backward to see you.

I will strike through to your spirit. I have the root
of your tree in my power.

SOUL CATCHER
FRANK HERBERT

SOUL CATCHER
FRANK HERBERT

BERKLEY BOOKS, NEW YORK

This Berkley book contains the complete
text of the original hardcover edition.
It has been completely reset in a typeface
designed for easy reading, and was printed
from new film.

SOUL CATCHER

A Berkley Book / published by arrangement with
G.P. Putnam's Sons

PRINTING HISTORY
G.P. Putnam's edition published 1972
Berkley edition / July 1979
Sixth printing / December 1983

ISBN: 0-425-07128-6

A BERKLEY BOOK ® TM 757,375
Berkley Books are published by The Berkley Publishing Group,
200 Madison Avenue, New York, New York 10016.
The name "BERKLEY" and the stylized "B" with design
are trademarks belonging to Berkley Publishing Corporation.
PRINTED IN THE UNITED STATES OF AMERICA

For RALPH and IRENE SLATTERY,
without whose love and guidance this book
would never have been

WHEN THE boy's father arrived at Six Rivers Camp, they showed him a number of things which they might not have revealed to a lesser person. But the father, as you know, was Howard Marshall and that meant State Department and VIP connections in Washington, D.C.; so they showed him the statement from the professor and the interviews with the camp counselors, that sort of thing. Of course, Marshall saw the so-called kidnap note and the newspaper clippings which some of the FBI men had brought up to the camp that morning.

Marshall lived up to expectations. He spoke with the measured clarity of someone to whom crises and decisions were a way of life. In response to a question, he said:

"I know this Northwest Coast country very well, you understand. My father was in lumber here. I spent

1

many happy days in this region as a child and young man. My father hired Indians whenever he could find ones who would work. He paid them the same wages as anyone else. Our Indians were well treated. I really don't see how this kidnapping could be aimed at me personally or at my family. The man who took David must be insane."

◻

STATEMENT OF Dr. Tilman Barth, University of Washington Anthropology Department:

I find this whole thing incredible. Charles Hobuhet cannot be the mad killer you make him out to be. It's impossible. He could not have kidnapped that boy. You must not think of him as criminal, or as Indian. Charles is a unique intellect, one of the finest students I've ever had. He's essentially gentle and with a profoundly subtle sense of humor. You know, that could just be our situation here. This could be a monstrous joke. Here, let me show you some of his work. I've saved copies of everything Charles has written for me. The world's going to know about him someday....

❑

FROM A news story in the Seattle *Post-Intelligencer:*

The most intensive manhunt in Washington history centered today on the tangled rain forest and virtually untouched wilderness area of the Olympic National Park.

Law enforcement officials said they still believe Charles Hobuhet, the Indian militant, is somewhere in that region with his kidnap victim, David Marshall, 13, son of the new United States Undersecretary of State.

Searchers were not discounting, however, the reports that the two have been seen in other areas. Part of the investigation focused on Indian lands in the state's far northwest corner. Indian trackers were being enlisted to assist in the search and bloodhounds were being brought from Walla Walla.

The manhunt began yesterday with discovery at the exclusive Six Rivers boys' camp that young Marshall was missing and that a so-called kidnap note had been left behind. The note reportedly was signed by Hobuhet with his pseudonym "Katsuk" and threatened to sacrifice the boy in an ancient Indian ceremony.

❑

THE NOTE left at Cedar Cabin, Six Rivers, by Charles Hobuhet-Katsuk:

3

I take an innocent of your people to sacrifice for all of the innocents you have murdered. The Innocent will go with all of those other innocents into the spirit place. Thus will sky and earth balance.

I am Katsuk who does this to you. Think of me only as Katsuk, not as Charles Hobuhet. I am something far more than a sensory system and its appetites. I am evolved far beyond you who are called hoquat. I look backward to see you. I see your lives based on cowardice. Your judgments arise from illusions. You tell me unlimited growth and consumption are good. Then your biologists tell me this is cancerous and lethal. To which hoquat should I listen? You do not listen. You think you are free to do anything that comes into your minds. Thinking this, you remain afraid to liberate your spirits from restraint.

Katsuk will tell you why this is. You fear to create because your creations mirror your true selves. You believe your power resides in an ultimate knowledge which you forever seek as children seek parental wisdom. I learned this while watching you in your hoquat schools. But now I am Katsuk, a greater power. I will sacrifice your flesh. I will strike through to your spirit. I have the root of your tree in my power.

❏

ON THE day he was to leave for camp, David Marshall had awakened early. It was two weeks after his thirteenth birthday. David thought about being thirteen as he stretched out in the morning warmth of his bed. There was some internal difference that came with being thirteen. It was not the same as twelve, but he couldn't pin down the precise difference.

For a time he played with the sensation that the ceiling above his bed actually fluttered as his eyelids resisted opening to the day. There was sunshine out in that day, a light broken by its passage through the big-leaf maple which shaded the window of his upstairs bedroom.

Without opening his eyes, he could sense the world around his home—the long, sloping lawns, the carefully tended shrubs and flowers. It was a world full of slow calm. Thinking about it sometimes, he felt a soft drumbeat of exaltation.

David opened his eyes. For a moment, he pretended the faint shadow marks in the ceiling's white plaster were a horizon: range upon range of mountains dropping down to drift-piled beaches.

Mountains ... beaches—he'd see such things tomorrow when he went to camp.

David turned, focused on the camp gear piled across chair and floor where he and his father had arranged the things last night: sleeping bag, pack, clothing, boots. ...

There was the knife.

The knife stimulated a feeling of excitement. That was a genuine Russell belt knife made in Canada. It had been a birthday gift from his father just two weeks ago.

A bass hum of wilderness radiated into his imagination from the knife in its deer-brown scabbard. It was a man's tool, a man's weapon. It stood for blood and darkness and independence.

His father's words had put magic in the knife:

"That's no toy, Dave. Learn how to use it safely. Treat it with respect."

His father's voice had carried subdued tensions. The adult eyes had looked at him with calculated intensity and there had been a waiting silence after each phrase.

Fingernails made a brief scratching signal on his bedroom door, breaking his reverie. The door opened. Mrs. Parma slid into the room. She wore a long blue and black sari with faint red lines in it. She moved with silent effacement, an effect as attention-demanding as a gong.

David's gaze followed her. She always made him feel uneasy.

Mrs. Parma glided across to the window that framed the maple, closed the window firmly.

David peered over the edge of the blankets at her as she turned from the window and nodded her awareness of him.

"Good morning, young sir."

The clipped British accent never sounded right to him coming from a mouth with purple lips. And her eyes bothered him. They were too big, as though stretched by the way her glossy hair was pulled back into a bun. Her name wasn't really Parma. It began with Parma, but it was much longer and ended with a strange clicking sound that David could not make.

He pulled the blankets below his chin, said: "Did my father leave yet?"

"Before dawn, young sir. It is a long way to the capital of your nation."

David frowned and waited for her to leave. Strange woman. His parents had brought her back from New Delhi, where his father had been political adviser to the embassy.

In those years, David had stayed with Granny in San Francisco. He had been surrounded by old people with snowy hair, diffident servants, and low, cool voices. It had been a drifting time with diffused stimulations. *"Your grandmother is napping. One would not want to disturb her, would one?"* It had

6

worn on him the way dripping water wears a rock. His memory of the period retained most strongly the whirlwind visits of his parents. They had descended upon the insulated quiet of the house, breathless, laughing, tanned, and romantic, arms loaded with exotic gifts.

But the chest-shaking joy of being with such people had always ended, leaving him with a sense of frustration amidst the smells of dusty perfumes and tea and the black feeling that he had been abandoned.

Mrs. Parma checked the clothing laid out for him on the dresser. Knowing he wanted her to leave, she delayed. Her body conveyed a stately swaying within the sari. Her fingernails were bright pink.

She had shown him a map once with a town marked on it, the place where she had been born. She had a brown photograph: mud-walled houses and leafless trees, a man all in white standing beside a bicycle, a violin case under his arm. Her father.

Mrs. Parma turned, looked at David with her startling eyes. She said: "Your father asked me to remind you when you awoke that the car will depart precisely on time. You have one hour."

She lowered her gaze, went to the door. The sari betrayed only a faint suggestion of moving legs. The red lines in the fabric danced like sparks from a fire.

David wondered what she thought. Her slow, calm way revealed nothing he could decipher. Was she laughing at him? Did she think going to camp was a foolishness? Did she even have a geographical understanding of where he would go, the Olympic Mountains?

He had a last glimpse of the bright fingernails as she went out, closed the door.

David bounced from bed, began dressing. When he came to the belt, he slipped the sheathed knife onto it, cinched the buckle. The blade remained a heavy presence at his hip while he brushed his teeth and combed his blond hair straight back. When he leaned close to the mirror, he could see the knife's dark handle with the initials burned into it: DMM, David Morgenstern Marshall.

Presently, he went down to breakfast.

❑

STATEMENT OF Dr. Tilman Barth, University of Washington Anthropology Department:

The word *katsuk* is very explicit in Hobuhet's native tongue. It means "the center" or the core from which all perception radiates. It's the center of the world or of the universe. It's where an aware individual stands. There has never been any doubt in my mind that Charles is aware. I can understand his assuming this pseudonym.

You've seen those papers he wrote. That one where he compares the Raven myth of his people to the Genesis myth of Western civilization is very disturbing. He has perceived the link between dream and reality— how we seek to win a place in destiny through rebellion, the evil forces we built up only to destroy, the Great Conquests and Great Causes to which we cling long after they've been exposed as empty glitter. Here... notice his simile for such lost perceptions:

"... the fish eyes like gray skimmed milk that stare at you out of things which are alive when they shouldn't be."

8

This is the observation of someone who is capable of great things, as great as any achievements in our Western mythology.

❏

IT HAD begun when his name still was Charles Hobuhet, a good *Indian* name for a *Good Indian*.

The bee had alighted, after all, on the back of Charles Hobuhet's left hand. There had been no one named Katsuk then. He had been reaching up to grasp a vine maple limb, climbing from a creek bottom in the stillness of midday.

The bee was black and gold, a bee from the forest, a bumblebee of the family Apidae. It's name fled buzzing through his mind, a memory from days in the white school.

Somewhere above him, a ridge came down toward the Pacific out of the Olympic Mountains like the gnarled root of an ancient spruce clutching the earth for support.

The sun would be warm up there, but winter's chill in the creek bottom slid its icy way down the watercourse from the mountains to these spring-burgeoning foothills.

Cold came with the bee, too. It was a special cold that put ice in the soul.

Still Charles Hobuhet's soul then.

But he had performed the ancient ritual with twigs and string and bits of bone. The ice from the bee told him he must take a name. Unless he took a name immediately, he stood in peril of losing both souls, the soul in his body and the soul that went high or low with his true being.

The stillness of the bee on his hand made this obvious. He sensed ugent ghosts: people, animals, birds, all with him in this bee.

He whispered: "Alkuntam, help me."

The supreme god of his people made no reply.

Shiny green of the vine maple trunk directly in front of him dominated his eyes. Ferns beneath it splayed out fronds. Condensation fell like rain on the damp earth. He forced himself to turn away, stared across the creek at a stand of alders bleached white against heavy green of cedar and fir on the stream's far slope.

A quaking aspen, its leaves adither among the alders, dazzled his awareness, pulled his mind. He felt abruptly that he had found another self which must be reasoned with, influenced, and understood. He lost clarity of mind and sensed both selves straining toward some pure essence. All sense of self slipped from his body, searched outward into the dazzling aspen.

He thought: *I am in the center of the universe!*

Bee spoke to him then: "I am Tamanawis speaking to you...."

The words boomed in his awareness, telling him his name. He spoke it aloud:

"Katsuk! I am Katsuk."

Katsuk.

It was a seminal name, one with potency.

Now, being Katsuk, he knew all its meanings. He was Ka-, the prefix for everything human. He was -tsuk, the bird of myth. A human bird! He possessed roots in many meanings: bone, the color blue, a serving dish, smoke... brother and soul.

Once more, he said it: "I am Katsuk."

Both selves flowed home to the body.

10

He stared at the miraculous bee on his hand. A bee had been the farthest thing from his expectations. He had been climbing, just climbing.

If there were thoughts in his mind, they were thoughts of his ordeal. It was the ordeal he had set for himself out of grief, out of the intellectual delight in walking through ancient ideas, out of the fear that he had lost his way in the white world. His native soul had rotted while living in that white world. But a spirit had spoken to him.

A true and ancient spirit.

Deep within his innermost being he knew that intellect and education, even the white education, had been his first guides on this ordeal.

He thought how, as Charles Hobuhet, he had begun this thing. He had waited for the full moon and cleansed his intestines by drinking seawater. He had found a land otter and cut out its tongue.

Kuschtaliute—the symbol tongue!

His grandfather had explained the way of it long ago, describing the ancient lore. Grandfather had said: "The shaman becomes the spirit-animal-man. God won't let animals make the mistakes men make."

That was the way of it.

He had carried *Kuschtaliute* in a deer scrotum pouch around his neck. He had come into these mountains. He had followed an old elk trail grown over with alder and fir and cottonwood. The setting sun had been at his back when he had buried *Kuschtaliute* beneath a rotten log. He had buried *Kuschtaliute* in a place he never again could find, there to become the spirit tongue.

All of this in anguish of spirit.

He thought: *It began because of the rape and pointless death of my sister. The death of Janik-taht . . . little Jan.*

11

He shook his head, confused by an onslaught of memories. Somewhere a gang of drunken loggers had found Janiktaht walking alone, her teen-aged body full of spring happiness, and they had raped her and changed her and she had killed herself.

And her brother had become a walker-in-the-mountains.

The other self within him, the one which must be reasoned with and understood, sneered at him and said: "Rape and suicide are as old as mankind. Besides, that was Charles Hobuhet's sister. You are Katsuk."

He thought then as Katsuk: *Lucretius was a liar! Science doesn't liberate man from the terror of the gods!*

Everything around him revealed this truth—the sun moving across the ridges, the ranges of drifting clouds, the rank vegetation.

White science had begun with magic and never moved far from it. Science continually failed to learn from lack of results. The ancient ways retained their potency. Despite sneers and calumny, the old ways achieved what the legends said they woud.

His grandmother had been of the Eagle Phratry. And a bee had spoken to him. He had scrubbed his body with hemlock twigs until the skin was raw. He had caught his hair in a headband of red cedar bark. He had eaten only the roots of devil's club until the ribs poked from his flesh.

How long had he been walking in these mountains?

He thought back to all the distance he had covered: ground so sodden that water oozed up at each step, heavy branches overhead that shut out the sun, undergrowth so thick he could see only a few body lengths in any direction. Somewhere, he had come through a tangled salmonberry thicket to a stream flowing in a canyon, deep and silent. He had followed

that stream upward to vaporous heights...upward
...upward. The stream had become a creek, this
creek below him.

This place.

Something real was living in him now.

Abruptly, he sensed all of his dead ancestors lusting
after this living experience. His mind lay pierced by
sudden belief, by unending movement beneath the
common places of life, by an alertness which never
varied, night or day. He knew this bee!

He said: "You are Kwatee, the Changer."

"And what are you?"

"I am Katsuk."

"*What* are you?" The question thundered at him.

He put down terror, thought: *Thunder is not angry.
What frightens animals need not frighten a man. What
am I?*

The answer came to him as one of his ancestors
would have known it. He said: "I am one who followed
the ritual with care. I am one who did not really expect
to find the spirit power."

"Now you know."

All of his thinking turned over, became as unsettled
as a pool muddied by a big fish. *What do I know?*

The air around him continued full of dappled
sunlight and the noise and spray from the creek. The
mushroom-punk smell of a rotten log filled his nostrils.
A stately, swaying leaf shadow brushed purple across
the bee on his hand, withdrew.

He emptied his mind of everything except what he
needed to know from the spirit poised upon his hand.
He lay frozen in the-moment-of-the-bee. Bee was
graceful, fat, and funny. Bee aroused a qualm of
restless memories, rendered his senses abnormally
acute. Bee....

An image of Janiktaht overcame his mind. Misery

13

filled him right out to the skin. Janiktaht—sixty nights dead. Sixty nights since she had ended her shame and hopelessness in the sea.

He had a vision of himself moaning beside Janiktaht's open grave, drunk with anguish, the swaying wind of the forest all through his flesh.

Awareness recoiled. He thought of himself as he had been once, as a boy heedlessly happy on the beach, following the tide mark. He remembered a piece of driftwood like a dead hand outspread on the sand.

Had that been driftwood?

He felt the peril of letting his thoughts flow. Who knew where they might go? Janiktaht's image faded, vanished as though of its own accord. He tried to recall her face. It fled him through a blurred vision of young hemlocks ... a moss-floored stand of trees where nine drunken loggers had dragged her to ... one after another, to....

Something had happened to flesh which his mind no longer could contemplate without being scoured out, denuded of everything except a misshapen object that the ocean had cast up on a curve of beach where once he had played.

He felt like an old pot, all emotion scraped out. Everything eluded him except the spirit on the back of his hand. He thought:

We are like bees, my people—broken into many pieces, but the pieces remain dangerous.

In that instant, he realized that this creature on his hand must be much more than Changer—far, far more than *Kwatee.*

It is Soul Catcher!

Terror and elation warred with him. This was the greatest of the spirits. It had only to sting him and he would be invaded by a terrible thing. He would become the bee of his people. He would do a terrifying thing, a dangerous thing, a deadly thing.

Hardly daring to breathe, he waited.

Would Bee never move? Would they remain this way for all eternity? His mind felt drawn tight, as tense as a bow pulled to its utmost breaking point. All of his emotions lay closed up in blackness without inner light or outer light—a sky of nothingness within him.

He thought: *How strange for a creature so tiny to exist as such spirit power, to be such spirit power— Soul Catcher!*

One moment there had been no bee on his flesh. Now, it stood there as though flung into creation by a spray of sunlight, brushed by leaf shadow, the shape of it across a vein, darkness of the spirit against dark skin.

A shadow across his being.

He saw Bee with intense clarity: the swollen abdomen, the stretched gossamer of wings, the pollen dust on the legs, the barbed arrow of the stinger.

The message of this moment floated through his awareness, a clear flute sound. If the spirit went away peacefully, that would signal reprieve. He could return to the university. Another year, in the week of his twenty-sixth birthday, he would take his doctorate in anthropology. He would shake off this terrifying wildness which had invaded him at Janiktaht's death. He would become the imitation white man, lost to these mountains and the needs of his people.

This thought saddened him. If the spirit left him, it would take both of his souls. Without souls, he would die. He could not outlast the sorrows which engulfed him.

Slowly, with ancient deliberation, Bee turned short of his knuckles. It was the movement of an orator gauging his audience. Faceted eyes included the human in their focus. Bee's thorax arched, abdomen tipped, and he knew a surge of terror in the realization that he had been chosen.

The stinger slipped casually into his nerves, drawing his thoughts, inward, inward....

He heard the message of Tamanawis, the greatest of spirits, as a drumbeat matching the beat of his heart: "You must find a white. You must find a total innocent. You must kill an innocent of the whites. Let your deed fall upon this world. Let your deed be a single, heavy hand which clutches the heart. The whites must feel it. They must hear it. An innocent for all of our innocents."

Having told him what he must do, Bee took flight.

His gaze followed the flight, lost it in the leafery of the vine maple copse far upslope. He sensed then a procession of ancestral ghosts insatiate in their demands. All of those who had gone before him remained an unchanging field locked immovably into his past, a field against which he could see himself change.

Kill an innocent!

Sorrow and confusion dried his mouth. He felt parched in his innermost being, withered.

The sun crossing over the high ridge to keep its appointment with the leaves in the canyon touched his shoulders, his eyes. He knew he had been tempted and had gone through a locked door into a region of terrifying power. To hold this power he would have to come to terms with that other self inside him. He could be only one person—Katsuk.

He said: "I am Katsuk."

The words brought calm. Spirits of air and earth were with him as they had been for his ancestors. He resumed climbing the slope. His movements aroused a flying squirrel. It glided from a high limb to a low one

16

far below. He felt the life all around him then: brown movements hidden in greenery, life caught suddenly in stop-motion by his presence.

He thought: *Remember me, creatures of this forest. Remember Katsuk as the whole world will remember him. I am Katsuk. Ten thousand nights from now, ten thousand seasons from now, this world still will remember Katsuk and his meaning.*

❏

FROM A wire story, Seattle dateline:

The mother of the kidnap victim arrived at Six Rivers Camp about 3:30 P.M. yesterday. She was brought in by one of the four executive helicopters released for the search by lumber and plywood corporations of the Northwest. There were tearstains on her cheeks as she stepped from the helicopter to be greeted by her husband.

She said: "Any mother can understand how I feel. Please, let me be alone with my husband."

❏

AN IRRITANT whine edged his mother's voice as David sat down across from her in the sunny breakfast room that overlooked their back lawn and private stream. The scowl which accompanied the whine drew sharp lines down her forehead toward her nose. A vein on her left hand had taken on the hue of rusty iron. She wore something pink and lacy, her yellow hair fluffed up. Her lavender perfume enveloped the table.

She said: "I wish you wouldn't take that awful knife to camp, Davey. What in heaven's name will you do with such a thing? I think your father was quite mad to give you such a dangerous instrument."

Her left hand jingled the little bell to summon the cook with David's cereal.

David stared down at the table while cook's pink hand put a bowl there. The cream in the bowl was almost the same yellow as the tablecloth. The bowl gave off the odor of the fresh strawberries sliced into the cereal. David adjusted his napkin.

His mother said: "Well?"

Sometimes her questions were not meant to be answered, but *"Well?"* signaled pressure.

He sighed. "Mother, everyone at camp has a knife."

"Why?"

"To cut things, carve wood, stuff like that."

He began eating. One hour. That could be endured.

"To cut your fingers off!" she said. "I simply refuse to let you take such a dangerous thing."

He swallowed a mouthful of cereal while he studied her the way he had seen his father do it, letting his mind sort out the possible countermoves. A breeze shook the trees bordering the lawn behind her.

"Well?" she insisted.

"What do I do?" he asked. "Every time I need a knife I'll have to borrow one from one of the other guys."

He took another mouthful of cereal, savoring the acid of the strawberries while he waited for her to assess the impossibility of keeping him knifeless at camp. David knew how her mind worked. She had been Prosper Morgenstern before she had married Dad. The Morgensterns always had the best. If he was going to have a knife *anyway*....

She put flame to a cigarette, her hand jerking. The smoke emerged from her mouth in spurts.

David went on eating.

She put the cigarette aside, said: "Oh, very well. But you must be extremely careful."

"Just like Dad showed me," he said.

She stared at him, a finger of her left hand tapping a soft drumbeat on the table. The movement set the diamonds on her wristwatch clasp aflame. She said: "I don't know what I'll do with both of my men gone."

"Dad'll be halfway to Washington by now."

"And you in that awful camp."

"It's the best camp there is."

"I guess so. You know, Davey, we all may have to move to the East."

David nodded. His father had moved them to the Carmel Valley and gone back into private practice after the last election. He commuted up the Peninsula to the city three days a week. Sometimes Prosper joined him there for a weekend. They kept an apartment in the city and a maid-caretaker.

But yesterday his father had received a telephone call from someone important in the government. There had been other calls and a sense of excitement in the house. Howard Marshall had been offered an important position in the State Department.

David said: "It's funny, y'know?"

"What is, dear?"

"Dad's going to Washington and so am I."

She smiled. "Different Washingtons."

"Both named for the same man."

"Indeed they were."

Mrs. Parma glided into the breakfast room, said: "Excuse me, madam. I have had Peter put the young sir's equipage into the car. Will there be anything else?"

"Thank you, Mrs. Parma. That will be all."

David waited until Mrs. Parma had gone, said: "That book about the camp said they have some Indian counselors. Will they look like Mrs. Parma?"

"Davey! Don't they teach you *anything* in that school?"

"I know they're different Indians. I just wondered if they, you know, looked like her, if that's why we called our Indians...."

"What a strange idea." She shook her head, arose. "There are times when you remind me of your grandfather Morgenstern. He used to insist the Indians were the lost tribe of Israel." She hesitated, one hand lingering on the table, her gaze focused on the knife at David's waist. "You *will* be careful with that awful knife?"

"I'll do just like Dad said. Don't worry."

❏

SPECIAL AGENT Norman Hosbig, Seattle Office, FBI:

Yes, in answer to that, I believe I can say that we do have some indications that the Indian may be mentally deranged. Let me emphasize that this is only a possibility which we are not excluding in our assessment of the problem. There's the equal possibility that he's pretending insanity.

❑

HANDS CLASPED behind his head, Katsuk had stretched out in the darkness of his bunk in Cedar Cabin. Water dripped in the washbasin of the toilet across the hall. The sound filled him with a sense of rhythmic drifting. He closed his eyes tightly and saw a purple glow behind his eyelids. It was the spirit flame, the sign of his determination. This room, the cabin with its sleeping boys, the camp all around—everything went out from the center, which was the spirit flame of Katsuk.

He drew in the shallow breaths of expectation, thought of his charges asleep in the long barracks room down the hall outside his closed door: eight sleeping boys. Only one of the boys concerned Katsuk. The spirits had sent him another sign: the perfect victim, the Innocent.

The son of an important man slept out there, a person to command the widest attention. No one would escape Katsuk's message.

To prepare for this time, he had clothed himself in a loincloth woven of white dog hair and mountain goat wool. A belt of red cedar bark bound the waist. The belt held a soft deerhide pouch which contained the few things he needed: a sacred twig and bone bound with cedar string, an ancient stone arrowhead from the beach at Ozette, raven feathers to fletch a consecrated arrow, a bowstring of twisted walrus gut, elk-hide thongs to bind the victim, a leaf packet of spruce gum...down from sea ducks...a flute....

A great aunt had made the fabric of his loincloth

21

many years ago, squatting at a flat loom in the smoky shadows of her house at the river mouth. The pouch and the bit of down had been blessed by a shaman of his people before the coming of the whites.

Elkhide moccasins covered his feet. They were decorated with beads and porcupine quills. Janiktaht had made them for him two summers ago.

A lifetime past.

He could feel slow tension spreading upward from those moccasins. Janiktaht was here with him in this room, her hands reaching out from the elk leather she had shaped. Her voice filled the darkness with the final screech of her anguish.

Katsuk took a deep, calming breath. It was not yet time.

There had been fog in the evening, but it had cleared at nightfall on a wind blowing strongly from the southwest. The wind sang to Katsuk in the voice of his grandfather's flute, the flute in the pouch. Katsuk thought of his grandfather: a beaten man, thick of face, who would have been a shaman in another time.

A beaten man, without congregation or mystery, a shadow shaman because he remembered all the old ways.

Katsuk whispered: "I do this for you, grandfather."

Each thing in its own time. The cycle had come around once more to restore the old balance.

His grandfather had built a medicine fire once. As the blaze leaped, the old man had played a low, thin tune on his flute. The song of his grandfather's flute wove in and out of Katsuk's mind. He thought of the boy sleeping out there in the cabin—David Marshall.

You will be snared in the song of this flute, white innocent. I have the root of your tree in my power. Your people will know destruction!

He opened his eyes to moonlight. The light came

22

through the room's one window, drew a gnarled tree shadow on the wall to his left. He watched the undulant shadow, swaying darkness, a visual echo of wind in trees.

The water continued its drip-drip-drip across the hall. Unpleasant odors drifted on the room's air. Antiseptic place! Poisonous! The cabin had been scoured out with strong soap by the advance work crew.

I am Katsuk.

The odors in the room exhausted him. Everything of the whites did that. They weakened him, removed him from contact with his past and the powers that were his by right of inheritance.

I am Katsuk.

He quested outward in his mind, sensed the camp and its surroundings. A trail curved through a thick stand of fir beyond the cabin's south porch. Five hundred and twenty-eight paces it went, over roots and boggy places to the ancient elk trace which climbed into the park.

He thought: *That is my land! My land! These white thieves stole my land. These* hoquat! *Their park is my land!*

Hoquat! Hoquat!

He mouthed the word without sound. His ancestors had applied that name to the first whites arriving off these shores in their tall ships. *Hoquat—something that floated far out on the water, something unfamiliar and mysterious.*

The hoquat had been like the green waves of winter that grew and grew and grew until they smashed upon the land.

Bruce Clark, director of Six Rivers Camp, had taken photographs that day—the *publicity* pictures he took every year to help lure the children of the rich. It

23

had amused Katsuk to obey in the guise of Charles Hobuhet.

Eyes open wide, body sweating with anticipation, Katsuk had obeyed Clark's directions.

"Move a little farther left, Chief."

Chief!

"That's good. Now, shield your eyes with your hand as though you were staring out at the forest. No, the right hand."

Katsuk had obeyed.

The photographs pleased him. Nothing could steal a soul which Soul Catcher already possessed. The photographs were a spirit omen. The charges of Cedar Cabin had clustered around him, their faces toward the camera. Newspapers and magazines would reproduce those pictures. An arrow would point to one face among the boys—David Marshall, son of the new Undersecretary of State.

The announcement will come on the six-o'clock news over the rec room's one television. There will be pictures of the Marshall boy and his mother at the San Francisco airport, the father at a press conference in Washington, D.C.

Many hoquat would stare at the pictures Clark had taken. Let them stare at a person they thought was Charles Hobuhet. The Soul Catcher had yet to reveal Katsuk hidden in that flesh.

By the moon shadow on the wall, he knew it was almost midnight. *Time.* With a single motion, he arose from the bunk, glanced to the note he had left on the room's tiny desk.

"I take an innocent of your people to sacrifice for all the innocents you have murdered, an innocent to go with all of those other innocents into the spirit place."

Ahhh, the words they would pour upon this

message! All the ravings and analysis, the hoquat logic. . . .

The light of the full moon coming through the window penetrated his body. He could feel the weighted silence of it all along his spine. It made his hand tingle where Bee had left the message of its stinger. The odor of resin from the rough boards of the walls made him calm. Without guilt.

The breath of his passion came from his lips like smoke: "I am Katsuk, the center of the universe."

He turned and, in a noiseless glide, took the center of the universe out the door, down the short hall into the bunk room.

The Marshall boy slept in the nearest cot. Moonlight lay across the lower half of the cot in a pattern of hills and valleys, undulant with the soft movement of the boy's breathing. His clothing lay on a locker at the foot of the cot: whipcord trousers, a T-shirt, light sweater and jacket, socks, tennis shoes. The boy was sleeping in his shorts.

Katsuk rolled the clothing into a bundle around the shoes. The alien fabric sent a message into his nerves, telling of that mechanical giant the hoquat called civilization. The message dried his tongue. Momentarily, he sensed the many resources the hoquat possessed to hunt down those who wounded them.

Alien guns and aircraft and electronic devices. And he must fight back without such things. Everything hoquat must become alien and denied to him.

An owl cried outside the cabin.

Katsuk pressed the clothing bundle tightly to his chest. The owl had spoken to him. In this land, Katsuk would have other powers, older and stronger and more enduring than those of the hoquat.

He listened to the room: eight boys asleep. The

sweat of their excitement dominated this place. They had been slow settling into sleep. But now they slept even deeper because of that slowness.

Katsuk moved to the head of the boy's cot, put a hand lightly over the sleeping mouth, ready to press down and prevent an outcry. The lips twisted under his hand. He saw the eyes open, stare. He felt the altered pulse, the change in breathing.

Softly, Katsuk bent close, whispered: "Don't waken the others. Get up and come with me. I have something special for you. Quiet now."

Hesitant thoughts fleeing through the boy's mind could be felt under Katsuk's hand. Once more, Katsuk whispered, letting his words flow through his spirit powers: "I must make you my spirit brother because of the photographs." Then: "I have your clothes. I'll wait in the hall."

He felt the words take effect, removed his hand from the boy's mouth. Tension subsided.

Katsuk went into the hallway. Presently, the boy joined him, a thin figure whose shorts gleamed whitely in the gloom. Katsuk thrust the clothing into his hands, led the way outside, waiting for the boy at the door, then closing it softly.

Grandfather, I do this for you!

❏

FRAGMENT OF a note by Charles Hobuhet found at Cedar Cabin:

Hoquat, I give you what you prayed for, this good

arrow made clean and straight by my hands. When I give you this arrow, please hold it in your body with pride. Let this arrow take you to the land of Alkuntam. Our brothers will welcome you there, saying: "What a beautiful youth has come to us! What a beautiful hoquat!" They will say to one another: "How strong he is, this beautiful hoquat who carries the arrow of Katsuk in his flesh." And you will be proud when you hear them speak of your greatness and your beauty. Do not run away, hoquat. Come toward my good arrow. Accept it. Our brothers will sing of this. I will cover your body with white feathers from the breasts of ducks. Our maidens will sing your beauty. This is what you have prayed for from one end of the world to the other every day of your life. I, Katsuk, give you your wish because I have become Soul Catcher.

❏

DAVID, HIS mind still drugged with sleep, came wide awake as he stepped out the door into the cold night. Shivering, he stared at the man who had awakened him—*the Chief.*

"What is it, Chief?"

"Shhhh." Katsuk touched the roll of clothing. "Get dressed."

More from the cold than any other reason, David obeyed. Tree branches whipped in the wind above the cabin, filled the night with fearful shapes.

"Is it an initiation, Chief?"

"Shhh, be very quiet."

"Why?"

"We were photographed together. We must become spirit brothers. There is a ceremony."

"What about the other guys?"

"You have been chosen."

Katsuk fought down sudden pity for this boy, this Innocent. *Why pity anyone?* He realized the moonlight had cut at his heart. For some reason, it made him think of the Shaker Church where his relatives had taken him as a child—hoquat church! He heard the voices chanting in his memory: *"Begat, begat, begat. . . ."*

David whispered: "I don't understand. What're we doing?"

The stars staring down at him, the wind in the trees, all carried forboding. He felt frightened. A gap in the trees beyond the porch revealed a great bush of stars standing out against the night. David stared into the shadows of the porch. Why wasn't the Chief answering?

David tightened his belt, felt the knife in its sheath at his waist. If the Chief were planning something bad, he'd have removed the knife. That was a real weapon. Daniel Boone had killed a bear with a blade no bigger than this one.

"What're we going to do?" David pressed.

"A ceremony of spirit brotherhood," Katsuk said. He felt the truth in his words. There would be a ceremony and a joining, a shape that occurred out of darkness, a mark on the earth and an incantation to the real spirits.

David still hesitated, thinking this was an Indian. They were strange people. He thought of Mrs. Parma. Different Indian, but both mysterious.

David pulled his jacket close around him. The cold air had raised goose pimples on his skin. He felt both frightened and excited. An Indian.

He said: "You're not dressed."

"I'm dressed for the ceremony."

Silently, Katsuk prayed: *"O Life Giver, now that you have seen the way a part of your all-powerful being goes. . . ."*

David sensed the man's tensions, the air of secrecy. But no place could be safer than this wilderness camp with that cog railroad the only way to get here.

He asked: "Aren't you cold?"

"I am used to this. You must hurry after me now. We haven't much time."

Katsuk stepped down off the porch. The boy followed.

"Where are we going?"

"To the top of the ridge."

David hurried to keep in step. "Why?"

"I have prepared a place there for you to be initiated into a very old ceremony of my people."

"Because of the photographs?"

"Yes."

"I didn't think Indians believed in that stuff anymore."

"Even you will believe."

David tucked his shirt more firmly into his belt, felt the knife. The knife gave him a feeling of confidence. He stumbled in his hurry to keep up.

Without looking back, Katsuk felt the boy's tensions relax. There had been a moment back on the porch when rebellion had radiated from the Innocent. The boy's eyes had been uncertain, wet and smooth in their darkness. The bitter acid of fear had been in the air. But now the boy would follow. He was enthralled. The center of the universe carried the power of a magnet for that Innocent.

David felt his heart beating rapidly from exertion.

He smelled rancid oil from the Chief. The man's skin glistened when moonlight touched it, as though he had greased his body.

"How far is it?" David asked.

"Three thousand and eighty-one paces."

"How far is that?"

"A bit over a mile."

"Did you have to dress like that?"

"Yes."

"What if it rains?"

"I will not notice."

"Why're we going so fast?"

"We need the moonlight for the ceremony. Be silent now and stay close."

Katsuk felt brass laughter in his chest, picked up the pace. The smell of newly cut cedar drifted on the air. The rich odor of cedar oils carried an omen message from the days when that tree had sheltered his people.

David stumbled over a root, regained his balance.

The trail pushed through mottled darkness—black broken by sharp slashes of moonlight. The bobbing patch of loincloth ahead of him carried a strange dream quality to David. When moonlight reached it, the man's skin glistened, but his black hair drank the light, was one with the shadows.

"Will the other guys be initiated?" David asked.

"I told you that you are the only one."

"Why?"

"You will understand soon. Do not talk."

Katsuk hoped the silence brought by that rebuke would endure. Like all hoquat, the boy talked too much. There could be no reprieve for such a one.

"I keep stumbling," David muttered.

"Walk as I walk."

Katsuk measured the trail by the feeling of it

30

underfoot: soft earth, a dampness where a spring surfaced, spruce cones, the hard lacery of roots polished by many feet. . . .

He began to think of his sister and of his former life before Katsuk. He felt the spirits of air and earth draw close, riding this moonlight, bringing the memory of all the lost tribes.

David thought: *Walk as he walks?*

The man moved with sliding panther grace, almost noiseless. The trail grew steep, tangled with more roots, slippery underfoot, but still the man moved as though he saw every surface change, every rock and root.

David became aware of the wet odors all around: rotting wood, musks, bitter acridity of ferns. Wet leaves brushed his cheeks. Limbs and vines dragged at him. He heard falling water, louder and louder—a river cascading in its gorge off to the right. He hoped the sound covered his clumsiness but feared the Chief could hear him and was laughing.

Walk as I walk!

How could the Chief even see anything in this dark?

The trail entered a bracken clearing. David saw peaks directly ahead, snow on them streaked by moonlight, a bright sieve of stars close overhead.

Katsuk stared upward as he walked. The peaks appeared to be stitched upon the sky by the stars. He allowed this moment its time to flow through him, renewing the spirit message: *"I am Tamanawis speaking to you. . . ."*

He began to sing the names of his dead, sent the names outward into Sky World. A falling star swept over the clearing—another, then another and another until the sky flamed with them.

Katsuk fell silent in wonder. This was no

astronomical display to be explained by the hoquat magic science; this was a message from the past.

The boy spoke close behind; "Wow! Look at the falling stars. Did you make a wish?"

"I made a wish."

"What were you singing?"

"A song of my people."

Katsuk, the omen of the stars strong within him, saw the charcoal slash of path and the clearing as an arena within which he would begin creating a memory maker, a death song for the ways of the past, a holy obscenity to awe the hoquat world.

"Skagajek!" he shouted. "I am the shaman spirit come to drive the sickness from this world!"

David, hearing the strange words, lost his footing, almost fell, and was once again afraid.

❏

FROM KATSUK'S announcement to his people:

I have done all the things correctly. I used string, twigs, and bits of bone to cast the oracle. I tied the red cedar band around my head. I prayed to Kwahoutze, the god in the water, and to Alkuntam. I carried the consecrated down of a sea duck to scatter upon the sacrificial victim. It was all done in the proper way.

❏

THE IMMENSITY of the wilderness universe around David, the mystery of this midnight hike to some strange ritual, began to tell on him. His body was wet with perspiration, chilled in every breeze. His feet were sopping with trail dew. The Chief, an awesome figure in this setting, had taken on a new character. He walked with such steady confidence that David sensed all the accumulated woods knowledge compressed into each movement. The man was Deerstalker. He was Ultimate Woodsman. He was a person who could survive in this wilderness.

David began dropping farther and farther behind. The Chief became a gray blur ahead.

Without turning, Katsuk called: "Keep up."

David quickened his steps.

Something barked "Yap-yap!" in the trees off to his right. A sudden motion of smoky wings glided across him, almost touched his head. David ducked, hurried to close the gap between himself and that bobbing white loincloth.

Abruptly, Katsuk stopped. David almost ran into him.

Katsuk looked at the moon. It moved over the trees, illuminating crags and rock spurs on the far slope. His feet had measured out the distance. This was the place.

David asked: "Why'd we stop?"

"This is the place."

"Here? What's here?"

Katsuk thought: *How is it the hoquat all do this? They always prefer mouth-talk to body-talk.*

33

He ignored the boy's question. What answer could there be? This ignorant Innocent had failed to read the signs.

Katsuk squatted, faced the trail's downhill side. This had been an elk trail for centuries, the route between salt water and high meadows. The earth had been cut out deeply by the hooves. Ferns and moss grew from the side of the trail. Katsuk felt into the growth. His fingers went as surely as though guided by sight. Gently, gently, he pulled the fronds aside. Yes! This was the place he had marked out.

He began chanting, low-voiced in the ancient tongue:

"Hoquat, let your body accept the consecrated arrow. Let pride fill your soul at the touch of my sharp and biting point. Your soul will turn toward the sky...."

David listened to the unintelligible words. He could not see the man's hands in the fern shadows, but the movements bothered him and he could not identify the reason. He wanted to ask what was happening but felt an odd constraint. The chanted words were full of clickings and gruntings.

The man fell silent.

Katsuk opened the pouch at his waist, removed a pinch of the consecrated white duck down. His fingers trembled. It must be done correctly. Any mistake would bring disaster.

David, his eyes adjusting to the gloom, began to make out the shadowy movement of hands in the ferns. Something white reflected moonlight there. He squatted beside the man, cleared his throat.

"What're you doing?"

"I am writing my name upon the earth. I must do that before you can learn my name."

"Isn't your name Charlie something?"

"That is not my name."

"Oh?" David thought about this. Not his name? Then: "Were you singing just now?"

"Yes."

"What were you singing?"

"A song for you—to give you a name."

"I already *have* a name."

"You do not have a secret name given between us, the most powerful name a person can have."

Katsuk smoothed dirt over the pinch of down. He sensed *Kuschtaliute*, the hidden tongue of the land otter, working through his hand upon the dirt, guiding each movement. The power grew in him.

David shivered in the cold, said: "This isn't much fun. Is this all there is to it?"

"It is important if we are to share our names."

"Am I supposed to do something?"

"Yes."

"What?"

Katsuk arose. He sensed tensions in his fingers where Kuschtaliute still controlled his muscles. Bits of dirt clung to his skin. The spirit power of this moment went all through his flesh. *"I am Tamanawis speaking to you. . . ."*

He said: "You will stand now and face the moon."

"Why?"

"Do it."

"What if I don't?"

"You will anger the spirits."

Something in the man's tone dried David's mouth. He said: "I want to go back now."

"First, you must stand and face the moon."

"Then can we go back?"

"Then we can go."

35

"Well...okay. But I think this is kind of dumb."

David stood. He felt the wind, a foreboding of rain in it. His mind was filled suddenly with memories of a childish game he and his friends had played among the creekside trees near his home: *Cowboys and Indians.* What would that game mean to this man?

Scenes and words tumbled through David's mind: *Bang! Bang! You're dead! Dead injun cowboy injun dead.* And Mrs. Parma calling him to lunch. But he and his friends had scratched out a cave in the creek bank and had hidden there, suppressing giggles in the mildew smell of cave dirt and the voice of Mrs. Parma calling and everything stirring in his head—memory and this moment in the wilderness, all become one—moon, dark trees moved by the wind, moonlit clouds beyond a distant hill, the damp odor of earth....

The man spoke close behind him: "You can hear the river down there. We are near water. Spirits gather near water. Once, long ago, we hunted spirit power as children seek a toy. But you hoquat came and you changed that. I was a grown man before I felt Tamanawis within me."

David trembled. He had not expected words of such odd beauty. They were like prayer. He felt the warmth of the man's body behind him, the breath touching his head.

The voice continued in a harsh tone:

"We ruined it, you know. We distrusted and hated each other instead of our common foe. Foreign ideas and words clotted our minds with illusion, stole our flesh from us. The white man came upon us with a face like a golden mask with pits for eyes. We were frozen before him. Shapes came out of the darkness. They were part of darkness and against it—flesh and antiflesh—and we had no ritual for this. We mistook immobility for peace and we were punished."

David tried to swallow in a dry throat. This did not have the sound of ritual. The man spoke with an accent of education and knowledge. His words conveyed a sense of accusation.

"Do you hear me?" Katsuk asked.

For a moment, David failed to realize the question had been directed at him. The man's voice had carried such a feeling of speaking to spirits.

Katsuk raised his voice: "Do you hear me?"

David jumped. "Yes."

"Now, repeat after me exactly what I say."

David nodded.

Katsuk said: "I am Hoquat."

"What?"

"I am Hoquat!"

"I am Hoquat?" David could not keep a questioning inflection from his voice.

"I am the message from Soul Catcher," Katsuk said.

In a flat voice, David repeated it: "I am the message from Soul Catcher."

"It is done," Katsuk said. "You have repeated the ritual correctly. From this moment, your name is Hoquat."

"Does it mean something?" David asked. He started to turn, but a hand on his shoulder restrained him.

"It is the name my people gave to something that floats far out on the water, something strange that cannot be identified. It is the name we gave to your people because you came that way to us from the water."

David did not like the hand on his shoulder, but feared saying anything about it. He felt that his being, his private flesh, had been offended. Opposing forces struggled in him. He had been prepared for an event which he could almost see, and this ritual failed to satisfy him.

He asked: "Is that all there is to it?"

"No. It is time for you to learn my name."

"You said we could go."

"We will go soon."

"Well...what's your name?"

"Katsuk."

David fought down a shudder. "What's that mean?"

"Many, many things. It is the center of the universe."

"Is it an Indian word?"

"Indian! I am sick with being Indian, with living out a five-hundred-year-old mistake!"

The hand on David's shoulder gripped him hard, shook him with each word. David went very still. Suddenly, he knew for the first time he was in danger. *Katsuk.* It had an ugly sound. He could not understand why, but the name suggested deadly peril. He whispered: "Can we go now?"

Katsuk said: "Mamook memaloost! Kechgi tsuk achat kamooks...."

In the old tongue, he promised it all: *I will sacrifice this Innocent. I will give him to the spirits who protect me. I will send him into the underplaces and his eyes will be the two eyes of the worm. His heart will not beat. His mouth...."*

"What're you saying?" David demanded.

But Katsuk ignored him, went on to the end of it. *Katsuk makes this promise in the name of Soul Catcher."*

David said: "I don't understand you. What was all that?"

"You are the Innocent," Katsuk said. "But I am Katsuk. I am the middle of everything. I live everywhere. I see you hoquat all around. You live like dogs. You are great liars. You see the moon and call it a

38

moon. You think that makes it a moon. But I have seen it all with my good eye and recognize without words when a thing exists."

"I want to go back now."

Katsuk shook his head. "We all want to go back, Innocent Hoquat. We want the place where we can deal with our revelation and weep and punish our senses uselessly. You talk and your world sours me. You have only words that tell me of the world you would have if I permitted you to have it. But I have brought you here. I will give you back your own knowledge of what the universe knows. I will make you know and feel. You really will understand. You will be surprised. What you learn will be what you thought you already knew."

"Please, can't we go now?"

"You wish to run away. You think there is no place within you to receive what I will give you. But it will be driven into your heart by the thing itself. What folly you have learned! You think you can ignore such things as I will teach. You think your senses cannot accept the universe without compromise. Hoquat, I promise you this: you will see directly through to the thing at its beginning. You will hear the wilderness without names. You will feel colors and shapes and the temper of this world. You will see the tyranny. It will fill you with awe and fear."

Gently, David tried to pull away from the restraining hand, to put distance between himself and these terrifying words of almost-meaning. Indians should not speak this way!

But the hand shifted down to his left arm, held it painfully.

No longer trying to conceal his fear, David said: "You're hurting me!"

39

FRANK HERBERT

The pressure eased, but not enough to release him.
Katsuk said: "We have shared names. You will
stay."

David held himself motionless. Confusion filled his
mind. He felt that he had been kicked, injured in a way
that locked all his muscles. Katsuk released his arm.
Still David remained fixed in that position.

Fighting dryness in his mouth, David said: "You're
trying to scare me. That's it, isn't it? That's the
initiation. The other guys are out there waiting to
laugh."

Katsuk ignored the words. He felt the spirit power
grow and grow. *"I am Tamanawis speaking to you. . . ."*
With slow, deliberate movements, he took an elkhide
thong from his pouch, whipped it over the boy's
shoulders, bound his arms tightly to his body.

David began twisting, struggling to escape. "Hey!
Stop that! You're hurting me!"

Katsuk grabbed the twisting hands, pinioned the
wrists in a loop of the thong.

David struggled with the strength of terror, but the
hands tying him could not be resisted. The thong bit
painfully into his flesh.

"Please stop it," David pleaded. "What're you
doing?"

"Shut up, Hoquat!"

This was a new and savage voice, as powerful as the
hands which held him.

Chest heaving, David fell silent. He was wet with
perspiration and the moment he stopped struggling,
the wind chilled him. He felt his captor remove the
knife and sheath, working the belt out with harsh,
jerking motions, then reclasping the belt without
putting it into its loops.

Katsuk bent close to the boy, face demoniac in the
moonlight. His voice was a blare of passion: "Hoquat!

Do what I tell you to do, or I will kill you immediately."
He brandished David's knife.

David nodded without control of the motion, unable to speak. A tide of bitter acid came into his throat. He continued to nod until Katsuk shook him.

"Hoquat, do you understand me?"

He could barely manage the word: "Yes."

And David thought: *I'm being kidnapped! It was all a trick.*

All the horror stories he'd heard about murdered kidnap victims flooded into his mind, set his body jerking with terror. He felt betrayed, shamed at his own stupidity for falling into such a trap.

Katsuk produced another thong, passed it beneath David's arms, around his chest, knotted it, and took the free end in one hand. He said: "We have a long way to go before daylight. Follow me swiftly or I will bury your body beside the trail and go on alone."

Turning, Katsuk jerked the rope, headed at a trot toward the dark wall of trees across the bracken clearing.

David, the stench of his own fear in his nostrils, stumbled into motion to keep from being pulled off his feet.

❑

STATEMENT OF Bruce Clark, chief counselor at Six Rivers Camp:

Well, the first night we make the boys write a letter home. We don't give them any dinner until they've written. We hand them paper and pencil there in the rec room and we tell them they have to write the letter before they can eat. They get their meal cards when they hand in the letter. The Marshall boy, I remember him well. He was on the six-o'clock news and there was a kind of hooraw about it when his father's picture came on and it was announced that the father was the new Undersecretary of State. The Marshall boy wrote a nice long letter, both sides of the paper. We only give them one sheet. I remember thinking: There's probably a good letter. His folks'll enjoy getting that.

❑

ABOUT AN hour after sunrise, Katsuk led Hoquat at a shambling trot to the foot of the shale slope he had set as his first night's goal. The instant they stopped, the boy collapsed on the ground. Katsuk ignored this and concentrated on studying the slope, noting the marks of a recent slide.

At the top of the slope a stand of spruce and willow concealed a notch in the cliff. The trees masked a cave and the spring which fed the trees. The cliff loomed as a gray eminence behind the trees. The slide made it appear no one could climb to the notch.

Katsuk felt his heart beating strongly. Vapor formed at his mouth when he breathed. The morning was cold, although there would be sunlight here below the cliff later. The sharp smell of mint scratched at his awareness. Mint fed by the runoff of the spring protruded from rocks at the bottom of the slide. The odor reminded Katsuk that he was hungry and thirsty.

That would pass, he knew.

Even if the searchers used dogs, Katsuk did not believe they would get this far. He had used a scent-killer of his own making many times during the night, had broken trail four times by wading into streams, starting one way, killing the scent, then doubling back.

The low light of morning set the world into sharp relief. Off to his right at the edge of the rockslide red fireweed plumes swayed on the slope. A flying squirrel glided down the slope into the trees. Katsuk felt the flow of life all around him, glanced down at Hoquat sprawled in a bracken clump, a picture of complete fatigue.

What a hue and cry would be raised for this one. What a prize! What headlines! A message that could not be denied.

Katsuk glanced up at the pale sky. The pursuers would use helicopters and other aircraft, of course. They would be starting out soon. Just about now, they would be discovering at the camp what had been done to them. The serious, futile hoquat with their ready-made lives, their plastic justifications for existence, would come upon something new and terrifying: a note from Katsuk. They would know that the *place of safety* in which their spirits cowered had been breached.

He tugged at the thong that linked him to Hoquat, got only a lifted head and questioning stare from eyes bright with fear and fatigue. Tear streaks lined the boy's face.

Katsuk steeled himself against sympathy. His thoughts went to all the innocents of his own people who had died beneath guns and sabers, died of starvation, of germ-laden blankets deliberately sold to the tribes to kill them off.

"Get up," Katsuk said.

43

Hoquat struggled to his feet, stood swaying, shivering. His clothes were wet with trail dew.

Katsuk said: "We are going to climb this rock slope. It is a dangerous climb. Watch where I put my feet. Put your feet exactly where I have. If you make a mistake, you will start a slide. I will save myself. You will be buried in the slide. Is this understood?"

Hoquat nodded.

Katsuk hesitated. Did the boy have sufficient reserves of strength to do this? The nod of agreement could have been fearful obedience without understanding.

But what did it matter? The spirits would preserve this innocent for the consecrated arrow, or they would take him. Either way, the message would be heard. There was no reprieve.

The boy stood waiting for the nightmare journey to continue. A dangerous climb? All right. What difference did it make? Except that he must survive this, must live to escape. The madman had called him Hoquat, had forced him to answer to that name. More than anything else, this concentrated a core of fury in the boy.

He thought: *My name is David. David, not Hoquat. David-not-Hoquat.*

His legs ached. His feet were wet and sore. He felt that if he could just close his eyes right here he could sleep standing up. When he blinked, his eyelids felt rough against his eyes. His left arm was sore where a long red abrasion had been dragged across his skin by the rough bark of a tree. It had torn both his jacket and shirt. The madman had cursed him then: a savage voice out of darkness.

The night had been a cold nightmare in a black pit of trees. Now he saw morning's rose vapors on the peaks, but the nightmare continued.

Katsuk gave a commanding tug on the thong,

studied the boy's response. Too slow. The fool would kill them both on that slide.

"What is your name?" Katsuk asked.

The voice was low, defiant: "David Marshall."

Without change of expression, Katsuk delivered a sharp backhand blow to the boy's cheek, measuring it to sting but not injure. "What is your name?"

"You *know* my name!"

"Say your name."

"It's Dav—"

Again, Katsuk struck him.

The boy stared at him, defiant, fighting back tears.

Katsuk thought: *No reprieve ... no reprieve....*

"I know what you want me to say," the boy muttered. His jaws pulsed with the effort of holding back tears.

No reprieve.

"Your name," Katsuk insisted, touching the knife at his waist. The boy's eyes followed the movement.

"Hoquat." It was muttered, almost unintelligible.

"Louder."

The boy opened his mouth, screamed: "Hoquat!"

Katsuk said: "Now, we will climb."

He turned, went up the shale slope. He placed each foot with care: now on a flat slab jutting from the slide, now on a sloping buttress which seemed anchored in the mountain. Once, a rock shifted under his testing foot. Pebbles bounded down into the trees while he waited, poised to jump if the slope went. The rocks remained in place, but he sensed the trembling uncertainty of the whole structure. Cautiously, he went on up.

At the beginning of the climb, he watched to see that Hoquat made each step correctly, found the boy occupied with bent-head concentration, step for step, a precise imitation.

Good.

Katsuk concentrated on his own climbing then.

At the top, he grasped a willow bough, pulled them both into the shelter of the trees.

In the shaded yellow silence there, Katsuck allowed the oil-smooth flow of elation to fill him. He had done this thing! He had taken the Innocent and was safe for the moment. He had all the survival seasons before him: the season of the midge, of the cattail flowering, of salal ripening, of salmonberries, the season of grubs and ants—a season for each food.

Finally, there would be a season for the vision he must dream before he could leave the Innocent's flesh to be swallowed by the spirits underground.

Hoquat had collapsed to the ground once more, unaware of what waited him.

Abruptly, a thunderous flapping of wings brought Katsuk whirling to the left. The boy sat up, trembling. Katsuk peered upward between the willow branches at a flight of ravens. They circled the lower slopes, then climbed into the sunlight. Katsuk's gaze followed the birds as they swam in the sky sea. A smile of satisfaction curved his lips.

An omen! Surely an omen!

Deerflies sang in the shadows behind him. He heard water dripping at the spring.

Katsuk turned.

At the sound of the ravens, the boy had retreated into the tree shadows as far as the thong would allow. He sat there now, staring at Katsuk, and his forehead and hair caught the first sunlight in the gloom like a trout flashing in a pool.

The Innocent must be hidden before the searchers took to the sky, Katsuk thought. He pushed past the boy, found the game trail which his people had known here for centuries.

"Come," he said, tugging at the thong.

46

Katsuk felt the boy get up and follow.

At the rock pool where the spring bubbled from the cliff, Katsuk dropped the thong, stretched out, and buried his face in the cold water. He drank deeply.

The boy sprawled beside him, would have pitched head foremost into the pool if Katsuk had not caught him.

"Thirsty," Hoquat whispered.

"Then drink."

Katsuk held the boy's shoulder while he drank. Hoquat gasped and sputtered, coming up at last with his face and blond hair dripping.

"We will go into the cave now," Katsuk said.

The cave was a pyramidal black hole above the pool, its entrance hidden from the sky by a mossy overhang which dripped condensation. Katsuk studied the cave mouth a moment for sign that an animal might be occupying it, saw no sign. He tugged at the thong, led Hoquat up the rock ledge beside the pool and into the cave.

"I smell something," the boy said.

Katsuk sniffed: There were many old odors—animal dung, fur, fungus. All of them were old. Bear denned here because it was dry, but none had been here for at least a year.

"Bear den last year," he said.

He waited for his eyes to adjust to the gloom, found a rock spur too high up on the cave's wall for the boy to reach with his tied hands, secured the end of the thong on the spur.

The boy stood with his back against the rock wall. His gaze followed every move Katsuk made. Katsuk wondered what he was thinking. The eyes appeared feverish in their intensity.

Katsuk said: "We will rest here today. There is no one to hear you if you shout. But if you shout, I will kill you. I will kill you at the first outcry. You must learn to obey me completely. You must learn to depend on me for your life. Is that understood?"

The boy stared at him, unmoving, unspeaking.

Katsuk gripped the boy's chin, peered into his eyes, met rage and defiance.

"Your name is Hoquat," Katsuk said.

The boy jerked his chin free.

Katsuk put a finger gently on the red mark on Hoquat's cheek from the two blows at the rockslide. Speaking softly, he said: "Do not make me strike you again. We should not have that between us."

The boy blinked. Tears formed in the corners of his eyes, but he shook them out with an angry gesture.

Still in that soft voice, Katsuk said: "Answer to your name when I ask you. What is your name now?"

"Hoquat." Sullen, but clear.

"Good."

Katsuk went to the cave mouth, paused there to let his senses test the area. Shadows were shortening at the end of the notch as the sun climbed higher. Bright yellow skunk cabbages poked from the shadowed water at the lower end of the spring pool.

It bothered him that he had struck Hoquat, although strong body-talk had been required then.

Do I pity Hoquat? he wondered. *Why pity anyone?*

But the boy had showed surprising strength. He had spirit in him. Hoquat was not a whiner. He was not a coward. His innocence lay within a real person whose center of being remained yet unformed but was gaining power. It would be easy to admire this Innocent.

Must I admire the victim? Katsuk wondered.

That would make this thing all the more difficult. Perhaps it would occur, though, as a special test of Katsuk's purpose. One did not slay an innocent out of casual whim. One who wore the mantle of Soul

48

Catcher dared not do a wrong thing. If it were done, it must fit the demands of the spirit world.

Still, it would be a heavy burden to kill someone you admired. Too heavy a burden? Without the need for immediate decision, he could not say. This was not an issue he wanted to confront.

Again, he wondered: *Why was I chosen for this?*

Had it occurred in a way similar to the way he had chosen Hoquat? Out of what mysterious necessities did the spirit world act? Had the behavior of the white world become at last too much to bear? Certainly that must be the answer.

He felt that he should call out from the cave mouth where he stood, shouting in a voice that could be heard all the way to the ocean:

"You down there! See what you have done to us!"

He stood lost in reverie and wondered presently if he might have shouted. But the hoard of life all around gave no sign of disturbance.

If I admire Hoquat, he thought, *I must do it only to strengthen my decision.*

❏

FROM THE speech Katsuk made to his people:

Bear, wolf, raven, eagle—these were my ancestors. They were men in those days. That's how it was. It really was. They celebrated when they felt happy about the life within them. They cried when they were sad. Sometimes, they sang. Before the hoquat killed us, our songs told it all. I have heard those songs and seen the carvings which tell the old stories. But carvings cannot talk or sing. They just sit there, the eyes staring and dead. Like the dead, they will be eaten by the earth.

❏

DAVID SHUDDERED with aversion to his surroundings. The gray-green gloom of the cave, the wet smoothness of rock walls at the sunlit mouth which his thong leash would not permit him to reach, the animal odors, the dance of dripping water outside—all tormented him.

He was a battleground of emotions: something near hysteria compounded of hunger, dread, shuddering uncertainty, fatigue, rage.

Katsuk came back into the cave, a black silhouette against sunlight. He wore the Russell knife at his waist, one hand on the handle.

My knife, David thought. He began to tremble.

"You are not sleeping," Katsuk said.

No answer.

"You have questions?" Katsuk asked.

"Why?" David whispered.

Katsuk nodded but remained silent.

The boy said: "You're holding me for ransom, is that it?"

Katsuk shook his head. "Ransom? Do you think I could ransom you for an entire world?"

The boy shook his head, not understanding.

"Perhaps I could ransom you for an end to all hoquat mistakes," Katsuk said.

"What're you...."

"Ahhh, you wonder if I'm crazy. Drunk, maybe. Crazy, drunken Indian. You see, I know all the clichés."

"I just asked why." Voice low.

"I'm an ignorant, incompetent savage, that's why. If I have a string of degrees after my name, that must be an accident. Or I probably have white blood in me, eh? Hoquat blood? But I drink too much. I'm lazy. I don't like to work and be industrious. Have I missed anything? Any other clichés? Oh, yes—I'm blood-thirsty, too."

"But I just—"

"You wonder about ransom. I think you have made all the mistakes a hoquat should be permitted."

"Are you . . . crazy?"

Katsuk chuckled. "Maybe, just a little."

"Are you going to kill me?" Barely whispered.

"Go to sleep and don't ask stupid questions." He indicated the cave floor, clumps of dry moss which could be kicked into a bed.

The boy took a quavering breath. "I don't want to sleep."

"You will obey me." Katsuk pointed to the floor, kicked some of the moss into position at the boy's feet.

Every movement a signal of defiance, Hoquat knelt, rolled onto his side, his tied hands pressed against the rock wall of the cave. His eyes remained open, glaring up at Katsuk.

"Close your eyes."

"I can't."

Katsuk noted the fatigue signs, the trembling, the glazed eyes. "Why can't you?"

"I just can't."

"Why?"

"Are you going to kill me?" Stronger that time.

Katsuk shook his head.

51

"Why are you doing this to me?" the boy demanded.

"Doing what?"

"Kidnapping me, treating me like this."

"Treating you like what?"

"You know!"

"But you have received ordinary treatment for an *Indian*. Have our hands not been tied? Have we not been dragged where we would rather not go? Have we not been brutalized and forced to take names we did not want?"

"But why me?"

"Ahhhh, why you! The cry of innocence from every age."

Katsuk pressed his eyes tightly closed. His mind felt damned with evil sensations. He opened his eyes, knew he had become that *other person*, the one who used Charles Hobuhet's education and experiences, but with a brain working in a different way. Ancient instincts pulsed in his flesh.

"What'd I ever do to you?" the boy asked.

"Precisely," Katsuk said. "You have done nothing to me. That is why I chose you."

"You talk crazy!"

"You think I have caught the hoquat disease, eh? You think I have only words, that I must find words to pin down what cannot be cut into word shapes. Your mouth bites at the universe. You give tongue to noises. I do not do that. I send another kind of message. I draw a design upon the emotions. My design will rise up inside people where they have no defenses. They will not be able to shut their ears and deny they heard me. I tell you, they will hear Katsuk!"

"You're crazy!"

"It is odd," Katsuk mused. "You may be one of the few people in the world who will not hear me."

"You're crazy! You're crazy!"

"Perhaps that's it. Yes. Now, go to sleep."

"You haven't told me why you're doing this."

"I want your world to understand something: That an innocent from your people can die just as other innocents have died."

The boy went pale, his mouth in a rigid grimace. He whispered: "You're going to kill me."

"Perhaps not," Katsuk lied. "You must remember that the gift of words is the gift of illusion."

"But you said. . . ."

"I say this to you, Hoquat: Your world will feel my message in its balls! If you do as I tell you, all will go well with you."

"You're lying!"

Anger and shame tore at Katsuk. "Shut up!" he shouted.

"You are! You're lying—you're lying." The boy was sobbing now.

"Shut up or I'll kill you right now," Katsuk growled.

The sobs were choked off, but the wide-open eyes continued to stare up at him.

Katsuk found his anger gone. Only shame remained. I *did lie.*

He realized how undignified he had become. To allow his own emotion such wild expression! He felt shattered, seduced into the word ways of the hoquat, isolated by words, miserable and lonely.

What men gave me this misery? he wondered.

Barren sorrow permeated him. He sighed. Soul Catcher gave him no choice. The decision had been made. There could be no reprieve. But the boy had learned to detect lies.

Speaking as reasonably as he could, Katsuk said: "You need sleep."

"How can I sleep when you're going to kill me?"

A reasonable question, Katsuk thought.

He said: "I will not kill you while you sleep."

"I don't believe you."

"I swear it by my spirits, by the name I gave you, by my own name."

"Why should I believe that crazy stuff about spirits?"

Katsuk pulled the knife partly from its sheath, said: "Close your eyes and you live."

The boy's eyes blinked shut, snapped open.

Katsuk found this vaguely amusing but wondered how he could convince Hoquat. Every word scattered what it touched.

He asked: "If I go outside, will you sleep?"

"I'll try."

"I will go outside then."

"My hands hurt."

Katsuk took a deep breath of resignation, bent to examine the bindings. They were tight but did not completely shut off circulation. He released the knots, chafed the boy's wrists. Presently, he restored the bindings, added a slip noose to each arm above the elbows.

He said: "If you struggle to escape now, these new knots will pull tight and shut off the circulation of blood to your arms. If that happens, I will not help you. I'll just let your arms drop off."

"Will you go outside now?"

"Yes."

"Are you going to eat?"

"No."

"I'm hungry."

"We will eat when you waken."

"What will we eat?"

"There are many things to eat here: roots, grubs. . . ."

"You'll stay outside?"

"Yes. Go to sleep. We face a long night. You will have to keep up with me then. If you cannot keep up, I will be forced to kill you."

"Why're you doing this?"

"I told you."

"No, you didn't."

"Shut up and go to sleep."

"I'll wake up if you come back."

Katsuk could not suppress a grin. "Good. I know what to do when I want to awaken you."

He stood up, went down to the spring pool, pushed his face into the water. It felt cold and fresh against his skin. He squatted back on his heels, allowed his senses to test the silences of this place. When he was sure of his surroundings, he made his way out to the edge of the trees where the shale slope began. He sat there for a time, quiet as a grouse crouching in its own shadow. He could see the trail his people had beaten down for centuries. It skirted the trees far down below the slide. The trail remained quite visible from this height, although forest and bracken had reclaimed it.

He told himself: *I must be strong now. My people have need of me. Our trails are eaten by the forest. Our children are cursed and slaughtered. Our old men do not speak to us anymore in words we can understand. We have withstood evil heaped upon evil but we are dying. We are landless in our own land.*

Quietly, to himself, Katsuk began singing the names of his dead: *Janiktaht . . . Kipskiltch. . . .* As he sang, he thought how all of the past had been woven into the spirit of his people's songs and now the songs, too, were dying.

A black bear came out of the trees far below him, skirted the slide, and went up the fireweed slope eating kinnikinnick. It gave the shale a wide berth.

We need not hurry here, Katsuk thought.

Presently, he crept under the wide skirt of a fat spruce, deep into the shadows of the low boughs. He lay down facing the shale slope and prepared to sleep with the smell of the forest floor in his nostrils.

Soon, he thought, *I must replace the hoquat knife with a proper blade, one that is fit to touch the bow and arrow I will make.*

❑

FROM A letter to his parents by David Marshall:
Dear Mother and Dad: I am having a lot of fun. The airplane was early in Seattle. A man from camp met me there. We got on a small bus. The bus drove for a long time. It rained. It took us to a thing they call a cogwheel train. The train comes up the mountain to the camp. They chased a bear off the tracks. My counselor is a Indian, not like Mrs. Parma. He was born by the ocean he said. His name is Charles something. We call him Chief. We do not have tents to sleep in. Instead, we sleep in cabins. The cabins have names. I am in Cedar Cabin. When you write, put Cedar Cabin on the letter. One of the guys in my cabin was here last year. He says the Chief is the best counselor. Mr. Clark is the camp director. He took our picture with the Chief. I will send you one when he gets them. Eight of us sleep in our cabin. The chief has his own room at the back near the toilet. Please send me six rolls of film and some insect repelent. I need a new flashlight. My other one got broken. A boy cut his hand on the train. There are lots of trees here. They have good sunsets. We will go on a

two day hike Sunday. Thanks for the package of goodies. I found them on the train. After I passed my cookies around to all my friends half of them were gone. I haven't opened the peanuts yet. We are waiting for dinner right now. They are making us write before we eat.

❏

DAVID AWAKENED.

For a moment his only awareness was of hunger cramps and the dry, hot thirst rasping his throat. Then he felt the thongs around his wrists and arms. He experienced surprise that he had slept. His eyes felt rough and heavy. Katsuk's warning against fighting the thongs came back to him. The cave light was a green grayness. He had scattered the cushioning moss. Coldness from the rock beneath him chilled his flesh. A moment of shivering overcame him. When it passed, his gaze went up the thong to the loop secured around the rock spur. It was much too high.

Where was that crazy Katsuk?

David struggled to a sitting position. As he moved, he heard a helicopter pass across the rock slope directly opposite the cave's mouth.

He recognized the sound immediately and hope surged through him. Nothing else made quite that sound: *Helicopter!*

David held his breath. He remembered the handkerchief he had dropped below the slide. He had carried the handkerchief for miles during the nightmare journey, wondering where to drop it. The handkerchief carried his monogrammed initials—a distinctive *DMM*.

He had wormed the handkerchief from his pocket soon after thinking about it, wadded the cloth into a ball, and held it—waiting . . . waiting. There had been no sense dropping it too soon. Katsuk had led them up and down streams, confusing their trail. David had thought of tearing the cloth into bits, dropping the pieces like a paper chase, but the monogram occupied only one corner and he had felt certain Katsuk would hear cloth ripping.

At the rock slope, David had been moved as much by fatigue and desperation as any other motive. Katsuk was sure to hide them during daylight. The ground below the slope was open to the sky. No trail crossed that area. A handkerchief in an unusual place *could* attract attention. And Katsuk had been so intent on the slide, so confident, he had not been watching his back trail.

Surely, the men in the helicopter out there now had seen the handkerchief.

Again, the noisy racket of rotors swept across the mouth of the notch and its concealed cave. What were they doing? Would they land?

David wished he could see the slope.

Where was that crazy Katsuk? Had he been seen? David's throat burned with thirst.

Again, the helicopter passed the notch. David strained to hear any telltale variation in sound. Was rescue at hand?

He thought of the long night's march, the fears which had blocked his thoughts, the dark paths full of root stumbles. Hunger and terror cramped him now, doubled him over. He stared down at the cave's rock floor. The bear smell of the place came thickly into his nostrils.

Again, the machine sound flooded the cave.

David tried to recall the appearance of the slope. Was there a place for a helicopter to land? He had been so tired when they had emerged from the trees, so thirsty and hungry, so filled with desperation about where to leave the telltale handkerchief, he had not really seen the area. The blind feelings of the night with its stars cold and staring clogged his memory. He recalled only the confused surge of bird cries at dawn, falling upon senses amplified by hunger and thirst.

What were they doing in that helicopter? Where was Katsuk?

David tried to recall riding in a helicopter. He had traveled with his parents to and from airports in helicopters. That sound had to be a helicopter. But he had never paid much attention to what landing place a helicopter required, except to know it could land on a small space. Could it land on a slope? He didn't know.

Perhaps the rockslide kept the machine from landing. Katsuk had warned about that danger. Maybe Katsuk had a gun now. he could have hidden one here and recovered it. He could be out there waiting to shoot down the helicopter.

David shook his head from side to side in desperation.

He thought of shouting. No one in the helicopter would hear him above that engine noise. And Katsuk had warned that death would follow any outcry.

David recalled his own knife in its sheath at Katsuk's waist—the Russell knife from Canada. He imagined that knife being pulled from its sheath by Katsuk's dark hand—one hard thrust. . . .

He'll kill me sure if I shout.

The clatter of the machine circling in and out of the clearing around the rockslide confused David. The cave and its masking trees baffled the sound. He could not tell when the helicopter flew low into the slope or when it hovered above the cliff—only that it was out there, louder sometimes than at other times.

Where was Katsuk?

David's teeth chattered with cold and terror. Hunger and thirst chopped time into uneven bits. The dusty yellow light outside the cave told him nothing. No matter how hard he listened, straining to identify what was happening, he could not interpret the sounds into meaning.

There was only the single fact of the helicopter. The sound of it filled the cave once more. This time it came as an oddly distorted noise building slowly into a rumbling roar louder than thunder. The cave trembled around him.

Had they crashed?

He held his breath as the terrifying noise went on and on and on... louder, louder. It built to a climax, subsided. The noise of a raven flock became audible. The helicopter had faded to a distant background throbbing.

He could still hear the machine, though. The rotors' *beat-beat-beat* mingled with drifts of cold green light within the cave to dominate David's awareness. He swallowed dry terror, listened with an intensity which began in the middle of his back. The sound of the helicopter faded... faded... vanished. He heard ravens calling and the dull clap of their wings.

The arch of the cave mouth was filled by Katsuk's black silhouette, its edges blurred by dusty light from outside. Katsuk advanced without a word, removed the thongs from the rock, untied the boy's wrists and arms.

David wondered: *Why doesn't he say something? What happened out there?*

Katsuk felt David's hip pocket.

David thought: *The handkerchief!* He tried to swallow, stared at his captor, begging for a clue to what was happening.

"That was very clever," Katsuk said, his voice conversational. He began massaging the boy's wrists. "Very, very clever; so very clever."

The sound of Katsuk speaking low, a voice like smoke in the cave, filled David with more fear than if the man had betrayed rage.

If he calls me Hoquat, David thought, *I must remember to answer and not anger him.*

Katsuk released David's wrists, sat down facing the boy. He said: "You will want to know what happened. I will tell it."

I am Hoquat, David reminded himself. *I must keep him calm.*

David watched Katsuk's lips, eyes, listened for any change of tone, any sign of emotion. Words came slow cadence from Katsuk's mouth: "Raven...giant bird...devil machine...."

The words carried odd half-meanings. David felt he was hearing some fanciful story, not about a helicopter but about a giant bird called Raven and Raven's victory over evil.

Katsuk said: "You know, when Raven was young, he was the father of my people. He brought us the sun and the moon and the stars. He brought us fire. He was white then, like you, but fire smoke blackened his feathers. It was that Raven who came back today and hid me from your devil machine—black Raven. He saved me. Do you understand?"

David trembled, unable to comprehend or to answer.

61

Katsuk's eyes reflected cobalt glints in the cave's half-light. The sunlight pouring in the entrance behind him put a honey glow on his skin, made him appear larger.

"Why are you trembling?" Katsuk asked.

"I . . . I'm cold."

"Are you hungry?"

"Y-yes."

"Then I will teach you how to live in my land. Many things are provided here to sustain us—roots, sweet ants, fat grubs, flowers, bulbs, leaves. You will learn these things and become a man of the woods."

"A w-woodsman?"

Katsuk shook his head from side to side. "A man of the woods. That is much different. You are sly and have a devil in you. These make the man of the woods."

The words made no sense to David, but he nodded.

Katsuk said: "Raven said to me we can travel by daylight. We will go now because the hoquat will be sending men on foot. They will come to this place because of your sly handkerchief."

David ran his tongue over his lips. "Where are we going?"

"Far into the mountains. We will find the valley of peace, perhaps, where my ancestors put all the fresh water once."

David thought: *He's crazy, pure crazy.* And he said: "I'm thirsty."

"You can drink from the spring. Stand up now."

David obeyed, wondered if the thongs would be tied on his wrists. His side hurt where he had slept on the rock floor of the cave. He looked at the light flaring outside. *Travel by daylight . . . with a helicopter out there somewhere?*

Was pursuit close on their heels? Was crazy Katsuk running in daylight because searchers were near?

Katsuk said: "You think your friends will fly to us in their devil machine and rescue you."

David stared at the cave floor.

Katsuk chuckled. "What is your name?"

"Hoquat." Without looking up.

"Very good. But your friends will not see us, Hoquat."

David looked up into staring dark eyes. "Why not?"

Katsuk nodded at the cave mouth. "Raven spoke to me out there. He told me he will conceal us from all searchers in the sky. I will not even bind you. Raven will keep you from running away. If you try to escape, Raven will show me how to kill you. Do you understand me, Hoquat?"

"Y-yes. I won't try to escape."

Katsuk smiled pleasantly. "That is what Raven told me."

❑

GENESIS ACCORDING to Charles Hobuhet, from a paper for Anthropology 300:

And therefore a man shall leave his father and shall leave his mother and he shall cling to the spirit which binds him to his flesh, being naked before this flesh as he can be naked before no other. And were he not ashamed before this nakedness, aware of this bone from his bones, then shall his flesh be closed and made whole. Then the heavy sleep shall fall upon this man, though he built a god. And finding no other helper, all the names of man shall be his. And his god shall cause the heavens to fall that every beast of the field might call the man, seeking a soul. A living soul is its name. All the cattle, all the fowl, every creature shall be brought unto the man to see what was formed from the primal substance into a living soul. And man, to his separation from that which formed him, will say only its name, thinking this his helper of helpers. But Alkuntam has said: "Not being good, thou shalt die. And all things that live shall become flesh of your flesh, and a separation from the heavens—and therefore a man."

❏

THE NOISE of a helicopter had awakened Katsuk shortly after noon. He lay motionless in the shadow of the spruce, locating the sound before he lifted his head. Even then, he moved slowly, as an alerted animal, aware that the low limbs concealed him, but avoiding any disturbance to attract a searcher's attention.

The helicopter came in over the trees below the rock slope, climbed to circle above his hiding place, went out and around once more. The *thwock-thwock* of its rotors dominated all other sounds around Katsuk as the machine circled over the cliff above him and back over the open ground of the slope.

Katsuk peered upward through the concealing limbs. Sunlight flashed from the helicopter's bubble canopy. The machine was green and silver with Park Service markings on its sides. Under the sound of its rotors it made a greedy hissing noise which set perspiration flowing in Katsuk's palms.

Why did they keep circling? What attracted them?

He knew the spruce hid him, but the abrasive presence of the searchers sank into his nerves, sent his mind leaping to escape.

Around and around the helicopter went, circling the open slope with its boundaries of cliff and trees.

Katsuk thought of the boy in the cave. The men in the helicopter would have to land and shut down their machine before they could hear a shout. They could not land atop the cliff, though: Stunted trees grew from the rocks up there. And the slope below the slide was too steep.

What were they doing here?

Katsuk tore his attention from the circling machine, scanned the slope. Presently, his gaze focused on something out of place. Far down the slope below the slide, in the narrow strip of grass and bracken before the trees, something unnaturally white glistened.

Where all else should be gray and green an odd whiteness lay draped in the bracken. A sharp woodsman's eye in that helicopter had seen it.

Katsuk studied the white thing as the helicopter made another pass. What was it? The wind of the rotors disturbed the thing, set it fluttering.

Awareness exploded in him: *Handkerchief!*

Hoquat had slipped a handkerchief out of his pokcet and let it fall there. Again, the wind from the helicopter stirred the square of cloth, betrayed its alien nature.

The thing shouted to an observer that something man-made lay there in the wilderness, far off the usual trails. Such a thing here would arouse a searcher's curiosity.

Once more, the helicopter came in over the trees below the rock slope. It flew dangerously low, tipped to give the man beside the pilot an opportunity to study the white object through binoculars. Katsuk saw sunlight flash from the lenses.

If the searcher aimed his binoculars into the shadows beneath the spruce, he might even detect a human shape there. But experience worked against the men in the aircraft. They had recognized the nature of the rockslide. They could see wind from their craft raising dust in the shale. They would see the slide as a barrier to a man on foot, especially to a man encumbered by an inexperienced boy. They would *know* a man could not climb that slope.

The pilot tried to hover his craft over the slope, giving his observer a steady platform, but a strong wind beat across the cliff in turbulent eddies. The helicopter bounced, slipped, drifted close to the tree-tops. The engine roared as the machine climbed out over the rocks. It skidded in a gust of wind, went around for another circuit.

Katsuk crept farther back into the trees.

The pilot obviously was daring, but he would know the perils of attempting a landing near the white object which had attracted him. He must have radio, though. He would have reported the strange thing he had seen. Searchers on foot would be coming.

Again, the helicopter skimmed in low over the trees, dipped across the slope. Engine sound filled the air.

A slow, grinding rumble came from the rocks below Katsuk. The slide began to move as the helicopter's thunderous vibration loosed a key rock in that delicate balance on the slope. The movement of the slide built momentum with ponderous inevitability. Tufts of dust puffed in the tumbling gray. The rocks gathered speed, raised a storm noise that drowned out the mechanical intruder. The machine climbed out of the clearing just above a rising cloud of dust that lifted into the wind.

The odor of burnt flint drifted into the notch past Katsuk.

Abruptly, a flock of ravens that had perched silently in the grove behind Katsuk through all the disturbance took flight. Their wings beat the air. Their beaks opened. But no sound of them could be heard above the avalanche.

The entire slope was in motion now. A great tumbling maelstrom of rock roared downward into the trees, buried the bracken, hurled bark chips from the trunks. Smaller trees and brush snapped and were smothered beneath the onslaught.

As slowly as it began, the slide ended. A few last rocks bounded down the slope, leaped through drifting dust, crashed into the trees. The ravens could be heard now. They circled and clamored against this outrage in their domain.

From a circling path high over the clearing, the helicopter played background to the ravens.

Katsuk peered up through the limbs at all the motion.

The helicopter drifted out to the right, came in for another pass over the subsiding dust of the rockslide. The handkerchief was gone, buried beneath tons of rocks. Katsuk distinctly saw one of the men in the bubble canopy gesture toward the ravens.

The flock had opened its ranks, whirled, and called raucously around the intruder.

The machine slid across Katsuk's field of vision. It climbed out over the trees and its downdraft sent the birds skidding.

Some of the ravens settled into the trees above Katsuk while their mates continued dipping and feinting around the helicopter.

The machine climbed out westward, set a course toward the ocean. The sound of its engines faded.

Katsuk wiped wet palms on his loincloth. His arm brushed the knife at his waist, made him think of the boy in the cave.

A handkerchief!

The ravens had protected him—and the rockslide. The spirits might even have started the slide.

As certainly as if he had heard the man's voice, Katsuk knew the searcher who had gestured at the ravens had explained that the birds were a sure sign no human was around. The aircraft had gone elsewhere to search. Its occupants were secure in the message of the ravens.

Head bowed, Katsuk silently thanked Raven.

This is Katsuk who sends gratitude to Thee, Raven Spirit. I speak Thy praise in a place where Thy presence was made known. . . .

As he prayed, Katsuk savored appreciation of the ignorant hoquat beliefs. Whites did not know *The People* had sprung from Raven. Raven always guarded his children.

He thought about the handkerchief. There had been one in Hoquat's pocket. Surely, that was the one on the slope.

Instead of angering him, the defiant gesture ignited a sense of admiration. *Darling . . . clever . . . little Hoquat devil!* Even the most innocent remained sly and resourceful. Hands tied behind him, terror in his heart, he still had thought to leave a sign of his passage.

Awareness growing within him, Katsuk studied the small seed of admiration he now held for Hoquat. Where could such a feeling lead? Was there a point of admiration that might prevent Hoquat's death? How much were the spirits willing to test Katsuk?

The boy had almost succeeded with that handkerchief.

Almost.

This then was not the real test. This was a preliminary skirmish, preparation for something greater to come.

Katsuk felt wild awareness telling him why the boy had failed. Something was tempering them here—both of them. Katsuk sensed that his own thinking had changed once more, that these events had been anticipated. The blur of black wings, that waterfall of ravens, had seized upon his awareness. He was being watched and guarded.

Fear had searched all through him and left him clean.

What had it done to the boy?

The blue-gray panting of the rockslide, the dust cloud rising like steam, had set the wilderness in motion, had given it a new voice which Katsuk could understand.

Tamanawis, the being of his spirit power, had been reborn.

Katsuk rubbed his place on his hand where Bee had marked him. His flesh had absorbed that message and much more: a power that would not be stopped. Let the searchers send their most sophisticated machines against him. He was the Bee of his people, driven by forces no hoquat machine could conquer. All that lived wild around him helped and guarded him. The new voice of the wilderness spoke to him through every creature, every leaf and rock.

Now, he could remember Janiktaht with clarity.

Until this moment, Janiktaht had been a dream-sister: disheveled, drowned, eyes like torches among treacherous images. She had been a tear-clouded mystery, her perfume the rotting sea strand, her soul walled in by loneliness, a graceless memory, accusing, united with every witch enchantment of the night.

Now his fears lay buried in the rocklslide. He knew

the eyes of Charles Hobuhet had seen reality: Janiktaht dead, sodden and bloated on a beach, her hair tangled with seaweed, one with a welter of lost flotsam.

As though to put the seal on his revelation, the last of the raven flock returned from pursuit of the helicoper. They settled into the trees above Katsuk. Even when he emerged boldly from the spruce shadows and climbed to the cave where Hoquat lay captive, the ravens remained, talking back and forth.

❏

FRAGMENT OF a note left at the Sam's River shelter:

Your words perpetuate illusion. You clot my mind with foreign beliefs. My people taught that Man is dependent upon the goodwill of all other animals. You forbade the ritual which taught this. You said we would be punished for such thoughts. I ask you who is being punished now?

❏

AS THEY picked their way down the remnants of the rockslide and walked openly into the forest, David told himself the helicopter was sure to return. The men in it had seen his handkerchief. Katsuk as much as admitted that. What did all his insane talk about ravens have to do with anything real? The men had seen the handkerchief; they would return.

David looked over his shoulder at the cliff, saw a thin cloud above it clinging like a piece of lint to the clear-blown sky.

The helicopter would return. People would come on foot.

David strained to hear the sound of rotors.

❑

KATSUK HAD led him into solid shadows under trees, and David prayed now that the aircraft would come only when they were in a clearing or on a trail not shielded by trees.

Crazy Indian!

Katsuk felt the pressure of the boy's thoughts, but he knew the two figures in this forest gloom were not people. No people passed this way. They were primal elements who snagged their essence upon bits of time like animal fur caught on thorns. His own thoughts went as wind through grass, moving this world only after they had passed. And when they had passed, everything behind them resolved itself into silence, almost-but-not-quite the way it had been before their intrusion.

Yet—something changed.

They changed something essential that could be felt on the farthest star.

Once Katsuk stopped, faced the boy, and said:

"Therefore the flight shall perish from the swift, and the strong shall not strengthen his force, neither shall the mighty deliver himself. That's what it says in your hoquat book. It says he that is courageous among the mighty shall flee away naked in the day. You hoquat had some wise men once, but you never listened."

Another time, they rested and drank at a spring that bubbled from a ledge. A green river roared in its chasm below them. High clouds rippled the sky and there were hill shadows on gray rocks across the river.

Katsuk pointed down to the river. "Look."

David whirled, stared down, and in the quick rhythm of light flung by the river into the canyon's gloom he saw a brown deer swimming, its head thrusting at the far shore. The light and sound and animal movement roaring together dazzled his mind.

There was a dark chill in the wind, and as they left the spring David sensed the quick silence of the forest birds. More clouds had accumulated. A deerfly crouched on his arm. He watched it pause and take flight. He had long since given up hope that Katsuk would produce food from this wilderness. It had been talk, just talk—all those words about food in this place. Katsuk had said it himself: Words fooled you.

David's eyes was caught by the venturesome racing of a squirrel's feet along a high limb. He wondered only if the creature could be caught and eaten.

The day wore on. Sometimes Katsuk talked about himself and his people, fanciful stories indistinguishable from reality. They moved through damp woods, through sunlit clearings, beneath clouds, beneath dripping leaves. Always, there was the sound of their own footsteps.

David forgot about his hunger in the presence of great weariness. Where were they going? Why were there no more aircraft?

Katsuk did not think of a destination, saying, "Now we are here, and we will go there." He felt himself changing, sensed the ancient instincts taking over. He sensed blank places growing in his memory, things he no longer knew in the ways this hoquat world accepted.

Where would the changes in him lead?

The answer unfolded in his mind, the spirits revealing their wisdom: The workings of his brain would go through a deep metamorphosis until, at last, his mind lay like a drunk within his driven self. He would be Soul Catcher entirely.

There was a spring shadowed by a giant cottonwood. Deer tracks led up to it and all around. Katsuk stopped and they drank. The boy splashed his face and collar.

Katsuk watched him, thinking: *How powerful, this young human, how strange, drinking from that spring with his hands. What would his people think of such a lad in such a pose?*

There was a new grace in things the boy did. He was fitting himself into this life. When it was time for silence, he was silent. When it was time to drink, he drank. Hunger came upon him in its proper order. The spirit of the wilderness had seeped into him, beginning to say that it was right for such a one to be here. The rightness of it had not yet become complete, though. This was still a hoquat lad. The cells of his flesh whispered rebellion and rejection of the earth around him. At any moment he might strike out and become once more the total alien to this place. The thing lay in delicate balance.

Katsuk imagined himself then as a person who adjusted that balance. The boy must not demand food before its time. Thirst must be quenched only in the rhythm of thirst. The shattering intrusion of a voice must be prevented by willing it not to happen.

73

Bees weighted with pollen were working in fireweed on the slope below the spring. Katsuk thought: *They watch us. They are the spirit eyes from which we never escape.*

He stared through leaf-tattered light at the working creatures. They were fitted into the orderliness of this place. They were not many creatures, but one single organism. They were Bee, the spirit messenger who had brought him here.

The boy finished drinking at the spring, sat back on his heels, watchful, waiting.

For a glimmering instant, something in the set of the boy's head opened for Katsuk a glimpse of the man who had fathered this human. The adult peered out of youthful eyes, weighing, judging, planning.

Momentarily, it unnerved Katsuk to think of that man-and-father here. The father was no innocent. *He* would have all of the hoquat vices. *He* would have the powers, evil and good, which had given the hoquat dominion over the primitive world. That one must be kept in the background, suppressed.

How could it be done? The boy's flesh could not be separated from that which gave it life. A spirit power must be invoked here. Which spirit power? How? Could the man-father be driven away with his own guilt?

Katsuk thought: *My father should come to help me now.*

He tried to call up a vision of his father, but no face came, not even a voice.

Katsuk felt the seeds of panic.

There had been a father. The man had existed. He was back there walking the beaches, fishing, breeding two children. But he had taken the path of drink and inward rage and a death in the water. Were the hoquat to blame for that?

Where was his face, his voice? He was Hobuhet, the Riverman, whose people had lived on this land for twice a thousand years. He had fathered a son.

And Katsuk thought: *But I am no longer Charles Hobuhet. I am Katsuk. Bee is my father. I have been called to do a terrible thing. The spirit I must call upon is Soul Catcher.*

Silently, he prayed then, and saw at once how the boy's eyelids blinked, how his attention wandered. No power stood against Soul Catcher in this wilderness. Once more, Katsuk felt calm. The greatest of the spirits could not be doubted. The hoquat father had been driven back into the flesh. Only the Innocent remained.

Katsuk arose and strode off along the slope, hearing the boy follow. There had been no need for words of command. Soul Catcher had created a wake in the air which drew the boy into it as though he were caught on a tow line.

Now, Katsuk left the game trail he had been following and struck off through moss-draped hemlocks. There was a granite ledge up above them somewhere hemming in the river valley. Without ordering his feet to seek that place, Katsuk knew he could find it.

He came on the first outcroppings within the hour and moved out of the trees, climbing a slope of stunted huckleberry bushes toward rock shade. The boy followed, panting, pulling himself up by the bushes as he saw Katsuk doing. They emerged presently on a bald rock and there was the river valley spread out southward with sweet grass and elk grazing in a meadow.

A string of fat quail stuttered through sun-splashed shadows below him, catching Katsuk's attention. The quail reminded him of a hunger which he knew his body would feel if it were time for that sensation. But

75

he sensed no hunger, knowing by this that his flesh had accommodated itself to primitive ways.

The boy had sprawled out on sun-warmed rock. Katsuk wondered if Hoquat felt hunger or denied it. The lad also was accommodating to primitive ways. But how was he doing it? Was he immersed so deeply in each moment that only the needs of the moment called out to his senses? The climb had tired him and thus he rested. That was the correct way. But what else had changed in the hoquat flesh?

Carefully, Katsuk studied his captive. Perspiration had left damp darkness in the hair at the boy's neck. Stains of brown dirt marked the legs of his trousers. Streaks of mud were drying on his canvas shoes.

Katsuk smelled the boy's sweat, a youthful, musky sweetness in it which called up memories of school locker rooms. He thought:

It is a fact that the earth which marks us on the surface also leaves its traces within us.

There would come a moment when the boy was tied so firmly to this wilderness that he could not escape it. If the link were forged in the right way, innocence maintained, there would be a power in it to challenge any spirit.

I was marked by his world; now he is marked by mine.

This had become a contest on two levels—the straightforward capture of a victim and the victim's desire to escape, but beneath that a wrestling of spirits. The signs of that other contest were all around.

Katsuk looked out across the valley. There was an old forest on the far slope, fire dead, burned silver hacking the green background into brittle shapes.

The boy turned onto his back, threw a hand across his eyes.

Katsuk said: "We will go now."

"Can't we wait just a minute?" Without removing the hand from his eyes.

Katsuk chuckled. "You think I don't know what you've been doing?"

The boy took the hand away, looked up at Katsuk. "What do you...."

"You slow down when we're crossing a meadow. You trip when we ford the river, then you want me to build a fire. You think I don't know why you complained when we left the elk trail?"

Blood suffused the boy's cheeks.

Katsuk said: "Look where we are now, eh?" He pointed skyward. "Wide open to searching devil machines, huh? Or men could see us from the valley. They could identify us with binoculars."

The boy glared at him. "Why do you say *devil machines* instead of helicopters? You know what they are."

"True, I know what you think they are. But different people see things differently."

David turned away. He felt stubborn determination to prolong this moment in the open. Hunger and fatigue helped him now. They sapped his physical strength but fed his rage.

Abruptly, Katsuk laughed, sat down beside him.

"Very well, Hoquat. I will demonstrate Raven's power. We will rest here while it's warm. Stare at the sky all you wish. Raven will hide us even if a devil machine flies directly over us."

David thought: *He really believes that!*

Katsuk rolled onto his side, studied his captive. How strange that Hoquat didn't understand about Tamanawis. The boy would wait and wait, hoping, praying. But Raven had spoken.

The rock felt warm and soothing beneath him. Katsuk rolled onto his back, glanced around. A quaking aspen grew from the sunward side of their aerie. The quickness of the bright sun pulsing on the aspen's leaves made him think of Hoquat's life.

Yes, Hoquat is like that: trembling in every wind, now glittering bright, now shadowy, now innocent, now evil. He is the perfect Hoquat for me.

The boy said: "You don't really believe that raven stuff."

Katsuk spoke softly: "You will see."

"A guy at camp said you went to the university. They must teach you at the university how stupid that stuff is."

"Yes, I went to the hoquat university. They teach ignorance there. I could not learn ignorance, although everyone was studying it. Maybe I'm too stupid."

Katsuk grinned at the sky, his gaze aimlessly following an osprey which soared and circled high above them.

David watched his captor covertly, thinking how the man was like a big cat he'd seen at the San Francisco zoo—supine on the rock, reclining at ease, the tawny skin dulled by an overlay of dust, eyes blinking, flaring, blinking.

"Katsuk?"

"Yes, Hoquat."

"They're going to catch you and kill you."

"Only if Raven permits it."

"You were probably so stupid they wouldn't let you stay at the university!"

"Haven't I admitted it?"

"What do you know about anything?"

Katsuk heard the rage and fear in the boy's voice, wondered what kind of a son this one had been. It was easy to think of that stage in the boy's life as past—all done. This one would never live to a ripe and wrinkled fulfillment. He had accepted too many lies, this one.

Even without a Katsuk he would never have made it to a rich old time of quiet.

"You don't know anything!" the boy pressed.

Katsuk shrugged himself into a new position, selected a stem of grass growing from a crack in the rock. He slipped the grass free of its sheath, began to chew the sweet juices.

David tasted the sourness at the back of his throat, muttered: "You're just stupid!"

Slowly, Katsuk turned his head, studied the boy. "In this place, Hoquat, I am the professor and you are the stupid."

The boy rolled away, stared into the sky.

"Look up there all you wish," Katsuk said. "Raven hides us from searchers." He extracted another grassblade from its green sheath, chewed it.

"Professor!" the boy sneered.

Katsuk said: "And you are slow to learn. You are hungry, yet there is food all around us."

The young eyes jerked toward the grass in Katsuk's mouth.

"Yes, this grass. It has much sugar in it. Back when we crossed the river, you saw me take the roots of those reeds, wash them, and chew them. You saw me eat those fat grubs, but you only wondered out loud how we could catch fish."

David felt the words burn into his consciousness. Grass grew from the rock near his head. He yanked a stem. It came up by its roots.

Katsuk chuckled, selected a supple young shoot, showed how to draw out the tender stem—slowly, firmly—without disturbing the roots.

David chewed the grass, experimentally at first. Finding it sweet, he ground the stem in his teeth. Hunger knotted his stomach. He pulled another stem, another....

79

Katsuk interrupted: "You've learned one lesson. Come. We will go now."

"You're afraid your raven can't hide us."

"You want a conclusive scientific test, eh? Very well, just stay where you are."

Katsuk turned away, cocked his head to one side, listening.

The pose primed David's senses. He felt the sound of an engine in the air, realized Katsuk must have been hearing it for some time. So that was why he'd wanted to go!

Katsuk said: "You hear it?"

David held his breath. The sound grew louder. He felt his heart beating wildly.

Katsuk lay back without moving.

David thought: *If I jump up and wave, he'll kill me.*

Katsuk closed his eyes. He felt sheet lightning in his brain, an inner sky filled with fire. This was an ultimate test. He prayed for the inner sense of power. *This is Katsuk....* The sound of the helicopter weighed upon his senses.

David stared southwest across the aspen which shaded their rock. The sound was coming from there. It grew louder... louder.

Katsuk lay motionless, with his eyes closed.

David wanted to shout: "Run!" It was insane. But Katsuk would be caught if he stayed there. Why didn't he get up and run into the trees?

A fit of trembling overcame David.

Movement flickered in the sky above the aspen.

David stared, frozen.

The helicopter was high but in plain sight. His gaze followed its passage: a big helicopter flying through a patch of blue sky between clouds. It flew from right to left in the open sky perhaps a mile away. An occupant would only have to glance this way to see two figures on the high rock escarpment.

The big machine crossed the far ridge of the river valley. High trees there gradually concealed it. The sound diminished.

As it disappeared, a single raven flew over the rock where David lay, then another, another. . . .

The birds flew silently, intent upon some private destination.

Katsuk opened his eyes in time to see the last of them. The sound of the helicopter was gone. He looked at the boy. "You did not try to attract their attention. Why? I would not have stopped you."

David's glance flicked across the knife at Katsuk's waist. "Yes, you would."

"I would not."

David sensed an impulse in the words, a confidence that spoke of truth. He reacted with bitter frustration. It made him want to run and cry.

Katsuk said: "Raven hides us."

David thought of the birds which had flown overhead. They had arrived after the helicopter was gone. It made no real sense to him, but David felt the flight of birds had been a signal. He had the eerie sensation that the birds had spoken to Katsuk in some private way.

Katsuk said: "I don't have to kill you while Raven protects. Without Raven's protection . . . well. . . ."

David whirled away. Tears stung his eyes. *I should've jumped up and waved! I should've tried!*

In one supple motion, Katsuk arose, said: "We go now."

Without a backward glance to see if the boy followed, Katsuk crossed the open rock, plunged into the trees on the next slope. He sensed rain in that southwest wind. Tonight it would rain.

81

❏

From an editorial submitted to the University of Washington *Daily* by Charles Hobuhet:

In terms of the flesh, you whites act upon fragmented beliefs. You fall therefrom into lineliness and violence. You do not support your fellows, yet complain of being unsupported. You scream for freedom while rationalizing your own self-imposed limitations. You exist in constant tension between tyranny and victimization. Through all your fraudulent pretensions and roundabout self-trickery, you say you would risk anything to achieve equal happiness for all. But your words risk nothing.

❏

David fingered the two small pebbles in his pocket—one for each day. The second day with this madman. They had slept and dozed through the night beneath a ledge which sheltered them from the rain. Katsuk had refused to build a fire, but he had gone alone into the forest and returned with food: a gray mush in a bark bowl. David had wolfed it, savoring an acrid sweetness. Katsuk had explained then that it was lily roots chopped with grubs and sweet red ants.

At the look of revulsion on David's face, Katsuk had laughed, said: "Squeamishness can kill you out here as fast as anything else. That is good food. It has everything in it that you need."

The laughter had silenced David's objections more than any other argument. He had eaten the gray mush again as dawn glared over the trees.

He had been following Katsuk two hours this morning before his clothes dried.

There were hemlocks overhead now. Ancient blaze marks formed pitch-ringed scars on some of the tree trunks. Katsuk had recognized the marks and explained them: This was a way his ancestors had traveled. Ferns and moss lay in a tangled miniature wilderness under the trees, obscuring the ancient track, but Katsuk said this was the way.

The sky darkened. David wondered if it was going to rain again.

Up ahead, Katsuk paused, studied his surroundings. He turned, watched the boy plunging along behind—over mossy logs, around great clumps of fern.

Katsuk stared down the slope ahead of him. The ancient elk trail his people had used ran somewhere down there. He would cross it soon and follow the path of his wild brethren.

The boy came up to him, stood panting.

Katsuk said: "Stay closer to me."

He set out once more, skirted a mossy log, noted beneath it a tiny dewed spiderweb. All around him lay a forest of mossy limbs—every limb draped with moss like green wool hung out to dry. The light, now bright and now dull as clouds concealed the sun, alternately flattened the colors and then filled the world with green jeweled glowing. At one passage of muted green, the sun suddenly emerged and sent a rope of light plunging through the trees to the forest floor.

Katsuk walked through the light, then ducked under dark boughs. He heard limbs catching at the boy behind him, scratching, slithering.

Beyond the dark passage, Katsuk stopped, reached out a hand, and caught the boy from stepping past. The trail was directly in front of them about two feet down a steep bank. It sloped down to the left. Tracks of hiking boots marked the soft earth.

David saw the tension in Katsuk, listened for the sound of the hikers. The tracks appeared fresh. Water trickled down the trail but had not yet filled the tracks.

Katsuk turned, glanced at the boy, motioned flatly with one hand—back up the way they had come.

David shook his head. "What?"

Katsuk stared up the hill behind them, said: "That big log we came over. Go back there and hide behind it. If I hear or see any sign of your presence, I will kill you."

David stepped backward, turned, and climbed back to the log. It was a cedar, its bark hidden beneath moss, but live limbs climbed skyward along its length. Katsuk had pointed out another such fallen tree, calling it a nurse log. The limbs would be trees some day. David climbed back over the nurse log.

He sank to his heels there, stared through the shadows. His eyes looked for color, for movement. In his own silence, he grew aware of the constant sound of water dripping all around. He felt the dampness of this place. His feet were sopping and his trousers were dark with water almost to the waist. It was cold.

Katsuk stepped down to the trail, turned left in the direction of the hikers' tracks. He glided down the trail, moving with a wraith quality—brown skin, the white loincloth tugging at David's gaze.

The trail switched back to the right. Katsuk turned with it. Only his head and shoulders remained visible to the watching boy.

Abruptly, far down the hillside David saw color and movement—a group of hikers. As though vision opened the air to sound, he heard their voices then: no distinguishable words, but sudden laughter and a shout.

David sank farther down behind the log, peered out between a tangle of dead limbs. As he did it, he wondered: *Why am I hiding? Why don't I sneak around Katsuk and get to those hikers? They'd protect me from him.*

But he sensed his own destruction in any movement. Part of Katsuk remained focused on his captive, some inner sense. There might even be ravens around.

David crouched, tense and quivering.

Katsuk had stopped, head and shoulders visible above the trail embankment. He stared up toward David, then looked up the trail.

David heard noise up the trail then, tried to swallow in a dry throat. More hikers?

He thought: *I could shout.*

But he knew any outcry would bring Katsuk and the knife.

Slogging, heavy footsteps became audible.

A bearded young man came down the trail. A green pack rode high on his shoulders. His long hair was bound at the forehead by a red bandanna. It gave him a curiously aboriginal look. The hiker glanced neither right nor left but kept his attention on the trail. He walked with a stiff, heel-first stride that jarred the ground.

David felt giddy with fear. He no longer could see Katsuk but knew the man lay in wait down there somewhere. He would be watching the hiker from some hidden spot below.

David thought: *All I have to do is stand up and shout.*

The other hikers might not hear it, but this one would. He was just passing David's hiding place. The other hikers were a long way down there though. There was a stream down in that canyon. Its noise would hide any sound from up here.

David thought: *Katsuk would kill this guy ... and then me. He told me what he'd do ... and he meant it.*

The bearded hiker was at the switchback. He would see Katsuk momentarily, or pass right by without noticing anything.

What was Katsuk doing?

For several minutes, Katsuk had felt a test of purpose building to a climax. In that dark passage before he had reached the trail, he had felt an odd fear that he would find his secret name carved some place—on a tree or stump or log.

At the few open places, he had stared up at the sky—now gray, now bright as blue-green glass. It was a crystal without form, but ready to take any shape. Perhaps his name would be written there.

A bulbous gray quinine canker on an old stump had filled him with foreboding. He had thought of Hoquat following him like a pet on a leash. Then, wonderingly: *Soul Catcher has given me power over Raven, but that is not enough.*

He wondered if there were any *thing* in these mountains with the power to set his universe in perfect order once more. A vision of Janiktaht filled his mind: a head with sand on its cheeks, a head turned to seaweed shadows, the face broken upon its imperfections. The ghost of Janiktaht could not set things right.

Now he heard the voices and laughter of the hikers

below and thought it was people taunting him. He heard the lone straggler coming.

The forest was a dull green-gray world suddenly, lidded by a lead sky. The wind had gone down under the trees, and in that new silence of birds and a storm building, Katsuk thought he heard his own heart beating only when he moved, that it stopped when he stopped.

Hatred formed in him then. What right had these hoquat to play in his forest? He felt all the defeats of his people. Their sobs and oaths and lamenting echoed within him, a swarm of unavenged shadows.

The bearded hiker came around the switchback, his head down, the many signs of fatigue in his stride. The pack was too heavy, of course, filled with things he did not need here.

With a dull shock, Katsuk realized he had seen that bearded face before—on the university campus. He could put no name to the face, only a vague recognition that this was a student he had seen. It bothered him that he could not name the face.

In that instant, the hiker saw Katsuk crouched on the trail and jarred to a stop.

"Wha...." The young man shook his head, then: "Hey, It's Charlie the Chief! Hey, man, what're y' doing out here in that getup? You playing Indians and settlers?"

Katsuk straightened, thinking: *The fool doesn't know. Of course he doesn't. He's been in my forest without a radio.*

The hiker said: "I'm Vince Debay, remember? We were in that Anthro Three-hundred class together."

Katsuk said: "Hello, Vince."

Vince leaned his pack against the trail's uphill embankment, took a deep breath. His face betrayed the questions in his mind. He could not help but recognize the strangeness of this encounter. He might recognize the face, but he must know this was not the same Charlie the Chief of that Anthro 300 class. He must know it! Katsuk felt hate covering his face with a stale mask as dry and wrinkled as a discarded snakeskin. Surely, Vince could see it.

Vince said: "Man, am I tired. We've been all morning coming from the Kimta. We were hoping to make it to Finley Shelter by tonight, but it doesn't look like we're going to make it." He waved a hand. "Hey, I was just joking, you know—about Indians and settlers. No offense."

Katsuk nodded.

"You see the other guys?" Vince asked.

Katsuk shook his head.

Vince said: "Why the loincloth bit, man? Aren't you cold?"

"No."

"I stopped to blow a little grass. The other guys must be almost to the bottom by now." He peered around Katsuk. "I think I hear them. Hey, guys!" The last came out in a shout.

Katsuk said: "They can't hear you. They're too close to the river."

"I guess you're right."

Katsuk thought: *I must kill him without anger, an act of irony. I must cut a malignant and venomous thing from my forest. It will be an event in which the world may see itself.*

Vince said: "Hey, Chief, you're awfully quiet. You're not mad or anything?"

"I am not angry."

"Yeah... well, good. You want a little grass? I got half a lid left."

"No."

88

"It's high-grade stuff, man. I got it in Bellingham last week."

"I do not smoke your marijuana."

"Oh. What *are* you doing out here?"

"I live here. This is my home."

"Come on! In that getup?"

"This is what I wear when I search for a deformity of the spirit."

"A what?"

"A thing by which men may know sanity."

"You're putting me on."

Katsuk thought: *I must end it. He cannot be allowed to go and report that he has seen me.*

Vince rubbed his shoulder beneath a pack strap. "This pack sure is heavy."

Katsuk said: "You have not yet discovered that having too much is not better than having enough."

Nervous laughter jerked in Vince's throat. He said: "Well, I gotta catch up with the others. See you, Chief." He hunched his shoulders into the straps, taking the weight of it off the embankment, stepped past Katsuk. There was obvious fear in his movements.

Katsuk thought: *I cannot pity. That would make the earth fall away from beneath my feet. My knife must go cleanly into this walking youth.* He pulled the knife from its sheath, moved after Vince. *The knife must pay homage to his blood and break open the time of death. Birth must end with death, with eyes gone dull, memory gone, heart gone, blood gone, all the flesh gone—the miracle ended.*

As he thought, he moved: left hand into Vince's hair, yanking the head back, right hand whipping the knife around and across the exposed throat.

There was no outcry, just the body slumping back, guided by the hand in the long hair. Katsuk dropped to one knee, caught the weight of the pack on it, held the jerking figure upright. A jet of red gushed from the slashed throat, the lucid color of a young life spurting in a bright fountain onto the trail—a rose petal spurting, ebbing, softly now and now frothing, resurgent, the body twitching, then still.

It was done.

Katsuk felt that this moment had been following him all his life, now to catch up with him.

An ending and a beginning.

He continued to support the body, wondered how old this young man had been. Twenty? Perhaps. Whatever his age, it was ended here—the pleasure and the time passing, all a dream now. Katsuk felt his mind whirling with what he had done. Strange visions captured his awareness: all a dream, black and hidden, an evil profile, clouds under water, limbs of air moving with jade ripples, a green crystal, fluid carving traces in his memory.

This earth had green blood.

He felt the weight of the sagging body. This flesh had been a minor pattern in an overlarge universe. Now it faded. He allowed the body to fall on its left side, stood, and peered uphill toward the log where Hoquat lay hidden. It was a hillside suddenly full of green light as clouds exposed the sun.

Deep within himself, Katsuk prayed: *Raven, Raven, keep the edge on my hate. O Raven, keep me terrible in revenge. This is Katsuk, who lay three nights in thy forest, who heeded no thorn, but did thy bidding. This is Katsuk, thy torch, who will set this world afire.*

◻

SPECIAL AGENT Norman Hosbig, Seattle Office, FBI:

Just because we suspect he may have gone to some city doesn't mean we stop searching that wilderness. As of today, we have almost five hundred people in all phases of the search over there. We have sixteen aircraft still in the park—nine of them helicopters. I read in the morning paper where they are calling it a strange kind of contest, modern against primitive. I don't see it that way at all. I don't see how he could be walking those trails unseen with all the people we have searching.

◻

DAVID HAD watched the killing, standing up from his hiding place, his mind raddled by terror. That young hiker who had been so alive—nothing but a carcass now. Katsuk's eyes were fearful things, their gaze hunting through the gloom of the hillside. Were they seeking another victim?

David felt that Katsuk's eyes had been hidden in some far depth, coming now to the surface—brown and terrible and so deep from where they had been.

On trembling legs, David crept up the hill behind his hiding place. He knew his face was contorted with

91

terror, his breathing all out of pace, coming fast and shallow. But he had little control over his muscles.

All he wanted was release.

Slowly, he started, moving parallel with the trail. He had to find those other hikers! At last, he turned downhill, stumbling over logs and limbs. Movement restored some of his muscle control. He began to run, emerging from the trees onto a lower section of the trail.

There was no sight or sound of the other hikers or of Katsuk.

He was running all out now. There was nothing left to do but run.

In a trick of the light, Katsuk saw the running boy—hair flying, a winged head, a slow-motion being of solid light: ivory with inner brilliance, splendid and golden, swimming upon the green field of the forest and the air.

Only then did Katsuk realize that he, too, was running. Straight down the slope he went in great gulping strides. He burst out upon the switchback trail as Hoquat rounded a corner above him, caught the running boy in full stride, and swept him to the ground.

Katsuk lay there a moment, catching his breath. When at last he could speak, his words came out in a wild drumbeat with little meaning outside the angry syllables pounding.

"Damn! Damn! Damn! I told you! Stay down earth. . . ."

But Hoquat had been knocked unconscious, his head striking a log beside the trail.

Katsuk sat up, grinning, his anger evaporated. How foolish Hoquat had appeared—the stumbling flight of a recent nestling. Raven had, indeed, anticipated everything in the universe.

There was a bloody bruise on the side of Hoquat's head. Katsuk put a hand to the boy's breast, felt the heart beating, saw vapor form as the boy breathed. The heart, the breath . . . the two things were one.

Sadness overcame him. Those loggers on the La Push road! Look what they had done. They had killed Janiktaht. They had killed this boy beneath his arm here. Not this moment, perhaps . . . but eventually. They had killed Vince, growing cold up there on the trail. There would be no sons of Vince's making. No daughters. No laughter ringing after him. Not now. All killed by those drunken hoquat. Who knew how many they had killed?

How could the hoquat not understand these things they did with their own violence? They remained blind to the most obvious facts, unwilling to see the consequences of their behavior. An angel-spirit could come down from heaven and show them the key to their actions and they would deny that spirit.

What would the nine drunken hoquat say if they saw Vince's dead flesh up there on the trail? They would become angry. They would say: *"We didn't do that!"* They would say: *"We just had a little innocent fun."* They would say: *"Christ! It was just a little klooch! When did a bit of tail ever hurt one of them?"*

Katsuk thought of Vince walking on the campus—not innocent enough to satisfy Soul Catcher, but naïve in the rightness of his own judgments. A preliminary sacrifice, one to mark the way.

Vince had judged his own people harshly, had shared the petty rebellions of his time, but had never sent his thoughts ahead to seek out a way in his world. He had merely *reacted* his way into sudden death.

Katsuk climbed to his feet, threw the unconscious boy over his shoulder, trudged back up the hill. He thought:

I must not pity. I must hide Vince's body and then go on.

Hoquat stirred on Katsuk's shoulders, muttered: "My head...."

Katsuk stood the boy on his feet, steadied him. "You can walk? Very well. We will go on."

❑

PSALM OF KATSUK: written on the backs of trail registry blanks and left at Cedar Cabin:

You brought your foreign god who sets you apart from all other life. He presents you with death as His most precious gift. Your senses are bedazzled by His illusions. You would give His death to all the life that exists. You pursue your god with death, threatening Him with death, praying to take His deadly place.

You stamp the crucifix across the earth's face. Wherever it touches, there the earth dies. Ashes and melancholy shall be your lot all the rest of your days.

You are a blend of evil and magnificence. You torture with your lies. You trample the dead. What blasphemy resides in your deadly pretensions of love!

You practice your look of sincerity. You become a mask, transparent, a grimace with a skull behind it. You make your golden idols out of cruelty.

You disinherit me in my own land.

Yea, by the trembling and fear of my people, I blight you with all of the ancient curses. You will die in a cave of your own making, never again to hear birdsong or trees humming in the wind or the forest's harp music.

DAVID AWOKE in pale dawn light. He was trembling with cold and damp. Katsuk's hand gripped his shoulder, shaking, shaking. Katsuk wore clothes taken from the dead hiker's pack: jeans that were too tight for him over the loincloth, a plaid shirt. He still wore moccasins and the band of red cedar bark around his head.

"You must awaken," Katsuk said.

David sat up. A cold, gray world pressed around him. He felt the damp chill of that world all through his body. The clothing on Katsuk made him think of the hiker's death. Katsuk had murdered! And so swiftly!

That memory conveyed a deeper chill than anything in the creeping gray fog of this wilderness.

"We will go soon," Katsuk said. "You hear me, Hoquat?"

Katsuk studied the boy, seeing him with an odd clarity, as though the dull gray light around them were concentrated into a spotlight which illuminated every movement in the young face.

Hoquat was terrified. Some part of the boy's awareness had translated the hiker's death correctly. One death was not enough. The ritual of sacrifice must be carried through to its proper end. Hoquat must not let this awareness rise into his consciousness. He must know it while denying it. Too much terror could destroy innocence.

The boy shuddered, a sudden, uncontrollable spasm.

Katsuk squatted back on his heels, felt a sudden inward chill, but kept a hand on Hoquat's arm. The flesh pulsed with life beneath Katsuk's fingers. There was warmth in that life, a sense of continuity in it.

"Are you awake, Hoquat?" Katsuk pressed.

David pushed the man's hand away, flicked a glance across the sheathed knife at Katsuk's waist.

My knife, David thought. *It killed a man.*

As though his memory had a life of its own, it brought up the picture of his mother warning him to be careful with "that dreadful knife." He felt hysterical laughter in his throat, swallowed to suppress it.

Katsuk said: "I will be back in a few minutes, Hoquat." He went away.

David's teeth chattered. He thought: *Hoquat! I am David Marshall. I'm David Morgenstern Marshall. No matter how many times that madman calls me Hoquat, that won't change a thing.*

There had been a sleeping bag in the hiker's pack. Katsuk had made a ground cover of moss and cedar boughs, spread the bag over them. The bag had been pushed aside during the night and lay now in a damp wad. David pulled it around his shoulders, tried to still the chattering of his teeth. His head still ached where he had bruised it when Katsuk had hurled him to the ground.

David thought then about the dead hiker. After he had regained consciousness and before they crossed the river, Katsuk had forced his captive back up the trail to that bloody body, saying: "Hoquat, go back to where I told you to hide and wait there."

David had been glad to obey. As much as he wanted *not* to look at the dead youth, his eyes kept coming back to the gaping wound in the neck. He had climbed back to the mossy nurse log, hidden his face behind it, and lost himself to dry sobs.

Then Katsuk, who had called him after a long time, was carrying the pack. There had been no sign of body or bloody marks of a struggle on the trail.

They had stayed off the elk track for a time after that, climbing parallel to it, returning to the trail on the other side of a high ridge.

At dusk, Katsuk had built a crude cedar-bark shelter deep in trees above a river. He had brought five small fish from the river, cooked them over a tiny fire in the shelter.

David thought about the fish, tasting them in memory. Had Katsuk gone for food now?

They had crossed the river before building the shelter. There had been a well-marked hiking trail, a bridge above a flood-scoured bar. The boards of the bridge had been soft wet with a pocking of slush on the downstream lip, the air all around full of smoky spray.

Had Katsuk gone down there to get more fish?

There was a sign by the bridge: FOOT OR HORSE USE ONLY.

Game was thick along the river trail. They had seen two does, a spotted fawn, a brown rabbit running ahead of them for a space, then darting into the wet greenery.

David thought: *Maybe Katsuk put out a rabbit snare.*

Hunger knotted his stomach.

They had climbed under a drizzle of rain. It had come down in thin plumes from catch-basin leaves to bend the ferns flat. There was no rain now though.

Where *was* Katsuk?

David peered out of the shelter. It was a dawn world of cold and dampness with the sound of ducks quacking somewhere. It was a ghostly world, a dark dawn. No bright cords of light, just a twisted, incoherent gray.

He thought: *I must not think how that hiker was killed.*

But there was no escaping that memory. Katsuk had done it in full view of his captive. A splash of light on steel and then that great gout of blood.

David felt his chest shaking at the memory.

Why had Katsuk done that? Because the hiker had called him Chief? Surely not. Why then? Could it be the spirits Katsuk kept referring to? Had they commanded him to murder?

He was crazy. If he listened to spirits, they could order him to do anything.

Anything.

David wondered if he could escape in this foggy morning. But who knew where Katsuk was now? The hiker had tried to leave. Katsuk could be waiting even now for his captive to run.

After the murder, all during that day, David's mind had rattled with unspoken questions. Something had told him not to ask those questions of Katsuk. The death of the hiker must be put behind them. To recall it was to invite more death.

They had come a long way from that terrible place of murder. David's legs had ached with fatigue and he had wondered how Katsuk could keep up such a pace. Every time David had lagged behind, Katsuk had motioned with the hand which had wielded the knife.

David remembered how he had welcomed nightfall. They had stopped perhaps a half hour before dark. It had been raining. Katsuk had ordered the boy to wait beneath a cedar while the shelter was built. The river valley had filled with liquid darkness that flowed into it from shadowed hills. The sodden woods had fallen silent. At dark, the rain had stopped and the sky had cleared. Sounds had grown in the darkness. David had heard rocks laboring in the river bottom, the noises of a world become chaos.

Every time he had closed his eyes, his memory had filled with that blood-wet, gaping neck, the knife in its brittle flashing.

For a long time, he had kept his eyes open, peered out of the shelter into the bower of darkness. A gray bulk of rock had emerged, hanging on the river's far slope, released from the night by moonlight. David had stared at it. Somewhere in that fearful staring, he had gone to sleep.

What was Katsuk doing?

Dragging the sleeping bag around him, David crawled to the shelter's opening. He poked his head out: cold, drifting fog everywhere. There was only one thing outside, a bulk of surrounding gray, wet and full of dull shapes, as though the fog tried to hold onto the night.

Where had Katsuk gone?

The man materialized then out of one of the dull shapes. He walked from the fog as though brushing aside a curtain, thrust a rolled bark cone into David's hand, and said: "Drink this."

David obeyed, but his hands trembled so that he spilled part of the cone's milky liquid onto his chin. The stuff smelled of herbs and tasted bitter. He gasped as it went down. It was cold in his mouth at first, then burned. He gulped convulsively, almost vomited.

Shuddering, David held out the cup of bark, demanded: "What was that?"

Katsuk pulled the sleeping bag from David's shoulders, began rolling it. "That is Raven's drink. I prepared it last night." He stuffed the sleeping bag into the pack.

"Was it whiskey?" David asked.

"Hah! Where would I get the hoquat drink?"

"But what. . . ."

"It is made from roots. One of the roots is devil's club. It gives you strength."

Katsuk slipped the pack straps over his shoulders, stood up. "We go now."

David crawled out of the shelter, got to his feet. As he cleared the entrance, Katsuk kicked a supporting limb for the shelter. The Bark structure fell with a clatter, sending up a puff of ashes from the their fire pit. Katsuk took up a limb, went to an animal burrow above the shelter, scattered dirt over the area. When he was through, he had created the effect that the animal had moved the dirt.

A ball of heat radiated from the drink in David's stomach. He felt wide awake and full of energy. His teeth had stopped chattering.

Katsuk threw aside the digging stick, said: "Stay close behind me." He climbed around the animal burrow into the fog.

David, stopping to pick up a pebble—his third, to make the third day—thought of putting his footprints in the raw dirt. But Katsuk had stopped above him and was watching.

Skirting the burrow, David climbed toward his captor. Katsuk turned, resumed the climb.

Why do I just follow him? David wondered. *I could run away and hide in this fog. But if he found me, he'd kill me. He still has that knife.*

A vision of the slain hiker filled his mind.

He'd kill me sure. He's crazy.

Katsuk began reciting something in a language strange to David. It was a low chant that went over the same syllables again and again.

"Crazy Indian," David muttered.

But he spoke in a low voice which would not carry to Katsuk.

❏

CHIEF PARK Ranger William Redek:

Well, you have to realize how big and wild this country really is, especially in the Wilderness Area. For example, we know there are at least six small aircraft crashed somewhere in there. We've never found them, although we've searched. Have we *ever* searched! Not even a clue. And those aircraft aren't actively trying to hide from us.

❏

"WHY DO you pick up those rocks?" Katsuk asked.

David held up four pebbles in his left hand. "To count the days. We've been gone four days."

"We count by nights," Katsuk said.

And Katsuk wondered at himself, trying to teach this essential thing to a hoquat. Four pebbles for the days or four pebbles for nights, what difference could it make for a hoquat? Night and day were only separations between degrees of fear for this young man's people.

They sat in another bark shelter Katsuk had built, finishing off the last morsels of a grouse Katsuk had snared. The only light was from the fire in the center of

101

the shelter. It cast ruddy shadows on the crude structure over them, glistened on the knots tied in rope made from twisted willow which supported the framework.

It was full dark outside and there was a pond which had reflected molten copper in the sunset. Now it was a haunted pond full of captured stars.

Katsuk had taken the grouse from a giant hemlock near the pond. He had called it a roosting tree. The ground beneath it was white with grouse droppings. The grouse had come sleepily to the hemlock branches at dusk and Katsuk had snared one with a long pole and a string noose.

David belched, sighed, put the last of the grouse bones into the fire pit as Katsuk had instructed him. Pit and bones would be covered up and disguised in the morning.

Katsuk had spread cedar boughs under the sleeping bag. He stretched out under the bag with his feet toward the dying fire, said: "Come. We sleep now."

David crawled around the fire, slid under the bag. It felt clammy from not being hung to dry in the sun. There was an acid smell to it which mingled with the smoke and burned grease, perspiration, and cedar.

The fire burned itself down to a few coals. David felt the night close in around him. Sounds took on fearful shapes. He felt the cedar needles scratching. This was a place so utterly foreign to the sounds, sights, and smells of his usual life that he tried to recall things from other times which would fit here. All he could bring to mind were the tire-humming whine of a car crossing a steel bridge, the city's smoke, his mother's perfume . . . nothing fitted. One place rejected the other.

Softly, he slipped across the border of awareness and into sheep, there to dream. A giant face leaned over him. It was a face much like Katsuk's—broad, prominent cheekbones, a mane of thick black hair, wide mouth.

The mouth opened, said: "You are not yet ready. When you are ready, I will come for you. Pray then, and a wish will be granted you." The mouth closed, but the voice continued: "I will come for you ... come for you ... for you ... you!" It reverberated in his skull and filled him with terror. He awoke trembling, sweating, and with a feeling that the voice continued somewhere.

"Katsuk?"

"Go to sleep."

"But I had a dream."

"What kind of dream?" There was alertness in the man's voice.

"I don't know. It scared me."

"What did you dream?"

David described it.

His voice oddly withdrawn, Katsuk said: "You have a spirit dream."

"Was it your god?"

"Perhaps."

"What does it mean, Katsuk?"

"You are the only one who can tell."

Katsuk struggled with an empty feeling in his breast. *A spirit dream for Hoquat!* Was it Soul Catcher playing an evil game? There were stories about such things. What a disturbing dream! Hoquat had been granted the right to a wish—any wish. If he wished to leave the wilderness, Hoquat could do it.

"Katsuk, what's a spirit dream?"

"That's where you get a spirit guide for your other soul—in the dream."

"You said it could be a god."

"It can be a god or a spirit. He tells you what you must do, where you must go."

"My dream didn't tell me to go anywhere."

"Your dream told you that you aren't yet ready."

"Ready for what?"

"To go anywhere."

"Oh." Silence, then: "That dream scared me."

"Ahhh, you see—the hoquat science doesn't liberate you from the terror of the gods."

"Do you really believe that stuff, Katsuk?"

His voice low and tense, Katsuk said: "Listen to me! Every person has two souls. One remains in the body. The other travels high or low. It is guided by the kind of life you lead. The soul that travels must have a guide: a spirit or a god."

"That isn't what they teach in church."

Katsuk snorted. "You doubt, eh? Once, I doubted. It almost destroyed me. I no longer doubt."

"Did you get a guide?"

"Yes."

"Is Raven your guide?"

Katsuk felt Soul Catcher stirring within him, said: "You do not understand about guides, Hoquat."

David scowled into he darkness. "Can only Indians get—"

"Don't call me Indian!"

"But you're—"

"Indian is a fool's name. You gave it to us. You refused to admit you hadn't found India. Why must I live with your mistake?"

David recalled Mrs. Parma, said: "I know a real Indian from India. She works for us. My parents brought her from India."

"Everywhere you hoquat go, the natives work for you."

"She'd be starving if she still lived in India. I've heard my mother talk about it. People starve there."

"People starve everywhere."

"Do real Indians get guides?"

"Anyone can get a guide."

"Do you do it just by dreaming?"

"You go into the forest and you pray."

"We're in the forest. Could I pray now?"

"Sure. Ask Alkuntam to send you a guide."

"Is Alkuntam your name for God?"

"You could say that."

"Did Alkuntam give you your guide?"

"You don't understand it, Hoquat. Go to sleep."

"But how does your spirit guide you?"

"I explained that. It speaks to you."

David recalled the dream. "Right in your head?"

"Yes."

"Did your spirit tell you to kidnap me?"

Katsuk felt the boy's questions as a pressure, stirring up wild powers within him. Soul Catcher moved there, stretching.

David pressed the question: "Did your spirit tell you?"

Katsuk said: "Be silent or I will tie and gag you." He turned away, stretched his feet toward the warmth remaining in the rocks around the fire pit.

"I am Tamanawis speaking to you...."

Katsuk heard the spirit so loud he wondered that the boy could not hear it.

"You have been given the perfect innocent."

David said: "When does your spirit speak to you?"

"When there is something you need to know," Katsuk whispered.

"What do I need to know?"

"How to accept my sharp and biting point," Katsuk whispered.

"What?"

"You need to know how to live that you may die

105

correctly. First, you need to live. Most of you hoquat do not live."

"Does your spirit make you talk crazy like that?"

Katsuk felt hysterical laughter in his throat, said: "Go to sleep or I will kill you before you have lived."

David heard intensity in the words, began to tremble. The man was crazy. He could do anything. He had murdered.

Katsuk felt the trembling, reached back, and patted the boy's shoulder. "Do not worry, Hoquat. You will yet live. I promise it."

Still the boy's trembling continued.

Katsuk sat up, took the old flute from his belt pouch, blew softly into it. He felt the song go out, smoke-yearning sounds in the shelter.

For a few moments, Katsuk imagined himself in some old, safe place with a friend, with a brother. They would share music. They would plan the hunt for the morrow. They would preserve the dignity of this place and of each other.

David listened to the low music, lulled by it.

Presently, Katsuk stopped, restored the flute to its pouch. Hoquat breathed with the even rhythm of sleep. As though it were a thing of reality which could be seen and touched, Katsuk felt a bond being created between himself and this boy. Was it possible they were really brothers in that other world which moved invisibly and soundlessly beside the world of the senses?

My brother, Hoquat, Katsuk thought.

❑

FROM A paper by Charles Hobuhet for Philosophy 200:

Your language is filled with a rigid time sense which denies the plastic fluidity of the universe. The whole universe represents a single organism to my people. It is the raw material of our creation. Your language denies this with every word you utter. You break the universe into lonely pieces. My people recognize immediately that Whitehead's "bifurcation of nature" is illusion. It is a product of your language. The people who program your computers know this. They say: "Garbage In—Garbage Out." When they get garbage out, they look to the program, to the *language*. My language requires that I participate with my surroundings in everything I do. Your language isolates you from the universe. You have forgotten the origin of the letters in which your language is written. Those letters evolved from ideographs which stood for movements in the surrounding universe.

❑

IN THE low light of morning, David stood beneath a tall cedar, fingered the five pebbles in his pocket. There was dew on the grass outside the cedar's spread, as though each star from the night had left its mark upon the earth. Katsuk stood in the grass adjusting the straps of the pack. Morning's red glow remained on the peaks beyond him.

David asked: "Where are we going today?"

"You talk too much, Hoquat."

"You're always telling me to shut up."

"Because you talk too much."

"How'm I going to learn if I don't talk?"

"By opening your senses and by understanding what your senses tell you."

Katsuk pulled a fern frond from the ground, set off through the trees. He swung the fern against his thigh as he walked, listened to the world around him—the sounds of the boy following, the animals. . . . Quail ran through an opening off to his left. He saw the yellow-brown patch of an elk's rump far off through the moss-green light of the morning.

They were climbing steadily now, their breath puffing out in white clouds. Presently, they came to a saddleback filled with old-growth hemlock and went down into a gloomy valley where lichen grew like scabs on the trees.

Water ran down their trail, filling the deep elk tracks, exposing small rocks, splashing off the downhill side wherever a channel formed. The dominant sound around them was the fall of their own footsteps.

Once, they passed a squirrel's head left on a log by a predator. The head was being picked at by birds with black topknots and white breasts. The birds continued their feeding even when the two humans walked within a pace of them.

At the foot of the valley, they came out of the trees to the reed fringe of a small lake. There was a dun-blue skyline full of haze beyond the lake; wax-green trees came down to the far shore. A stretch of mud indicated shallows off to the right. Bird tracks were written in the mud, crisscrossing from food to food. Mergansers fed alertly along the far shore. As Katsuk and the boy emerged from the screening trees, the ducks fled, beating the water with a whistling in their wings, gaining flight at the last moment and circling back above the intruders.

David said: "Gosh. Has anybody ever been here before?"

"My people . . . many times."

Katsuk studied the lake. The ducks had been wary. That was not a good sign.

A windfall hemlock lay across the reeds into the lake. Its back was scarred by the passage of many hooves. Katsuk dropped the pack, stepped out onto the log. It trembled beneath him. He wove his way between upthrusting limbs to a flat space near the open water, hesitated. A black feather floated beside the log. Katsuk knelt, plucked the feather from the water. He shook away clinging moisture.

"Raven," he whispered.

It was a sign! He thrust the feather into his headband, steadied himself with one hand on a limb, immersed his face to drink from the lake. The water was cold.

The log trembled under him and he felt the boy approach.

Katsuk stood up and once more studied his surroundings. The boy made noisy splashings drinking. There was a marsh at the lake's upper end and a meadow beyond the marsh with a stream slashing through it. He felt the boy leave the log, turned.

The pack was an alien green mound beyond the

reeds. He thought of the food in it: a package of peanuts, two chocolate bars, tea bags, a bit of bacon, some cheese.

Katsuk considered these things, thought: *I am not yet hungry enough to eat hoquat food.*

The boy stood waiting beside the pack, staring at it. *He is hungry enough*, Katsuk thought.

A grasshopper went "Chrrrk! Chrrk!" in the reeds.

Katsuk returned to the boy, picked up the pack.

David said: "I thought you were going to fish."

"You would never survive alone in this country," Katsuk said.

"Why?"

"There is something wrong about this place and you do not even feel it. Come."

Katsuk settled his shoulders into the pack straps, went back into the trees to the game trail which ran parallel to the shore.

David followed, thinking: *Something wrong about this place?* He sensed only the biting cold, the way every leaf he touched left its deposit of moisture on him.

Katsuk turned left on the game trail, fell into a stalking pace—slow, alert, every motion fitted into the natural tempo of his surroundings. He felt himself caught up in the supernatural world of Soul Catcher, a movement of ecstasy within him, an ancient religious ritual described by every step he took.

The wilderness was too wakeful. Something had slipped out of place here ... a broken pattern, a special quality to the silences. It all focused on that meadow at the head of the lake.

David tried to match his movements to Katsuk's, thinking: *What's he seen?* The oppressive caution of their movements filled the forest around him with danger.

110

They passed a salmonberry patch, the fruit still hard and unripe. David watched Katsuk pause, study the bushes, saw how the leaves went swaying as though they were tongues telling him of this place: voices from the bushes, from the trees, from the lake—conversation all around but intelligible only to Katsuk.

Is it more hikers?

David stumbled on a root, finding himself possessed by both hope and dread.

The trail slanted up the hill beyond the salmonberry bushes. Katsuk heard the boy stumble, recover his balance, heard the crouched silence of the forest, a creek running in shallows down to the left. Trail dew had left streaks of moisture along the sleeves of the dead hiker's shirt he wore. He felt the damp chill against his skin, thought how it would be to have a sheepskin coat.

The thought shocked him to stillness, as though the forest had sent him a warning. *A hoquat coat!* He knew he never again would see s sheepskin coat or feel its warmth. That was hoquat nonsense. And he realized the essence of the warning: hoquat clothing weakened him. He would have to discard it before long or be destroyed.

Slowly, he resumed the stalking climb, heard the boy following. The trees were too thick below him for a view of the meadow, but he knew the danger lay there. He slid under a low branch, shifting the pack to prevent its rasping on wood.

The trail branched. One arm went down the hill toward the meadow. The trees were thinner below him, but still no vista of the meadow. Katsuk eased himself down the trail, around a thick spruce, and there was the meadow. The bright light of it was like a collision after the forest shadows. The creek sent a straight black gash through tall grass and patches of blue camas and bog laurel. Elk had beaten tracks across the lush pasture and had carved out a muddy ford across the stream.

Katsuk felt the boy ease up behind him. He studied the meadow. Abruptly, he cluthced the boy's arm to hold them both frozen. A dead elk calf lay in the meadow, steam still rising from it. The calf's head was twisted under its body, the neck broken. Great claw marks flowed along its flanks, red against the brown.

Katsuk moved only his eyes, searching for the big cat that had done this. It was not like a cat to leave such a meal. What had frightened it? He stared across the meadow, abruptly conscious of the discordant potential in the crouched boy beside him. Hoquat was not trained in silence. He could attract whatever had frightened away the cat. Katsuk felt his stomach as tight as a drumhead with tension.

Softly, as though without beginning, a wave motion traversed tall grass at the far side of the meadow. Katsuk sensed the cat shape within the grass. He felt his heart rolling, a stone beat in his breast. The wave of grass moved diagonally toward the upper end of the meadow where the creek emerged from a wall of trees.

What had frightened the beast?

Katsuk felt anger. Why was there no sign to specify the danger? He gripped Hoquat's arm tightly, began to drift backward up the trail, pulling the boy with him, heedless of the occasional snapped branch.

A grouse began to drum somewhere far up the hill behind him. Katsuk fixed his hearing on that sound, moved toward it. They were partly screened from the meadow by the trees now. He no longer could see the wave of grass. Katsuk's thoughts were one long pang of uncertainty: something wrong in that meadow, so wrong it shrieked at him. His lips felt cold to his tongue, cracked and cold.

David, frightened by Katsuk's silent probing and the sudden retreat, moved as quietly as he could, allowing himself to be hauled up the hill toward the drumming grouse. A bramble scratched his arm. He hissed with pain. Katsuk only tugged at him, urging more speed.

They glided around the uplifted root tangle of a nurse log, a long hemlock studded with young trees feeding on it.

Katsuk pulled the boy into a crouch behind the log. They peered over the log.

"What is it?" David whispered.

Katsuk put a hand over the boy's mouth to demand silence.

David pushed the hand away, and as he moved, the sharp crack of a rifle shot in the meadow sent echoes rolling back and forth across the lake valley.

Katsuk pulled the boy flat behind the nurse log, lay tense and listening, breathing in an even, shallow rhythm. *Poacher! It has to be a poacher. There is no hunting allowed in here.*

A hazelnut tree shaded the hiding place behind the log. Its yellow-green leaves filtered the sunlight, glistened on a spider casting its net between two ferns beside Katsuk's head. The nimble hunter with its silken web spoke to him of this place. *Poacher.* In this valley, the poacher would be one of his own people. Who else would dare use this place? Who else would know of the supplies hidden in buried steel drums, of the camouflaged huts, the cave that had been a mine?

Why were his people here? He had honored all the principal spirits. His deed was ready to be sung. The design of it lay in his mind where Soul Catcher had imprinted it. The thing was a tattoo needle to impress its shape upon the entire world!

113

Would his people try to stop him?

There could be no stopping. The hiker had been killed. His blood was a promise to this forest. The body might never be found, but Hoquat had seen the blood flow, had seen the young man die. Hoquat could not live now.

Katsuk shook his head, moving his eyes through the dappled light, seeing-but-not-seeing the silver wheel of the spiderweb.

No!

He could not think of the boy as a witness to the killing. Witness? That was hoquat thinking. What was a witness? Vince's death had not been murder. He had died because he was part of a larger design. His death was an imprint upon the *Perfect Innocent*, to prepare the way for the sacrifice.

A deep sigh shook Katsuk. He sensed Hoquat shivering beside him—a small forest creature caught in the web and almost resigned to its fate.

❑

SHERIFF MIKE PALLATT:

Look, this Indian lost his kid sister a couple months ago. He adored that kid. He was her family, understand? After their parents died he raised her almost by himself. She was raped by a gang of drunken bastards and went out and killed herself. She was a good kid. I'm not surprised Charlie went off his nut. This is what comes of sending an Indian to college. He studies how we've been giving his people the shitty end of the stick. Something happens... he reverts to savage.

❏

DAVID JERKED upright into empty blackness. He shivered with fear and cold. He hugged himslf to still the trembling, searched for something to place him in a world, any abrasive edge to convey reality. Where was he?

He knew why he had awakened. A dream had taken him, loping along the edge of wakening. It had confronted him with a black stone, then green water and rippling glass. The smell of rancid oil had tickled his awareness. Something had chased him. Something still ran close behind him, singing softly of things he knew but did not want to hear. Even the awareness that the song contained a meaning terrified him.

David exhaled a sobbing breath. Fear shimmered over him with a bass hum of sweat and running and the remembered dream. He felt the white gold pulsebeat of gods and firelight. The thing with meaning pressed close. It was right behind him. He felt his muscles wanting to run. His mouth tasted of rusty iron. He felt his throat jerking with sounds he could not make. The thing behind him was going to catch him! The words of its song draped over his mind, a white-gray whispering, smooth as glass, promising happiness while it presented him with terror.

The dream singing persisted.

David heard it and tasted bitter acid in his throat.

The dream terror washed around him in that faint tide of sound. He shuddered, wondering if he still dreamed, if the sensation of awakening was illusion.

A spark of orange light formed in the darkness. He heard movement near the light. Cautiously, he reached up with his left hand. His fingers encountered a rough wood surface.

Memory filled him—a dungeon cave with moldering plank walls. Katsuk had brought them here at dusk, searching out the way, exploring ahead while the boy crouched in shadows. This was a secret place used by his people when they broke the hoquat law and hunted game in these mountains.

The orange light was a remnant of the tiny fire Katsuk had built in the cave mouth. Movement of shadowy arms flickered across the light—Katsuk!

But the singing continued. Was it Katsuk? No . . . it seemed far away and full of words he could not understand—a whistling flute and a slow, walking rhythm on a drum. Katsuk had played his flute one night and this sounded like a distant parody of that playing.

David's fear ebbed. That was real singing, a real drum, and a flute like Katsuk's. There were several voices.

The poachers!

Katsuk had crept away in the first dark, returning much later to say he recognized the people camped in the trees at the edge of the meadow.

A groan came from near the fire. Was that Katsuk? David strained to hear what Katsuk was doing. He wondered: *Should I let him know I'm awake? Why did he groan?*

Again, the groan sounded.

David cleared his throat.

116

"You are awake!" Katsuk hurled the words at him from the cave's mouth.

David recoiled at the madness in Katsuk's voice, was unable to answer.

"I know you are awake," Katsuk said, calmer now and nearer. "It will be daylight soon. We go then."

David sensed the presence over him, blackness in blackness. He tried to swallow in a dry throat, managed: "Where will we go?"

"To my people."

"Is that them . . . singing?"

"There is no singing."

David listened. The forest outside the cave gave off only the soughing of wind in trees, faint drippings, stirrings, and rustlings. Katsuk pressed something hot beneath the boughs beside David: another heated rock.

"I heard singing," David said.

"You dreamed it."

"I heard it!"

"It is gone now."

"What was it?"

"Those of my people who have eaten spirits."

"What?"

"Try to sleep a little longer."

David remembered the dream. "No." He pressed against the moldering boards beside him. "Where are your people?"

"Everywhere around us."

"In the forest?"

"Everywhere! If you sleep, the spirit eaters may come to you and explain their song."

With sudden realization, David asked: "You're trying to tell me it was ghosts singing!"

"Spirits."

"I don't want to sleep."

"Have you prayed for your spirit?"

"No! What was that song?"

"It was a song asking for power over that which no human can defeat."

David groped in the darkness for the sleeping bag, pulled it around him. He leaned over the place where Katsuk had placed the heated rock. *Crazy Katsuk! He makes no sense.*

"You will not sleep?" Katsuk asked.

"How soon will it be daylight?" David countered.

"Within the hour."

Katsuk's hand came out of the dark, pressed David toward the warm rock. In a soothing tone, Katsuk said: "Go to sleep. You dreamed an important dream and ran from it."

David stiffened. "How do you know?"

"Sleep," Katsuk said.

David stretched out over the rock. His body drank the warmth. The musky, falling, swimming attraction of sleep radiated from the warmth. He did not even feel it when Katsuk's hand released him.

He lapsed into a state with no sharp edges. Magic and ghosts and dreams: They were gauze in an orange wind. Nothing completed a sensation of touch. Everything blended, one blur into another: warmth into the cedar boughs beneath him, Katsuk returning to the cave's mouth, the dream into the chill where the rock's warmth failed to reach him. Vagueness everywhere.

All blurred and faded.

He felt his childhood fading, thought: *I am becoming a man.* Memory treasures stored up against just such an awakening, receded into gray impressions—pictures he recalled pasting in a book, the rungs of a staircase where he had peered through to

118

watch guests arriving, being tucked into bed by a benign figure whose face was lost in a halo of silver hair.

David sensed warm orange firelight. Katsuk had built up the fire at the cave's mouth. He felt damp cold under his back. A night bird screamed twice. Katsuk groaned.

The groan sent a shock all through David.

Vagueness vanished, taking sleep and the dreams of his childhood. He thought: *Katsuk is sick. It's a sickness no one can heal. Katsuk has caught a spirit and eaten it. He has the power no human can defeat. That's what he meant about the song! The birds obey him. They hide us. He has gone into some place where humans can't follow. He has gone where the song is ... where I'm afraid to go.*

David sat up, wondered at such thoughts coming all unbidden into his mind. Those were not the thoughts of childhood. He had thought real things, penetrating things. They were thoughts from immediate pressures of life and death.

As though his thoughts had called it into being, the song started up once more. It began out of nothing, the words still unintelligible, even it's direction undefined ... somewhere outside.

"Katsuk?" David said.

"You hear the singing?" He spoke from near the fire.

"What is it?"

"Some of my people. They hold a sing."

"Why?"

"They try to call me out of the mountains."

"Do they want you to turn me loose?"

"They have eaten a small spirit, Hoquat. It is not as powerful as my spirit."

"What're you going to do?"

"When it is daylight, we will go to them. I will take you to them and show them the power of my spirit."

❏

FROM KATSUK'S speech to his people, as reported by his Aunt Cally:

This is the way it is with me. My mind was sick. My mind suffered the sickness of the hoquat. I lost my way without a spirit to guide me. Therefore, I had to beg medicine from anyone who would give it to me. I begged it from you, my people. I begged it from my grandfathers, my father's brothers, all the people we came from, all our ancestors, my mother's grandmothers and grandfathers, all the people. Their medicine words poured down upon me. I felt them within me. I feel them now. They are a fire in my breast. Raven leads me. Soul Catcher has found me.

❏

IN THE last of the darkness, Katsuk stood outside the cave which was an ancient mine shaft high on the hillside above the lake. He saw lights flickering in the

120

branches below him, campfires beneath the fog that veiled the valley. The lights glowed and swam as though they were moving phosphor in water, shapes blurred in fog ripples.

He thought: *My people.*

He had crept close and identified them in the night, not by their hoquat names but by their tribal names which were shared only with those who could be trusted. They were Duck Woman, Eyes on Tree, Hates Fish, Elk Jumping, One-ball Grandfather, Moon Water. . . . In his own tongue now, he said their names:

"Tchukawl, Kipskiltch, Ishkawch, Klanitska, Naykletak, Tskanay. . . ."

Tskanay was there, thinking of herself as Mary Kletnik, no doubt. He tried to summon a Charles Hobuhet memory of Mary Kletnik. Nothing came into his mind. She was there, but behind a veil. Why was she hiding? He sensed a lithe shape naked in firelight, a voice murmuring, fingers touching flesh, a softness which demanded dangerous things of him.

She was a threat.

He understood this now. Tskanay had been important to Charles Hobuhet. She might strike through to the center which was Katsuk. Women had powers. Soul Catcher must deal with her.

The sun came over the edge of the valley. Katsuk looked beyond the bowl of fog to the mountain suspended in the dawn. Black splotches of rock stood out against snow as white as a goat-hair blanket. The mountain was an ancient shape pressed hard against the sky and left hanging there.

Katsuk prayed then: *Soul Catcher protect me from that woman. Guard my strength. Keep my hatred pure.*

He went into the mine-cave then, awakened the boy, and fed him chocolate and peanuts from the pack.

Hoquat ate hungrily, unaware that Katsuk was not eating. The boy said nothing of his dream, but Katsuk recalled it, sensing the dangerous forces being gathered against him.

Hoquat had dreamed of a spirit who would grant any wish. The spirit had said he was not yet ready. Ready for what? For the sacrifice? It said something that Hoquat had a spirit in his dream. That didn't happen to everyone. That was a sign of real powers. How else could this be, though? The sacrifice must be a great thing to have any meaning. The *Innocent* must go into the spirit world with a great voice which could not be denied. Both worlds must hear him or the death would be meaningless.

Katsuk shook his head. It was disturbing, but this was no morning for dreams. This would be a day for testing the realities of the fleshly world.

He went back outside then and saw that the sun had burned part of the fog from the valley. The lake was a mirror catching the bright flare of sunlight. It filled the valley with pale clarity. A black bear came out into the meadow above the lake, drank the air with its tongue hanging like a dog's. It caught the scent of humans, whirled, and loped back into the trees.

Katsuk stripped off the hoquat clothing, stood in only the loincloth and the moccasins Janiktaht had made, the medicine pouch hanging at his waist.

The boy came out. Katsuk handed the hoquat clothing to him, said: "Put this in the pack. Stuff the sleeping bag on top, and hide the pack beyond where we slept."

"Why?"

"Do it and come back here."

David shrugged, obeyed. Presently, he returned, said: "I'll bet you're cold."

"I am not cold. Come. We go to my people now." He led the way at a fast walk which had the boy trotting to keep up.

They went down across a bracken slope, acid green with red-leaved vines creeping through the green. A gray prow of rock jutted from the slope. They went around the rock and plunged into a dark trail through trees.

David was panting by the time they splashed across rocky shallows in the creek. Katsuk seemed unaware of exertion, keeping up that steady, long stride. There were cottonwoods by the creek—pale, yellow-green moss on their trunks. The trail went through wet salal, emerged on a narrow ledge thick with spruce and cedar, a few tall hemlocks. Four crude huts, one of them as large as all the other three together, were spaced among the trees about fifty feet apart. All had been built of split cedar boards dug into the needle duff of the ground and lashed to a pole framework. David could see the lashings of twisted willow rope. The largest hut had a low door curtained by raw elk-hide.

As Katsuk and the boy came in sight of the door, the curtain lifted and a young woman emerged. Katsuk stopped, held his captive with a hand on the boy's shoulder.

The young woman came fully outside before she saw them. She stopped then, put a hand to her cheek. Recognition was obvious in her stare.

David stood locked under Katsuk's grip. He wondered what was in Katsuk's mind. Katsuk and the young woman just looked at each other without speaking. David studied the woman, his senses abnormally alert. Her hair was parted in the middle, hanging loosely over her shoulders. The ends were braided, tied with white string. Pockmarks disfigured her left cheek, showing around the hand she held there. Her cheeks were broad. They glistened, and her eyes were set deeply into the flesh. Her figure was full and slender beneath a red-purple dress which stopped just below her knees.

All the way down the mountain, David had told himself Katsuk's people would end this nightmare. The old days of Indians and white captives were gone forever. These people had come here as part of the search for Katsuk. Now David saw fear in the young woman's eyes and began to doubt his hopes.

She dropped her hand, said: "Charlie."

Katsuk gave no response.

She looked at David, back to Katsuk. "I didn't think it would work."

Katsuk stirred, said: "Didn't think *what* would work?" His voice sounded strained.

"The sing."

"You think I came because they sang me in?"

"Why not?"

Katsuk released David's shoulder, said: "Hoquat, this is Tskanay . . . an old friend."

Coming toward them, she said: "My name is Mary Kletnik."

"Your name is Tskanay," Katsuk said. "Moon Water."

"Oh, stop that nonsense, Charlie," she said. "You—"

"Do not call me Charlie."

Although he spoke softly, his tone stopped her. Again, she put a hand to her pockmarked cheek. "But. . . ."

"I have another name now: Katsuk."

"Katsuk?"

"You know what it means."

She shrugged "The center . . . kind of."

"Kind of," he sneered. He touched the boy. "This is Hoquat, the Innocent who will answer for all of our innocents."

"You don't really...."

"The reality I show you, it will be the only reality." Her glance went to the knife at his waist.

"Nothing that simple," Katsuk said. "Where are the others?"

"Most of them went out before dawn... searching."

"For me?"

She nodded.

David's heart leaped at her response. Katsuk's people *were* here to help. They were searching. He said: "My name is David Marshall. I—"

A stinging backhand blow sent him reeling.

Tskanay put both hands to her mouth, stifled a scream.

In a conversational tone, Katsuk said: "Your name is Hoquat. Do not forget again." He turned to the young woman. "We spent the night in the old mine. We even built a fire. Why did your searchers not search there?"

She lowered her hands, did not answer.

Katsuk said: "Do you still think your pitiful sing brought me in?"

Her throat convulsed with swallowing.

David, his cheek burning from the blow, glared angrily at Katsuk, but fear kept him rooted.

"Who is still in camp?" Katsuk asked.

Tskanay said: "Your Aunt Cally and old Ish, that I know of. Probably one or two of the younger boys. They don't like to go out in the cold too early."

"The story of our lives," Katsuk said. "Do you have a radio?"

"No."

The elkhide curtain behind her lifted. An old man emerged—long nose, gray hair to his shoulders, a crane figure. He wore bib overalls and a green wool shirt that flopped loosely on his thin frame. Caulked boots covered his feet. He carried a lever-action rifle in his right hand.

David, seeing the rifle, allowed his hopes to grow once more. He studied the old man: pale face full of wrinkles, eyes sunken above high cheeks. A dark, elemental spirit lay in the eyes. His hair was twisted together like old kelp that had dried and rotted on a beach.

"Been listening," the old man said. His voice was high and clear.

Katsuk said: "Hello, Ish."

Ish came fully out of the door, let the curtain drop. He moved with a limp, favoring his left foot. "Katsuk, eh?"

"That is my name." Katsuk spoke with a subtle air of deference.

"Why?" Ish asked. He advanced to a position beside Tskanay. A distance of about ten feet separated them from Katsuk and the boy.

David sensed the contest between these two, looked at Katsuk.

"We both know what opens the mind," Katsuk said.

"Solitude and suffering," Ish said. "So you think you're a shaman."

"You use the correct word, Ish. I'm surprised."

"I've had a *little* education, boy."

Katsuk said: "I sought the old ways. I suffered with hunger and cold in the high mountains. I gained a spirit."

"You're a woods Indian now, eh?"

In a cold, hard voice, Katsuk said: "Do not call me Indian."

126

"Okay," Ish said. He shifted his grip on the rifle.

David looked from the rifle to Katsuk, hardly dared to breathe, afraid he might call attention to himself.

Ish said: "You really think you got a spirit?"

Tskanay said: "Oh, this is idiot talk!"

Katsuk said: "I will not be disinherited by my own people in my own land. I know why you are here. My spirit tells me."

"Why are we here?" Ish asked.

"You used the excuse of hunting for me to *poach* in your own land. You came to break the hoquat laws, to kill game your families need to survive and which is ours by right!"

The old man grinned. "Didn't need a spirit to tell you that. You think we weren't really hunting for you?"

"I heard the sing," Katsuk said.

"It brought you in, too!" Tskanay said.

"Sure did," Ish agreed.

Katsuk shook his head. "No, uncle of my father, your sing did not bring me in. I came to show you my rank."

"You didn't even know I was here," Ish protested. "I heard you ask Mary."

"Tskanay," Katsuk corrected him.

"Mary, Tskanay—what's the difference?"

"You *know* the difference, Ish."

David realized suddenly that, despite his glib tone, the old man was terrified and trying to hide it. Why was he afraid? He had a rifle and Katsuk only had the knife. The fear was there, though—in the pallor, in the stiffness of his grin, the tension in his old muscles. And Katsuk knew it!

"So I know the difference," Ish muttered.

"I will show you," Katsuk said. He spread his arms, lifted his face to the sky. "Raven," he said, his voice low, "show them that my spirit is all powerful."

127

The old man sighed, said: "That sure as hell isn't why we sent you to the university."

"Raven," Katsuk said, louder this time.

"Stop calling your damned bird," Tskanay said. "Raven's been dead for a hundred years at least."

"Raven!" Katsuk screamed.

A wooden door banged in one of the huts off to the left. Two boys about David's age emerged, stood staring at the scene in the clearing.

Katsuk lowered his head, folded his arms.

David said: "I saw him bring the birds once." Immediately, he felt foolish. The others ignored him. Did they doubt him? "I *did*," he insisted.

Tskanay was looking at him now. She shook her head sharply. David saw that she, too, was fighting down terror. She was angry, also. Her eyes flashed with it.

Katsuk said: "I accept what Raven gives." He began singing, a low chant with harsh, clicking sounds.

Ish said: "Stop that!"

Tskanay looked puzzled. "That's just names."

"Names of his dead," the old man said. His eyes glittered as he glanced around the clearing.

Katsuk broke off his chant, said: "You felt them last night during your sing!"

"Don't talk nonsense," the old man growled, but there was fear in his voice. It trembled and broke.

"Felt *what?*" Tskanay demanded.

Cold gripped David's chest. He *knew* what Katsuk meant: There were spirits in this place. David sensed a dirge humming in the trees. He shivered.

"While you sang, I heard them here," Katsuk said. He touched his chest. "They said: 'We are the canoe people, the whale people. Where is our ocean? What are you doing here? This lake is not our ocean. You have run away. The whales taunt us. They spout only a spear's throw from the beach. Once, they would not have dared this.' That is what the spirits told me."

Ish cleared his throat.

Katsuk said: "Raven protects me."

The old man shook his head, started to lift the rifle. As he moved, a single raven flew in through the trees from the lake. Its pinions clattered in the clearing. It alighted on the ridge of the largest hut, tipped its head to stare at the people below it.

Ish and Tskanay had turned their heads to follow the flight. Tskanay turned back immediately. Ish took longer to study the bird before returning his attention to Katsuk.

David kept his attention on Katsuk. What a thing that was—to summon the raven.

Katsuk stared into the old man's eyes, said: "You will call me Katsuk."

Ish took a deep, shuddering breath, lowered the rifle.

Tskanay put both hands to her cheeks, lowered them guiltily when she saw David glance at her. Her eyes said: "I don't believe this and neither do you."

David felt sorry for her.

Katsuk said: "You, of all our people, Ish, must know what I am. You have seen the spirits work in men before this. I know it. My grandfather told me. You might have been a *shichta*, you, a great leader of our people."

Ish coughed, then: "Lot of damned nonsense. That bird's just a coincidence. I haven't believed in that stuff for years."

Softly, Katsuk asked: "How many years?"

Tskanay said: "Do any of you *really* believe he called that bird in here?"

David whispered: "He did."

"How many years?" Katsuk insisted.

"Since I saw the light of reason," Ish said.

"Hoquat reason," Katsuk said. "Ever since you fell for the hoquat religion."

"By God, boy...."

"That's it, isn't it?" Katsuk demanded. "You swallowed the hoquat religion like a halibut eating the bait. They pulled you right in. You swallowed it, even though you knew it took you out of all touch with our past."

"That's blasphemy, boy!"

"I am not *boy!* I am Katsuk. I am the center. I say *you* blaspheme! You deny the powers that are ours by right of inheritance."

"That's damned nonsense!"

"Then why don't you shoot me?" He screamed it, leaning toward the old man.

David held his breath.

Tskanay backed away.

Ish hefted the rifle. As he moved, the raven on the roof squawked once. Ish almost dropped the rifle in lowering it. His eyes reflected terror now, peering at Katsuk as though he were trying to see inside the younger man.

"Now, you know," Katsuk said. He waved his right arm.

At the gesture, the raven leaped into the air, flew back toward the lake.

"What is my name?" Katsuk demanded.

"Katsuk," the old man whispered. His shoulders sagged. The rifle dragged at his arm as though he wanted to drop it.

Katsuk gestured at David. "This is Hoquat."

"Hoquat," the old man agreed.

Katsuk strode between Ish and Tskanay, went to the elkhide curtain. He lifted the curtain, turned back to the girl. "Tskanay, you will keep watch on Hoquat. See that he doesn't try to run away. It is too soon for him to die." He went into the hut, dropping the curtain.

"He's crazy," David whispered. "He's wild crazy."

Tskanay turned on the old man. "Why did you cave in like that? The boy's right. Charlie's—"

"Shut up!" Ish snapped. "He's lost to you, Mary. Understand me? You'll never have him. I know. I've seen it before. He's lost to all of us. I've seen it."

"You've seen it," she sneered. "Why, you old fool, you just stood there with that rifle while he—"

"You saw the bird!"

"The bird!"

"It could just as well have been lightning to strike us dead!"

"You're as crazy as he is!"

"Are you blind, girl? I was just talking to keep up my nerve. I didn't even have to see him call that bird. You can feel the power in him. He didn't come in because of our sing. He came to show us his power."

She shook her head. "Then what're you going to do?"

"Going to wait for the others and tell them."

"What're you going to tell them?"

"That they better watch out before they go up against Katsuk. Where's Cally?"

"She went out before I did...about ten minutes."

"When she gets back, tell her to fix the house for a big meeting. And don't let that kid there get away from you. You do, Katsuk'll kill you."

"And you'd just stand there and let him!"

"Damned right I would. Don't catch me going up against a real spirit. Soul Catcher's got that one."

❏

SPECIAL AGENT Norman Hosbig, FBI:

Look, I told you media guys how much we appreciate your cooperation. We're giving you everything we can. I know how big a story this is, for Christ's sake. We're in complete charge and the sheriff is talking out of turn. We consider that note Hobuhet left to be a ransom note. As soon as that comes up, we automatically take jurisdiction. We're operating on the rebuttable presumption that the kid has been transported in interstate or foreign commerce. I know what the sheriff says, but the sheriff doesn't know everything. We're going to get another ransom demand before long. Hobuhet was a university student and we've reason to believe he was an Indian militant. He's going to demand that we cede Fort Lawton or Alcatraz or set up an independent Indian Territory somewhere else. Now, for God's sake, don't print any of this.

❏

DAVID WAS PERPLEXED. He knew he had a stake in what had just happened in this woods clearing. He had a life-and-death problem with Katsuk, but the contest between Katsuk and old Ish had gone beyond any question of a captive's fate. It had gone into another world, into the place of the spirit dreams. David knew this. It no longer was a problem of the world in which he lived with his body.

He wondered: *How do I know this?*

It went against everything he had been taught to believe before Katsuk. There were two problems, or one problem with two shapes. One involved his need to escape from the crazy Indian, to get back with people who were sane and could be understood. But there was another part of this thing—a force which tied together two people called Katsuk and Hoquat.

He thought: *I'm David, not Hoquat.*

But just by answering to Hoquat he knew he had formed a link of some kind. If he were to escape, he had to break both bonds. Ish had understood this, but Tskanay had not.

Tskanay still stood where Katsuk had left her. There was a worried look on her face as she studied the boy who had been put in her care. A wind from the lake ruffled her hair. She brushed a lock from her forehead. There was anger in the movement and frustration.

Ish had gone off into the forest with a purposeful, long-legged stride. It was her problem now.

Tskanay stood firmly in this world, David realized. She held only half the vision. It was like being blind. Ish was another matter. He could see both worlds, but he was afraid. Perhaps Ish felt fear *because* he could see both worlds.

David stilled a spasm of trembling.

Tskanay's long silence bothered David. He looked away from her toward the lake, disturbed by the steady pressure of those dark eyes. What was she thinking? The sun stood high over the hills now, throwing dappled light onto the floor of the clearing. Why was she staring like that? Why didn't she say something? He wanted to shout at her to say something or go away.

She was thinking about Katsuk.

133

He knew this as surely as though she had said it. She wanted to talk about Katsuk.

It was a dangerous to talk to her about Katsuk. He knew this now. But it had to be done. *The problem with Katsuk*. The danger had something to do with the spirit dream which Katsuk had experienced but refused to describe in detail. It had been a powerful dream. That was obvious. David wondered suddenly if his Hoquat-self had been caught up in Katsuk's dream. Could that happen? Could you take another human being into your dream and hold that person captive there?

With a chill shock of awareness, he realized that he had favored Katsuk over Ish in their contest. How could that be? The realization filled him with guilt. He had abandoned himself! He had weakened the David part. Somewhere, he had made a colossal mistake.

His mouth opened in dismay. What power had commanded that he strengthen the Hoquat-Katsuk bond?

Tskanay stirred, said: "Are you hungry?"

David wondered if he had heard her correctly. What did hunger have to do with anything real? Hungry? He thought about it for a moment.

"Have you eaten?" Tskanay insisted.

David shrugged. "I guess so. I had some peanuts and a chocolate bar."

"Come with me." She led the way across the clearing to a gray mound of ashes outside the end hut.

David, following her, noted there were several such ash mounds in the clearing. Some of them were smoking. Tskanay had chosen one that smoked. It had a charred log behind it and a pile of bark at one side.

As Tskanay walked, David noted the edges of her skirt were damp from dew. She had been out in the tall grass already this morning. The skirt showed dirt and stain marks all around the hem. She squatted by the ashes.

David asked: "What do I call you?"

"M—" She glanced at the hut where Katsuk had gone. "Tskanay."

"It means Moon Water," David said. "I heard him."

She nodded, picked up small branches from a stack beneath the bark, scraped coals into view, and piled the branches over them.

David moved around the charred log. "Have you known Katsuk very long?"

"Since we were kids." She leaned close to the coals, blew them into life. Flame climbed through the piled branches. She put bark around the flame.

"Do you know him very well?" David asked.

"I thought I was going to marry him."

"Oh."

She went into the end hut, returned with two old enamel pots. Water sloshed in one of them. Huckleberry leaves floated on the water. The other contained a gray-blue mush.

"Salal berries, tule roots, and tiger-lily bulbs," she told him when David asked what was in the mush.

David squatted by the fire, enjoying its warmth.

Tskanay put both pots into the coals. She went into the hut, returned with an enamel plate and cup, a tinned spoon. She wiped them on her skirt, served up the mush and a steaming cup of huckleberry-leaf tea.

David sat on an end of the charred log to eat. Tskanay sat on the other end, watched him silently until he had finished. He found the mush sweet and filling. The tea was bitter but left his mouth feeling clean.

"You like that food?" Tskanay asked. She took the utensils from him.

"Yes."

"That's Indian food."

"Katsuk doesn't like you to say Indian."

"To hell with Katsuk! Has he hit you very much?"

"No. Are you going to marry him?"

"Nobody's going to marry him."

David nodded. Katsuk had gone into a world where people didn't marry.

Tskanay said: "He was never cruel before."

"I know."

"He calls you his Innocent. Are you?"

"What?"

"Innocent!"

David shrugged. This trend in the conversation embarrassed him.

"I'm not," she said. "I was his woman."

"Oh." David looked away toward the lake.

"You know why he named you Hoquat?" she asked.

"Because I'm white."

"How old are you?"

"Thirteen." David looked toward the big hut. "What happened to Katsuk?"

"He hates."

"I know, but why?"

"Probably because of his sister."

"His sister?"

"Yeah. She committed suicide."

David looked at Tskanay. "Why'd she do that?"

"A bunch of white guys caught her alone out on the Forks road and raped her."

David read the hidden enjoyment in Tskanay's recital, wondered at it. He asked: "Is that why Katsuk hates whites?"

"I guess so. You never raped anyone, huh?"

David blushed, felt anger at himself for this betrayal of his feelings. He turned away.

"You know what it means, though," Tskanay said.

"Sure." His voice sounded too gruff.

"You really are innocent!"

"Yes." Defiant.

"You never even feel under a girl's skirt?"

Again, David felt his cheeks flame hot.

Tskanay laughed.

David turned, glared at her. "He's going to kill me! You know that? Unless you people stop him!"

She nodded, face suddenly sober. "Why don't you run away?"

"Where would I go?"

She pointed toward the lake. "There's a creek goes out the other end of the lake. Follow it. Lots of game trails. You come to a river. Turn left, downstream. You come to a regular park trail and a bridge. Go over the bridge. Got a sign there. Trail goes to a campground. That's where we left our cars."

Cars! David thought. The image of a car represented safety to him, release from this terrifying bondage.

"How far?"

She considered, then: "Maybe twenty miles. Took us two days coming in."

"Where would I rest? What would I eat?"

"If you hold to the north side of the river, you'll find an abandoned park shelter. Ish and some of his friends buried a steel drum in it. Got some blankets, beans, stuff to make fire. It's in the northeast corner of the shelter, I heard him say."

David stared out at the lake. *Shelter . . . blankets . . . bridge . . . cars . . .* He glanced at the hut where Katsuk had gone.

"He'll kill you if I escape."

"No, he won't."

"He might."

"He'll scream for his damned Raven!"

David thought: *He'll send his birds after me!*

"He won't hurt me," Tskanay said. "Don't you want to escape?"

"Sure."

137

"What're you waiting for?"

David got to his feet. "You're sure?"

"I'm sure."

David looked once more at the lake. He felt elation grow. *Follow the creek to the river. Go downstream to the park trail. Cross a bridge.*

Without a backward glance or thought for Tskanay, he strolled down to the lake, making it casual in case Katsuk was watching. At the lake, he found a flat stone. He skipped it into the reeds to make it appear he had just come down to the water to play. Another stone went into the reeds. It startled a drake from hiding. The duck went squawking out of the reeds, beating the water with its wings, settled at the far end of the lake. It shook its feathers, stretched.

David swallowed, forced himself not to look back at the camp. The drake had made a lot of noise and it had made him bird-conscious. Watching for ravens, he skirted the meadow, found a game trail with water running across a low spot. The wet grass around him was waist high. His knees and feet already were sopping. He hesitated at the edge of the trees. Once he entered the trees he was committed.

A raven called.

David whirled left, looked down the lake. A whole flock of ravens sat in a tall silver snag beside the lake. The trail would go directly under them!

He thought: *If I go close to them, they'll fly up. They'll make a big fuss and call Katsuk.*

Through the trees in front of him, he could see the hillside above the lake: no trail, a tangle of closely packed spruce and hemlock, roots, mossy logs.

Anything was preferable to the ravens.

David moved straight into the trees, up the hill. It was hard climbing—over logs, slipping on moss, falling between logs, getting himself caught on brush and broken limbs. He lost sight of the lake within two hundred steps. Once, he confronted a moss-topped stump with a grouse sitting atop it, blinking at him.

The bird twisted its head around to watch him pass.

Except for the constant sound of dripping, the forest felt silent to him. He thought: *When I get to the top of this hill, I'll turn left. That way, I'll come back to the lake or the creek.*

His feet hurt where the wet socks chafed them.

The hill was steeper now, trees smaller and thinner. There were blackberry vines to catch at his clothing. He came out into a small clearing with twisted black roots ahead of him. They snaked down over the foundations of a granite steeple—straight up! No way to climb it.

David sat down, panting. Roots and rock formed a cup, blocking his way to the left, but a narrow deer trail angled up to the right. He thought: *When I get to the top, then I can turn left.*

Taking a deep breath, he got up, climbed into the deer trail. Before he had climbed one hundred steps, he was confronted by a thick wall of brush. The wall ran up to his left toward the rock steeple, curved away from him on the downhill side. He tried to press into the brush, saw it was useless. Fur on a limb above the brush told him the deer had leaped this barrier.

Winded, frightened, he studied his surroundings. Downhill to the right was back to Katsuk . . . unless he crossed the valley above the Indian encampment. That way, he could go down the left side of the lake, away from the ravens. There was a trail there, too: He and Katsuk had come up that way.

Decision restored some of his hope. He angled downhill, trying to move with the caution he'd learned from watching Katsuk. It was no use: He continued to step on dead branches which broke with loud snappings; he continued to stumble through limbs and brush.

The trees were bigger now, more of them, more windfalls. He was thirsty and felt the beginning pangs of hunger.

Presently, he stumbled onto another deer trail. Within a few steps, it divided sharply. One arm went almost straight up the hill to his left, the other plunged steeply into green gloom.

David stared around him. He knew he was lost. If he went uphill, he felt sure he would come face to face with another part of that rock cliff. Downhill was the only way. He would find water to quench his thirst at least. He plunged into the green gloom. The trail switched back and forth, went almost straight down in places, avoided a tall curve of roots at the base of a fallen tree.

He went around the roots, found himself face to face with a black bear. The bear backed up, snorting. David leaped off the deer trail, downhill to his right, straight through brush and limbs, panic driving him in great, gulping strides. A low limb cut his forehead. He stumbled on a mossy log, fell hard into a narrow rivulet tinkling across black rocks. He got up, mud and water dripping from him, stared around. No sign of the bear. His chest and side ached where he had fallen.

He stood, listening, heard only wind in the trees, the sound of the tiny stream, his own gasping breaths. The sound of water recalled him to his thirst. He found a hollow in the rocks, stretched out and sank his face into the water to drink. His face dripped when he sat up, but he could find no dry part of his clothes to wipe away the water. He shook his head, scattering droplets.

There was a breeze blowing across the hillside. It chilled him. David felt his muscles trembling. He got up, followed the tiny stream downhill. It ran under logs, over shallows, dropped in miniature cataracts, growing larger and larger. Finally, it came out on flat, marshy ground, ran directly into a tangle of devil's club.

David stopped, looked at the sharp white spines of the thicket. No way to get through there. He looked to the right: That way must lead to the camp. He turned to the left, moved out across ground so spongy it sloshed and squirted with each step. The devil's club gave way to a stand of salal higher than his head. The ground became more solid.

A deer trail entered the salal. David stopped, examined his surroundings. He guessed he had been gone at least three hours. He was not even sure he still was in the valley of the lake. There was a trail. He peered into the dark hole through the salal. The ground was gray mud, pocked with deer tracks.

Fear crept through him. His teeth chattered with the cold.

Where did that trail go? Back to Katsuk?

The constant sound of water dripping from leaves wore on his nerves. His feet ached. He sensed the silent, fearful warfare of the plants and animals around him. His whole body shook with chill.

A distant cawing of ravens came to his ears. David turned his head, searching for the direction of the sound. It grew louder, a great clatter of wings and calling directly over him, hidden by the thick tree cover.

They could see him even through the trees!

In a panic even greater than when he had seen the bear, David sprinted into the salal, slipped, almost fell. He regained his balance, ran gasping and crying to himself through the heavy shadows. The trail twisted and turned. David skidded, burst from the thicket, desperate, incoherent, his mind filled with confusion, his body teetering.

Ish stood directly in front of him. The old man put out a hand to steady the boy.

"You lost, boy?"

David, his mouth open, panting, could only stare up at the wrinkled old face, the glittering birdlike eyes. There was a clearing behind Ish, a wide cirlce of trees all around. Sunlight poured into it. David blinked in the brightness.

Ish said: "Kind of figured you were lost when I heard you crashing down the hill a while back." He dropped his hand from David's shoulder, stepped back to get a full view. "You *are* a mess. Had you a time out there."

"I saw a bear," David managed. Even as he said it, he felt that was a stupid thing to say.

"Did you, now?" There was laughter in Ish's voice.

David blushed.

Ish said: "Came looking for you because of Tskanay."

"Did he hurt her?"

"Cast a spirit into her. Gave her a cramp and she fell down in a faint."

"He hit her!"

"Maybe so."

"I told her he would."

"You shouldn't run away, boy. Get yourself killed."

"What's the difference?"

Ish said: "Well, you had yourself a good walk. I'll show you the short way back to camp. Katsuk's expecting you." He turned, strode off across the clearing, a limping old man with the sun beating onto his gray head and shoulders.

David, too tired to cry, trailed after the old man like a puppy on a leash.

◻

FROM KATSUK'S "Red Power" letter to the United Indian Council:

You call yourselves Indians! Every time you do that you deny that you are People. Nehru was an Indian. Gandhi was an Indian. They knew what it was to be People. If you cannot listen to me, listen to Gandhi. He said: "Immediately the subject ceases to fear the despotic force, its power is gone." Do you hear that, you fearful subjects? Choose your own name!

◻

AN OLD woman stood just outside the curtained doorway of the big hut. She was talking to Katsuk as Ish and the boy entered the clearing. Ish held out a hand to stop the boy and they waited there just into the clearing.

"That's Cally, his aunt on his mother's side," Ish said.

She was a head shorter than Katsuk, heavy and solid in a black dress that stopped halfway between knees and ground. Low black socks and tennis shoes covered her feet. Her hair was shiny black streaked by gray, pulled tight and tied with a blue ribbon at the back. Below the ribbon, her hair sprayed out to her shoulder blades. She had a high forehead, cheeks that puffed out round and fat and dark. When she looked across the clearing at David, he saw remote brown eyes that told him nothing.

Cally motioned with her head for Ish to bring the boy closer. Katsuk turned at the gesture and a smile moved from his lips to his eyes.

"Come on, boy," Ish said. He led David to the pair at the doorway.

"You have a good walk, Hoquat?" Katsuk asked. And he thought: *It is true and real—the Innocent cannot escape me. Even when he runs away he is brought back.*

David looked at the ground. He felt miserable and lost.

There were other people around, squatting at the lake edge of the clearing, standing clustered in the door of another hut. David felt only a cold curiosity from them. He thought:

This can't be happening. These aren't wild Indians out of a history book. These people have gone to school and to church. They have cars. They have TV.

He felt his mind trying to draw points of similarity between himself and the people around him. It was a growing-up effort, a stretching of himself out of desperation. He focused on the tennis shoes that covered Cally's feet. Those shoes came from a store. She had been to a city and a store. Ish had a rifle. He wore clothes which came from a store...just like Cally's shoes did. They were people, not wild Indians.

And they were all afraid of Katsuk.

Katsuk glanced at the old woman, said: "Hoquat is tied to me, you understand? He cannot escape."

"You're talking crazy," she said, but there was no force in the words.

To David, Katsuk said: "This is Cally, my mother's sister. I don't expect you to understand that, Hoquat, but it is from my mother's people that I got my first power."

144

David thought: *He's talking to impress her, not me.*

David shot a penetrating glance at the old woman's face to gauge her reaction, found only a withdrawn measuring in remote brown eyes. With breath-choking realization, David saw that Cally was proud of Katsuk, proud of what Katsuk was doing, but had not admitted it to herself. She would never admit it.

Cally asked: "Are you all right, boy?"

David shrugged, still caught in realization of the power Katsuk held over this woman. She was proud. *What can I do?* David wondered. He blinked back tears. His shoulders sagged with despair. Only then did he realize how desperately he had hoped this woman would help him. He had thought a woman would have softness for a boy in trouble.

But she was proud . . . and afraid.

Cally put a hand on David's shoulder, said: "You got yourself all soaking and cut up out in that brush. Ought to get those clothes off you and dry them."

David peered up at her. Was she softening? No. She was only going through the motions. This would keep her from admitting how proud she was.

She glanced sideways at Katsuk, said: "What're you *really* going to do with him, son? Are you going to potlatch them?"

Katsuk frowned. "What?" He didn't like this tone in his aunt's voice. There was slyness in her now.

Cally said: "You tell me he's tied to you and you're the only one can cut him loose. Are you going to give him back to them?"

Katsuk shook his head, seeing his aunt's fear for the first time. What was she trying to do? She wasn't talking to Katsuk. She was trying to revive Charles Hobuhet! He put down a surge of rage, said: "Be quiet!" Even as he spoke, he knew it was pointless. He had brought this upon himself with his own thoughtless arrogance. He had said this was his aunt. Katsuk had no relatives. It was Charles Hobuhet who had been related to this woman.

"That'd be about the biggest gift anyone could give," Cally said. "They'd owe you."

Katsuk thought: *How sly she is. She appeals to the ancestors in me. Potlatch! But those aren't my ancestors. I belong to Soul Catcher.*

"What about it?" Cally demanded.

David tried to swallow in a dry throat. He sensed the struggle between Katsuk and this woman. But she wasn't trying to save a captive. What was she trying to do?

Katsuk said: "You want me to save my life by saving his."

It was an accusation.

David saw the truth in Katsuk's words. She was trying to save her nephew. She didn't care about any damned hoquat. David felt like kicking her. He hated her.

"Anything else doesn't make sense," Cally said.

David had heard enough. He screamed at her, fists clenched at his sides: "You can't save him! He's crazy!"

Unnervingly, Katsuk began to laugh.

Cally turned on the boy, said: "Be still!"

Katsuk said: "No, let him talk. Listen to my Innocent. He knows. You cannot save me." He stared across David's head at Ish. "Did you hear him, Ish? He knows me. He knows what I have done. He knows what i must do yet."

The old man nodded. "You've got a bloody look on you."

David felt himself frightened into stillness. His own actions terrified him. He had almost told about the hiker's murder. Katsuk had realized this. *"He knows what I have done."* Did all of these people know about the murder? Was that why they were afraid? No. They feared Katsuk's power from the spirit world. Even while some of them didn't admit it, that was what they feared.

Katsuk stared at Cally, asked: "How could we make the hoquat owe us more than they do already?"

David saw that she was angry now, fighting against the realization of her own pride. She said: "There's no sense crying over the past!"

"If we don't cry over it, who will?" Katsuk asked. He felt amusement at her weakness.

"The past is dead!" she said. "Let it be!"

"As long as I live it is not dead," Katsuk said. "I may live forever."

"That boy's right," she snapped. "You're crazy."

Katsuk grinned at her. "I don't deny it."

"You can't do this thing," she argued.

His voice low and reasonable, Katsuk asked: "What thing?"

"You know what I mean!"

Katsuk thought: *She knows and she cannot say it. Ahhh, poor Cally. Once our women were strong. Now they are weak.* He said:

"There is no human being who can stop me."

"We'll see about that," she said. Anger and frustration in every movement, she turned away, grabbed David's arm, hustled him down the line of huts to the end one. "Get in there," she ordered. "Take off your clothes and pass them out."

Katsuk called after her: "Indeed, we will see, Cally."

David said: "Why do you want my clothes?"

"I'm going to dry them. Get in there now. There're blankets in there. Wrap up in blankets until your things are dry."

The split plank door squeaked as David opened it. He wondered if Cally might yet try to save him—out of anger. There were no windows in the hut. Light came in the door. He stepped inside onto a dirt floor. The place smelled of fish oil and a wet mustiness that came from the fresh hide of a mountain lion pegged to the wall opposite the door. Thin strips of something dark hung from the rafters. There were a jumble of nets, burlap bags, rusty cans, and boxes on the dirt floor. A pole frame in one corner held a crumpled pile of brown-green blankets.

"Get a wiggle on," Cally said. "You'll catch your death in them wet clothes."

David shuddered. The hut repelled him. He wanted to run outside and beg the people there to save him. Instead, he stripped down to his shorts, passed the clothing out the door.

"Shorts, too," she said.

David wrapped up in one of the blankets, stripped off the shorts, and passed them out the door.

"These'll take a couple hours," she said. "Wrap up warm and get some rest." She closed the door.

David stood in the sudden darkness. Tears began running down his cheeks. All the alien strangeness of people and place weighed in upon him. The young woman had wanted him to escape. Old Cally seemed to want to help him. But none of them would really stand up to Katsuk. Katsuk's spirit was too powerful. David wiped his face on a corner of his blanket, stumbled through the confusion on the floor to the pole bed. Putting the blanket tightly around him, he sat down on the bed. It creaked.

As his eyes adjusted to the gloom, he saw that the door did not shut completely. There were cracks and holes all around to admit light. He heard people moving outside, low voices. At one point, there was a sound like young boys playing—the sound of a stick hitting a can.

Tears continued running down David's cheeks. He

stifled a sob. Anger at his own weakness overcame him. He thought: *I couldn't even escape!*

Katsuk had power over birds and people and his spirits all through the forest. There was no place to hide. Everything in the forest spied for crazy Katsuk! The people in this camp knew it and were afraid.

Now they held Katsuk's captive trapped without clothes.

David smelled smoke, meat cooking. There came a shout of laughter outside, quickly silenced. He heard wind in the trees, people moving about, low conversations with the words unintelligible. The blanket around him smelled of old perspiration. It was rough against his skin. Tears of despair ran down his cheeks. The sounds of activity outside gradually diminished. There came longer and longer silent periods. What wre they doing out there? Where was Katsuk? He heard footsteps approaching his hut. The door squeaked open. Tskanay entered with a chipped bowl in one hand. There was an angry furtiveness about her movements.

As the door opened wide and she stepped inside, the light revealed a blue bruise down her left jaw. She closed the door, sat down beside him on the pole bed, and offered the bowl.

"What's that?"

"It's smoked trout. Very good. Eat it."

David took the bowl. It was smooth and cold against his fingers. He stared at her bruised jaw. Light coming through the cracks in the wall drew stripes down across the mark on her skin. She appeared restless and uncomfortable.

David said: "He hit you, didn't he?"

"I fell down. Eat the trout." There was anger in her voice.

David turned his attention to the fish. It was hard and chewy with a light and oily fish flavor. At the first bite, he felt hunger knot his stomach. He ate a whole trout before speaking, then: "Where're my clothes?"

"Cally's drying them in the big house. Be another hour at least. Charlie and Ish and some of the others have gone out hunting."

David heard her words and wondered at them. She seemed to be saying one thing but trying to tell him something else. He said: "He doesn't like you calling him Charlie. Is that why he hit you?"

"Katsuk," she muttered. "Big deal." She looked toward the door as she spoke.

David ate another of the trout, licked his fingers. She was acting uncomfortable, shifting on the pole bed, picking at the blankets beneath them. He said:

"Why're you all afraid of him?"

"I'll show him," she whispered.

"What?"

Without answering, she took the bowl from David's hands, tossed it aside. He heard the clatter of it in the shadowy center of the hut.

"Why'd you do that?"

"I'm going to show that *Katsuk!*" She made the name sound like a curse.

David felt a surge of hope, quickly extinguished. What could Tskanay do? He said:

"None of you are going to help me. He's crazy and you're afraid of him."

"Crazy wild," she said. "He wants to be alone. He wants death. That's crazy. I want to be with someone. I want life. That's not crazy. I never thought he'd be a stick Indian."

"Katsuk doesn't like you to call him Indian."

She shook her head, setting the string-tied braids in motion. "Fuck Katsuk!" It was low and bitter.

David sat in shocked silence. He'd never heard an adult say that openly before. Some of his more daring friends said it, but never anyone such as this young woman. She was at least twenty years old.

"Shocks you, huh?" she asked. "You're an innocent, all right. You know what it means, though, or it wouldn't shock you."

David cleared his throat.

Tskanay said: "Big mean, crazy Indian thinks he has an innocent, huh! Okay. We'll show him." She got up, went to the door, closed it.

David heard her moving, the slither of clothing. He whispered: "What're you doing?"

She answered by sitting down beside him, finding his left hand and pressing it against her bare breast.

David hissed in surprise. She was naked! As his eyes adjusted to the gloom, he could see her beside him.

"We're going to play a game," she said. "Men and women play this game all the time. It's fun." She slid a hand beneath his blanket, caressing, touched his penis. "You got hair. You're man enough for this game."

David tried to push her hand away. "Don't."

"Why not?" She kissed his ear.

"Because."

"Don't you want to get away from Charlie-Katsuk?"

"Sure." Her skin was soft and exciting. He felt a strange eagerness in his loins, a hardness. He wanted to stop her and he did not want to stop her.

"He wants you innocent," she whispered. She was breathing fast now.

"Will he let me go?" David whispered. There was an odd milky smell about her that sent his pulse racing.

"You heard him." She guided his left hand, pressed it into the tangle of hair between her legs. "Doesn't that feel good?"

"Yes. But how do you know he'll. . . ."

"He said he wants you innocent."

Frightened and fascinated, David allowed her to

pull him down onto the pole bed. It creaked and stretched. Eagerly now, he did what she told him to do. They were showing that Katsuk! Crazy damned Katsuk.

"Right there," she whispered. "There! Ahhhhh. . . ." Then: "You've got a good one. You're good. Not so fast. There . . . that's right . . . that's right . . . ahhhh. . . ."

It seemed to David much later. Tskanay rubbed him down with a blanket while he stretched out, tingling and excited, but calm and relaxed, too. He thought: *I did it!* He felt alive, in direct contact with every moment. *Pretty Tskanay.* He reached up boldly, touched her left breast.

"You liked that," she said. "I told you it was fun." She stroked his cheek. "You're a man now, not a little innocent Katsuk can push around."

At the sound of Katsuk's name, David felt his stomach tighten. He whispered: "How will Katsuk know?"

She giggled. "He'll know."

"He's got a knife," David said.

She stretched out beside him, caressed his chest. "So what?"

David thought about the murdered hiker. He pushed her hand away, sat up. "He's crazy, you know." And he wondered if he could tell Tskanay about the murder.

She spoke languidly: "I can hardly wait to see his face when he—"

The door banged open, cutting her off and bringing a gasp from David.

Katsuk stepped inside, his face in black shadows from the back lighting. He carried David's shoes and clothing in a bundle. As the light from the doorway revealed the two naked figures on the pole bed, Katsuk stopped.

Tskanay began to laugh, then: "Hey, Charlie-boy! He's not your little innocent anymore! How about that?"

Katsuk stared at them, consternation tightening his throat. His hands went to the knife at his waist and he almost drew it. Almost. But the wisdom of Soul Catcher whispered to him and he saw the trickery in her woman power. She wanted the knife! She wanted death and the end of him by that death. She wanted the ancient ritual defeated. Ahhhh, the slyness of her. He threw the clothing at David, took one step forward, his face still in shadows and unreadable.

"You going to kill us, Charlie-boy?" she asked.

David sat frozen with terror. He expected the knife. It was the logical thing to happen—the *right* thing. His chest ached. His body felt even more exposed than its nakedness of flesh. There was no way to prevent the knife.

Katsuk said: "Don't think you will steal my spirit *that* way, Tskanay."

"But he's not your innocent little hoquat anymore." She sounded puzzled. Katsuk wasn't reacting the way she had expected. She wasn't sure precisely what she had expected, but certainly not this quietness. He should be raging and violent.

Katsuk glanced at the terrified boy. *Innocent?* Could sex make the difference? No. The quality of innocence was something else. It was tangled with intent and sensitivity. Was there selfishness in this hoquat? Was he indifferent to the fate of others? Was he capable of self sacrifice?

"Are you sure he's not innocent?" Katsuk asked.

She slid off the pole bed, stood up, angrily defiant in her nakedness, taunting him with it. "I'm damned sure!"

"I am not," Katsuk said.

"You want another performance for proof?" she demanded.

Slowly, David got his knees beneath him on the bed. He sensed that Katsuk was not completely in this room, that the man listened to voices from another world. Tskanay still could not see this. Katsuk was obeying his spirits or he would have struck out with the knife. He might hit Tskanay again if she continued to taunt him, but he wouldn't use the knife.

David said: "Katsuk, don't hurt her. She was only trying to help me."

"You see," Katsuk said. "You tried to use him against me, Tskanay, and still he doesn't want you hurt. Is that not innocence?"

"He's not!" she raged. "Damn you, he's not!"

David said: "Katsuk, she doesn't understand."

His voice oddly soft, Katsuk said: "I know, Hoquat. Get dressed now. There is your clothing all dry and clean and mended by Cally."

Tskanay whispered: "He's not, I tell you. He's not."

"But he is," Katsuk said.

David touched the clothing Katsuk had thrown onto the bed. Why couldn't Tskanay shut up? It was a stupid argument. He felt defiled, tied to Katsuk even more strongly than before. She hadn't been trying to help. She'd been trying to get back at Katsuk, but she couldn't reach that part of him in the spirit world.

Tskanay stood trembling now, her fists clenched, her face immobile. Her whole body spoke of failure. She had tied herself to something lost in this place and would carry the mark of it for the rest of her life and she knew it.

Katsuk said: "Hoquat, we are truly bound together now. Perhaps we are brothers. But which of us is Cain and which Abel?" He turned away, went out, leaving the door open.

In the clearing, Katsuk stood a moment thinking. *Innocence is not taken by being used.*

He looked at his right hand, the hand that had struck Tskanay earlier in anger. *It was wrong to strike her. There was a small bit of Charles Hobuhet remaining in me. That's who struck her. Now she has cleansed me of that. It was a hoquat thing to strike her. She has cleansed that away, too, and proved the innocence of my chosen victim. I am Katsuk who can smile at what she did and appreciate its value to me.*

In the hut, Tskanay said: "Damn him! Damn him! Damn him!" She was crying.

David put a hand on her calf, said: "Don't cry."

She put her hands to her face, sobbing harder.

David pleaded: "Please don't cry, Tskanay."

She jerked away, dropped her hands. "My name is Mary!"

Still crying, she found her clothes, pulled them on, not bothering to straighten the garments. She went to the door and, without looking back, said: "Well, you heard him. Get dressed!"

❏

HARLOW B. WATTS, teacher at Pacific Day School, Carmel, California:

Yes, David is one of my students. I'm very shocked by all this. He's a very good student, considerably ahead of most in his form. We use the British system here, you know. David is very sensitive the way he studies things. His reports and other papers often reveal this. He sometimes says odd things. He once remarked that Robert Kennedy had tried too hard to be a hero. When I questioned David about this, he would only say: "Well, look, he didn't make any mistakes." Don't you think that's an odd thing for a boy to say?

❑

IN THE afternoon, the sky darkened with a heavy overcast. A cold, raw wind began blowing from the southwest. It chilled David where he stood at the lake margin below the huts. He rattled the six pebbles in his pocket. Six days!

Most of the people in the camp, more than twenty of them, had gone into the big hut and built a fire there. They had two haunches of elk turning on a spit over the fire.

David felt that everyone in the camp must know what he and Tskanay had done. His cheeks felt hot every time he thought about it.

Two youths squatted at the timber's edge watching him unobtrusively. Tskanay was no longer his guard. He had not seen her since she had left the little hut. The two youths were his guards now. David had tried to talk to them. They had refused, turned away when he insisted. He heard them talking in low voices.

Barren frustration permeated him. Again, he thought of Tskanay. She had not changed a thing. Even worse, she had bound him tighter to Katsuk.

"Perhaps we are brothers now."

Katsuk had said that.

By forgiving, by denying anger, Katsuk had put a new burden on his captive. A link had been forged between them.

David tried to imagine Katsuk and Tskanay making love. It had happened. Tskanay admitted it. Katsuk as much as admitted it. David could not imagine them doing it. They had been two other people then—Mary and Charlie.

It was growing darker. Sunset conjured a bloody lake at the edge of the forest's green darkness. The wind was blowing hard up on the ridges, sweeping the clouds away. The moon emerged and David saw it as Katsuk would: the moon eaten, a curve of it gnawed out by Beaver. The moon was in the lake, too. He watched it there as it drifted against the reeds and was gone. But the reeds remained.

One of the youths behind him coughed. Why wouldn't they talk to him? David wondered. Was it Katsuk's command?

He heard distant aircraft engines. An airplane's green wing light moved off to the north. The engines flowed with the light, a cold, far sound in the sky. Sound and light gathered up David's hopes, bore them away. He chewed his lower lip. He could feel himself falling into emptiness, the whole sky opening to take him. That plane, the warmth, the light, the people—all vanished into another dimension.

Katsuk was speaking in the big hut, his voice rising and falling. The curtain had been thrown back. Light spilled into the clearing. David turned away from the lake, went toward the firelight. He passed the two youths in the dark, but they gave no indication of noticing him. David squatted just outside the range of the firelight, listened.

Katsuk, his powerful body clad in the loincloth and

moccasins, wore the red cedar band around his head, a single raven feather stuck into the band at the back. He stood with his back to the open door. The fire drew glowing outlines of his movements, his skin now amber, now bloody.

"Have I found this innocent in my belly like a woman?" Katsuk demanded. "Look you! I am Katsuk. I am the center, yet I live everywhere. I can wear the chief beads. What do you fear? The hoquat? They did not conquer us. Gun, steel, knife, hatchet, needle, wheel—these conquered us. Look you! I wear the chilkat cloth and moccasins made by a woman of our people."

He turned slowly, staring at each face in turn.

"I can see in your faces that you believe me. Your belief strengthens me, but that is not enough. We were the Hoh people. What are we now? Does any among you call himself a Christian man and sneer at me?"

His voice grew louder: "We lived on this coast more than fifteen thousand years! Then the hoquat came. Our cedar plank houses are almost gone from this land. We hide a few pitiful huts in this forest! Our salmon rivers are dying. I must tell you these things mostly in English because all of you do not speak our tongue."

He turned, stared out into the dark, whirled back.

"Ours is a beautiful tongue! English is simple beside it. Things have reality in our tongue! I go from one condition to another in my tongue and feel each condition. In English, I feel very little."

He fell silent, stared into the fire.

A woman shifted closer to the fire at the right and David thought at first it was Tskanay, youth and grace in her movements. But she turned, the light flaring briefly, and he saw it was the old aunt, Cally. Her face was a gaunt mask. The illusion shook him.

Katsuk said: "Look you at the preparations you

made for me. You brought body paints and a Soul Catcher rattle. Why do these things unless to honor me?"

He touched the knife at his waist. "I am Drukwara. I make war all around the world. I have only two dances. One of them is Bee."

Someone in the circle around the fire coughed.

Cally said: "Ish, answer him. A man must answer him."

Ish stood up directly across the fire from Katsuk. The old man's gangling frame appeared taller in the low light. His eyes reflected firelight.

He said: "You talk of old times, but these are not old times." Diffident voice, fear in it.

Katsuk said: "You mean we no longer bang a log drum until moonrise." He pointed to the ground beside Ish. "But you bring a flute and that wood rattle dressed with eagle feathers. Why?"

"Some of the old ways work," Ish said. "But those tribes were wild."

"Wild?" Katsuk shook his head. "They had their loyalties. Their world had shape. They worked it so."

"But they were wild."

"That is a hoquat word! Our woods, our animals, our people had loyalties and shape!"

"Shape," Ish said, shaking his head.

Katsuk said: "You came up the Hoh road. In cars, by damn! You parked your cars beside those of the hoquat and walked in here. You saw the signs of the new shapes: WATCH FOR TRUCKS. RANGE AREA—WATCH FOR LIVESTOCK. Whose trucks? Whose livestock? We drive their trucks to help destroy our land! That shingle mill down there at tidewater where they let you work . . . sometimes! That's the shape now!"

Ish said: "That what you learned at the university?"

"You're more right than you imagine, uncle. I am

the last chosen of my mother's clan. Once we were strong and could withstand any strain. We supported our people in their troubles. Now...."

"Now, you bring trouble on all of us," Ish said.

"Do I? Or do we merely live in hoquat trouble we have come to accept?" Katsuk pointed to the west. "The dragways of our whaling canoes, dug deep for those thousands of years, line the beaches down there. Yet we must petition a hoquat congress to tell us we can use one little piece of that land! Our land!"

"If you're talking about the old village at the beach," Ish said, "we'll get it back. The whites are beginning to understand our problems. They have—"

"Pity!" Katsuk shouted. "They throw us a bone out of pity—a tiny corner of all this that once was ours. We don't need their pity! They deprive us of the experience and responsibility of being human!"

Ish said: "Who cares why the whites do what we—"

"I care!" Katsuk touched his chest. "They come into our land—*our* land! They cut the underbrush to decorate their flower arrangements. They pile the logs high that should be left as trees. They take fish for sport that should feed our families. All the while, these hoquat do the one thing we must not forgive: They remain complacent in their evil. They are so satisfied that they are doing right. Damn these fiends!"

"Some of them were born here," Ish protested. "They love this land."

"Ahhhh," Katsuk sighed. "They love our land even while they kill it and us upon the land."

Guilt filled David. He thought: *I am Hoquat.*

His people had stolen this land. He knew Katsuk was speaking the truth.

We stole his land.

That was why the two youths set to guard him wouldn't speak to him. That was why the room full of pcople around Katsuk showed their sympathy with him even while they voiced fears and objections.

David felt himself hostage for all the sins of his kind. He had even sinned as his ancestors had, with a woman of these people. Thought of Tskanay weighted him down. He felt shattered, broken by the ruin of a life that once had seemed sweet and constant. He stared into the hut: ruddy shadows on rafters there, firelight in the crossbeams...all the people—honey-red skin, the sleek black hair, the gray hair, the old and tangled hair. He suddenly saw Tskanay almost directly behind Ish in the third row: round face, a purple blouse, fawn red of her skin in the firelight. David swallowed convulsively, remembering the slither of her clothing in the dark hut, the tangle of shadows.

Katsuk said: "You will not stop me. No one will stop me."

Cally stood up. She moved with slow stiffness now. She faced Katsuk. "We won't stop you. That's true. But if you kill that boy, you'll be like the worst of them. I won't want to live with that in my family." She turned away, walked into the shadows.

Ish said: "What's past is past." He sat down.

Katsuk straightened, glanced left and right. He did not appear to be looking at his audience but to be showing them his face.

He said: "All the past is in my words. If those words die, you will have forgotten the moaning and misery in our houses. You will forget what the hoquat did to us. You will forget what we were. But I will not forget. This is all I must say."

He turned, strode out of the house.

Before David could move, Katsuk was upon him. Katsuk grabbed the boy's arm, dragged him along. "Come, Hoquat. We go now."

❏

SHERIFF MIKE PALLATT:

Sure I think old Cally has seen her nephew. Why else would she come in with all that warning stuff? She and her gang were in the Wilderness Area. That's where I'm concentrating my men. I listened to her real good. Got a head on her shoulders, that old woman. She says we should call him Katsuk, we call him Katsuk. There's no more Charlie Hobuhet. Somebody calls him Charlie at the wrong moment, that could blow the whole show.

❏

IT BEGAN to rain intermittently soon after they left the clearing of the huts: rain, then moonlight, rain, moon. It was raining steadily and hard before they reached the old mine shaft. There was distant lightning and thunder. David, allowing himself to be dragged along in the darkness, wondered if Katsuk was creating the trail one step at a time out of his magic. Katsuk could not possibly see his way in the wet blackness.

All the way up the hill, Katsuk chanted and raged.

David, his heart palpitating, heard the word-ravenings and understood only the rage. Wet branches clawed at him. He tripped on roots, slipped in mud. He was drenched by the time they reached the shaft.

Katsuk's mind was in turmoil. He thought: *It was the truth. They know I told them truth. Still they fear. They do not give me all their thoughts. My own people are lost to me. They do not want the powers I could give them. My own people!*

He pulled Hoquat into the shelter of the mine shaft, released him. Water ran from them. Katsuk pressed his hands against the chilkat loincloth. Rivulets ran down his legs. He thought: *We must rest, then go on. Some of my people are fools. They could tell the hoquat where I am. There must be a reward. Some have the hoquat sickness. They could do it for money. My own people deny me a home in their thoughts. There is no home. My own people turn away. No one will come to meet me. I am truly homeless.*

How could he rest here? Katsuk wondered. He could feel his own people down there by the lake—restless, disturbed, divided, arguing. They had heard his words nad felt his meaning, but all in a language which blasphemed what he held scared.

No darkness will ever rest me. I will be a ghost spirit. Not even Tskanay supports me.

He thought of how Tskanay had looked at him. Her eyes had seen him and found him alien. She had given her body to the boy, trying to swallow innocence. She had thought to make Hoquat unfit. She had failed. Hoquat's shame reinforced his innocence. He was more innocent now.

Katsuk stared into the black emptiness of the old mine shaft. He sensed the dimensions of it with his memory, with his skin, his nose, his ears. There were ghost spirits here, too. The boy's teeth chattered. Hoquat's fear could almost be touched.

The boy whispered: "Katsuk?"

"Yes."

"Where are we?"

"In the cave."

"The old mine?"

"Yes."

"Are y-you g-going t-to b-build a f-f-fire?"

Lightning gave a brief flicker of illumination: the cave mouth, dripping trees, rain slanting down. Thunder followed, close, a crash that made the boy gasp.

Katsuk said: "Perhaps we have too much fire."

The world suddenly was shattered by a barren plume of lightning so close they smelled the hell fragrance of it as the thunder shook them.

The boy whirled, clung to Katsuk's arm.

Again, lightning flickered against wet blackness, this time near the lake. The thunderclap came like an echo of the one before it.

The boy trembled and shook against Katsuk.

"That was Kwahoutze," Katsuk said. "That was the god in water, the spirit of all the regions brought together by water."

"It was s-so close."

"He tells us this is still his land."

Again, the lightning flashed—beyond the lake now. Thunder followed, rumbling.

The boy said: "I don't want to steal your land."

Katsuk patted his shoulder. "And *I* was going to over-proud my enemies. This land does not know who owns it."

David said: "I'm sorry we stole your land."

"I know, Hoquat. You are truly innocent. You are one of the few who feel why this land is sacred to me. You are the immigrant invader. You have not learned how to worship this land. It is my land because I worship it. The spirits know, but the land does not know."

Silence fell between them. Katsuk freed himself

from the boy's grip, thinking: *Hoquat depends upon me for his strength, but that can be dangerous for me. If he takes strength from me, I must take strength from him. We could become one person, both of us Soul Catcher. Who could I sacrifice then?*

David listened to the sound of falling rain, the distant progression of lightning and thunder. Presently, he said: "Katsuk?"

"Yes."

"Are you going to kill me... like your aunt said?"

"I use you to send a message."

David chewed his lower lip. "But your aunt said...."

"Unless you tell me to do it, I will not kill you."

Relief flooded through David. He drew a deep breath. "But I'd never tell you to—"

"Hoquat! Why do you prefer mouth-talk to body-talk?"

Katsuk moved into the shaft.

Rebuked, David stood trembling. The old madness had returned to Katsuk's voice.

Katsuk found the pack by smelling the mustiness of it. He squatted, felt the fabric, removed matches, a packet of tinder. Presently, he had a small fire going. Smoke drifted in a gray line along the ceiling. The flame cast raw shadows on old beams and rock.

David approached, stood close to the fire, trembling, holding his hands out to the warmth.

Katsuk gathered the cedar boughs of their bed, spread the sleeping bag. He stretched out on the bag with his back against a rotting beam.

The boy stood with his head just beneath the smoke. The gray line above him was like a spirit essence drifting toward the dark entrance into the world.

Katsuk withdrew the willow flute from his waistband, touched it to his lips. He blew softly. The clear sound circled upward into the smoke, carrying his mind with it. He played the song of cedar, the song to placate cedar when they took bark for mats and clothing, for rope and net string. He blew the song softly. It was a bird singing deep in the shade of cedar boughs.

Sweetly on the song, he sensed a vision: Janiktaht carrying a basket piled with curling shreds of cedar bark. And he thought: *This is better for Janiktaht. I should not be forever seeking her face among the faces of strangers.*

The words of the song echoed in his mind: "Life maker cedar...fire maker cedar...."

The vision of Janiktaht moved within him. She grew larger, larger, older, uglier. The basket of cedar bark shriveled.

Sweat broke out on his forehead. His mind stumbled. He dropped the flute.

David asked: "Why did you stop?"

Katsuk sat up, stared at the evil flute beside him. He shook his head. The movement was like wind swaying cedar boughs. The cedar band around his head pressed into his skull. He knew it might crush his head. He could not remove the band.

"Keep that sickness away from me," he muttered.

"What?"

"I don't want to be killed by that sickness."

"What's wrong?"

Katsuk glared across the fire at the boy. "What has made me so unlucky?"

"Are you unlucky?" David didn't understand the conversation but felt his participation being demanded.

"I am overcome by it," Katsuk said. "I have been found by Short-Life-Maker."

"Katsuk, you're talking awfully funny."

"Evil words have been sent against me!"

"What words?"

"I have enemies. They have cursed me. They wish me to die quickly. My own people! They have no mercy."

David moved around the fire, squatted beside the sleeping bag. He touched Katsuk's flute. "I liked the music. Will you play some more?"

"No!"

"Why?"

"Because I have discovered my omen tree."

The boy stared at him, puzzled.

Katsuk closed his eyes. He pictured a cedar, a great cedar with bulging roots, glossy needles, a cedar deep in the forest, sucking at the earth's belly and piling its boughs high, a skirt of long boughs at the bottom that leaned outward into a thick bed of leaf mold.

"My omen tree," Katsuk whispered.

"What's an omen tree?" David asked.

Katsuk said: "I was my mother's firstborn." He opened his eyes, stared upward into the ruddy smoke. "Her brother carved a little canoe for me. He made a tiny fish spear. He made a rattle box. He made all of these things from cedar."

"That makes an omen tree?"

Katsuk spoke in a distant voice: "My parents were in a cedar canoe when they died. Janiktaht stole a cedar canoe when she. ... The splinter! I was very sick that time with the splinter in my knee. They said I could lose the leg. It was a cedar splinter. All this is very clear, Hoquat. Someone in my family has offended cedar. That is the end of me, then."

"Do you really believe that stuff?"

"Don't tell me what I believe!" He glared at the boy. David recoiled. "But. ..."

"We have burned cedar, carved her. We have made

167

rafts of cedar, kindling wood, long planks, and shakes to keep off the rain. But we did not show how thankful we were to her. Cedar's heart aches. We have stepped on her roots, bruised them, and never thought about it. I rest on cedar right now! How stupid!"

He leaped off the sleeping bag, jerked it aside, began gathering up the boughs. He carried them outside, stacked them in the rain. His skin glistened with water when he returned. He squatted, gathered the fallen needles, sweeping them together, searching out every one. When he had them all, he took them out into the rain, scattered them.

"Cedar!" he shouted. "I give you back what I took! I beg forgiveness! I ask my spirits to give you this message. I did not mean to harm you. Cedar, forgive me!"

David squatted by the fire, watched wide-eyed. Katsuk was insane!

Katsuk returned to the fire, put a damp spruce limb into the flame. "See," he said, "I do not burn cedar."

David stood, pressed his back against the rock wall.

Katsuk nodded his head to the flames. Falsetto whines came out of his throat, monotone grunts.

David said: "Are you praying?"

"I need a language to explain how I feel. I need a language that has never been heard before. Cedar must hear me and know my prayer."

David listened for words, heard none. The sounds were hypnotic. He felt his eyelids drooping. Presently, he went to the sleeping bag, wrapped himself in it, stretched out on the hard ground.

Katsuk went on with his odd noises, groaning, whining. Even after the fire had reduced itself to a glowing, orange eye, the sound went on and on and on. The boy heard it occasionally as he half awoke from sleep.

❏

FROM A note left by Katsuk in the abandoned shelter at Sam's River:

Hoquat is an innocent without father and mother. He says his father will pay me. But how can people who do not exist make payment? Besides, I do not ask ransom. I have the advantage over you. I understand your economics. You do not understand mine. My system goes by vanity, prestige, and ridicule, the same as the hoquat. But I see the vanity. I see the prestige. I see the ridicule. This is how my people made potlatch. The hoquat do not have potlatch. I know the names and shapes of everything I do. I understand the spirit powers and how they work. That is the way it is.

❏

THE FIRST thing David saw when he awoke was thin pillars of rain slanting across the mine entrance. The world outside was full of dawn's broken light, misty gray-white. Katsuk was nowhere to be seen, but ravens clamored somewhere outside.

David trembled at the sound.

He slid out of the sleeping bag, stood up. It was cold. Moisture filled the air. He went to the mouth of the shaft, stared around him, shivering.

The rain slackened.

David turned, peered into the shaft. Not likely Katsuk had gone back deeper into there. Where was he?

The ravens called from the trees down by the lake. Mist hid them. David felt hunger grip his stomach. He coughed.

The wind remained strong. It blew from the west, pushing clouds against the peaks beyond the lake valley. Branches whipped in the wind atop the ridge, chopped the light.

Should I go down to the huts? David wondered.

He could see the game trail they had climbed in the night. The rain stopped, but water dripped from every leaf he could see.

David thought of the huts, the people. They had allowed Katsuk to take his captive away. They wouldn't help. Cally had said as much.

He heard splashing on the game trail, grunting.

Katsuk climbed into view. He wore a loincloth and moccasins. The sheathed knife flopped against his side with every step. His body glistened with wetness, but he seemed unaware of water or cold. He climbed onto the ledge at the mouth of the mine and David saw that he carried a package. It was wrapped in dirty cloth.

Katsuk thrust the pakcage toward the boy, said: "Smoked fish. Cally sent it."

David took the package, opened it with cold-stiffened fingers. The fish was bright red, oily, and hard. He broke off a piece, chewed. It tasted salty and sweet. He swallowed and immediately felt better.

He took another mouthful of fish, spoke around it: "You went down to see your friends?"

"Friends," Katsuk said, his voice flat. He wondered if a shaman ever had friends. Probably not. You went outside human associations when you gained spirit powers. Presently, he glanced at the boy, said: "You didn't try to escape again."

"I thought about it." Defiant.

"Why didn't you try?"

"I heard the ravens."

Katsuk nodded. It was logical. He said: "That lightning last night—it hit the big spruce beside the house where my *friends* were talking. They were arguing whether to turn me over to the hoquat police when pieces of the tree smashed through the roof." He smiled without mirth.

David swallowed a bite of fish. "Was anybody hurt?"

"A fish rack fell on Tskanay. It bruised her arm. Ish was burned. He tried to jump across the fire. They were not hurt much, but they no longer discuss what to do with me."

David chewed silently, studying his captor, trying not to betray awe at this revelation. It was one more thing to confirm the powers Katsuk controlled. He could bring down the lightning.

Katsuk said: "They don't want me to send more lightning."

David sensed something cynical and doubting in Katsuk's tone, asked: "Did you make the lightning?"

"Maybe. I don't know. But that's what they think."

"What did you tell them?"

"I told them an owl's tongue will bring rain. I told them Raven can create fire. They know this, but they've been taught the hoquat ways of doubting their own past. Have you had enough of that fish?"

"Yes." David nodded numbly. To have lightning silence those who could harm you! To know what would bring rain and fire! What powers those were.

Katsuk took the package of fish from the boy's hand, wrapped it tightly, thrust it into his pouch. He said: "Will you follow, or will you try to escape?"

David swallowed a lump in his throat. Escape? Where could he run that Katsuk's powers would not follow? But there had to be some way out of this nightmare. There must be some way to break free of Katsuk.

"Answer me," Katsuk ordered.

David thought: *He'll know if I try to lie to him.* He said: "If I find a way to get away from you, I will."

The honesty of innocence, Katsuk thought. Admiration for this hoquat youth rose in him. What a magnificent sacrifice Hoquat would make. Truly, this was the Great Innocent, one to answer for all of those the hoquat had slain.

Katsuk asked: "But will you follow me now?"

"I'll follow." Sullen. "Where're we going?"

"We will climb today. We will go over the mountain into another valley where there are no man trails."

"Why?"

"I am pulled in that direction."

"Shall I get the pack and the sleeping bag?"

"Leave them."

"But won't we. . . ."

"I said leave them!" There was wildness in his voice. David backed up into the mine.

Katsuk said: "I must discard hoquat things. Come."

He turned to his right, went up around the mine shaft on a deer trail. David darted into the open, followed.

Katsuk said: "Follow close. You will get wet. Never mind that. The climb will keep you warm."

They stayed on the deer trail until the sun began to break through the overcast. Tiny cones like deer droppings covered the trail. Ferns blanketed the ground on both sides. Moss obscured all the downed trees. The trail dipped and climbed. Water ran in the low spots.

As the sun came out, Katsuk took to the ferns and moss, climbing straight up a steep ridge side to another trail. He turned right on this and soon they encountered snow on the ground. It had collected along the hill margins of the trail but had melted away on the downhill side. They walked the thin strip of open ground. Urine-colored lichen poked through the snow in the thinner places.

Once, they heard an aircraft flying low under the broken clouds. It could not be seen through the heavy tree cover.

As they climbed, the trees began to thin. The deer track crossed a park trail with a signboard. The sign pointed left: KIMTA PEAK.

Katsuk turned right.

They began encountering long stretches of snow on the trail. There were old footprints in the snow. The flat inner surfaces of the prints had almost lost their foot shape. Rain pocked the prints. Some of them showed mud stains.

Once, Katsuk pointed to the prints, said: "They were going over Kimta Peak. It was last week."

David studied the tracks. He couldn't tell toe from heel. "How do you know?"

"Do you see how we leave mud in the snow? It is always after we cross open ground. They left mud on the downhill side. The tracks have melted for at least a week."

"Who was it, do you suppose?"

"Hoquat searching for us, perhaps."

David shivered as the wind gusted. The air carried the chill of snow and ice. Even the effort of keeping up with Katsuk failed to warm him. He wondered how Katsuk could endure it in only loincloth and moccasins. The moccasins were dark with water. The loincloth appeared soggy. David's tennis shoes sloshed with each step. His feet were numb with cold.

They came to another sign: THREE PRUNE SHELTER. It pointed downhill to the right.

Katsuk left the park trail there, took to a deer path that went straight up the hill. David was pressed to keep up.

Whenever he could see up through the trees, the sky showed blue patches. David prayed they would come out into warm sunshine. The backs of his hands were wet and cold. He tried to put them into his jacket pockets, but the jacket was soaking.

They came to a rocky ridgetop. Katsuk followed it, climbing toward a mountain which lifted itself against clouds directly ahead. Trees on both sides of the ridge were gnarled, stunted, wind-bent. Wrinkled patches of lichen marked the rocks.

Katsuk said: "We are near timberline. We will go down soon."

He spoke above the sound of water roaring in a deep gorge to the right. They came to an elk trail which angled down toward the sound. Katsuk scrambled down onto the elk trail. David followed, slipping, avoiding snow where he could. Katsuk was covering the ground in great long strides. David ran to catch up, almost overran Katsuk. An outthrust arm stopped him.

"Dangerous to run down such a hill," Katsuk said. "You could run right off a cliff."

David nodded, shivered. He felt the cold seep through him. It was that way every time they stopped. How could Katsuk stand it?

"Come," Katsuk said.

Again, they went down the trail. Presently, they came out on a granite ledge above the river. The roaring milky water below them filled the air with cold mist. Katsuk turned left, upstream. Soon, the stunted trees gave way to tiny clumps of huckleberry bushes.

They encountered smaller and smaller bushes until there were none. Lichen lay on the bare rocks. Tufts of greenery speared through snow patches. The river became narrower, gray rocks thrusting out of it. The sound of it was loud beside them. The water was gray-green with snowmelt, no more than six feet across. Patches of vapor drifted on its surface.

Katsuk came to the place he had been seeking—rocks like stepping stones across the river. Water piled high against the upstream sides of the rocks. He looked upstream. There was the ice wall from which this tumbling water flowed. He stared at the cold, dirty-white fountainhead of all that water. Ice . . . ice. . . .

The boy stood behind him, huddled up, shivering with the cold. Katsuk glanced at Hoquat a moment, then peered down to the right where the river plunged into the trees—far, far down there. The sun came through the clouds. He saw a deep pool in the river's middle distance: scintillant water, its current pulled taut against the deep unrest beneath. He felt the river ceaselessly churning in its depth. Who counted that water or cut it into bits? The water was bound together, one end connected to the other.

"Why're we waiting?" David asked.

Katsuk did not hear him. He thought: *All things start downstream from this place. Here is the beginning.*

There were river spirits here. The spirits permitted no leisure for this torrent of water or the torrent in his own breast. Each would run until it broke its energy into other forms. All was movement, energy, and currents—never ceasing.

He found a deep, calming, enjoyment in this thought. His mind had taken a leap, not asking why, but how?

How?

The spirits told him: "Never ceasing, one energy into another."

"Come," he said, and crossed the stream, jumping from rock to rock.

The boy followed.

❑

SHERIFF PALLATT:

Hell, I know the FBI thinks he's gone underground in some city. That's nuts! That twisty-minded, god-damned Indian's in there someplace. I'm sure he crossed the Hoh. I saw tracks. Could've been a man and a boy. Right up near the middle fork. How they got across there, though, with the river that high, I'll never know. Maybe he's a woods devil. I guess if you're crazy enough you do impossible things.

❑

A VINE maple shadow stretched out into the river below Katsuk. The maple leaves above his head shone as though polished. He squatted beside an old elk trail whose edges had tumbled into the water, stared at the tree shadow, thinking.

The boy lay stetched out, belly down, on a thin strip

of grass upstream. The grass blended gradually into a moss-covered ledge of rock which the elk trail skirted. The inevitable blade of grass protruded from the boy's mouth and he was picking red ants out of the grass, nipping off their heads, and eating them. He had told Katsuk he was going to try *not* thinking.

David thought: *That's a very strange thing. How do you get a nonthought into your head?*

Katsuk had started this queer train of thinking. He had accused the boy of thinking too much in words and had said this was a failing of all hoquat.

David glanced at Katsuk. The man obviously was thinking right now—squatting there, thinking. Did Katsuk use words?

They had spent most of a day coming down into the lowlands after crossing the high ridge and the river. There were seven pebbles in David's pocket—seven days, a week. They had spent the night in an abandoned park shelter. Katsuk had dug up a poacher's cache of blankets and tallow-dipped cans of food. He had built a small fire in the shelter and they had eaten beans and slept on spruce boughs over the ashes.

It had been a long hike from the shelter. David glanced up at the sun: early afternoon. Not too long, then. He hadn't really thought about the time.

The trail into the lowlands had followed a watercourse. It had plunged through salal thickets, forded the river, followed dry sloughs. Once, they had surprised a cow elk poking her nose from an alder copse. Her fur had glistened.

David gave up attempting to not-think. He began mouthing "David" silently to himself. He wanted to say his name aloud but knew this would only excite the craziness in Katsuk.

He thought: *I'm David, not Hoquat. I'm a hoquat,*

but my name is David, not Hoquat.

The thought rolled through his mind: *David-not-Hoquat, David-not-Hoquat. . . .*

The trail from the high ridge had crossed well-traveled park trails twice. One of the trails had carried a pattern of recent boot tracks in mud. Katsuk had avoided the mud, had taken them up a game trail that angled across an old burn. They had crossed another river beyond the burn and Katsuk had said there would be no more man trails now.

Katsuk seemed to go on and on without tiring. There was a nervous, sweaty energy in him even now as he squatted beside the river. He had brought the blankets from the poacher's cache, one of them rolled and tied at his waist, the other carried loose over his shoulders. He had discarded the blankets when he had squatted beside the river. His dark, flat-cheeked face remained immobile in thought. His eyes glistened.

David thought: *I am David-not-Hoquat.*

Was that another name? he wondered. Was it a halfway identity, David-not-quite-Hoquat? He recalled that his mother had called him Davey. His father had occasionally called him *Son*. Grandmother Morgenstern had called him David, though. Names were odd. How could he be Hoquat in his own mind?

He thought: *What's Katsuk thinking?*

Was it possible Katsuk knew how to not-think?

David raised himself on his elbows, pushed the chewed blade of grass from his mouth with his tongue, said: "Katsuk, what're you thinking?"

Without looking up from the river, Katsuk said: "I am thinking how to make a bow and arrow in the old way. Do not disturb my thinking."

"The old way? What's that?"

"Be still."

David heard the edge of insanity in Katsuk's voice, lapsed into sullen silence.

178

Katsuk studied the river, a milky-green surge. He noted the shadows on a tumbling twig.

An uprooted stump came twisting through the current which boiled under the vine maple shadow. The stump was an old one with dark, red-brown punk wood in the root end. It turned slowly, end over end, roots up like clutching hands, then falling over, sinking beneath the slick water, the cut end rising into the afternoon sunlight. Water drained from it and the whole cycle started once more as it passed.

The stump made a sound in its turning—*klug-slumk-hub-lub*.

Katsuk listened, wondering at the language of the stump. He felt the stump was talking to him, but it was no language he understood. What could it be saying? The cut end was gray with age. It was a hoquat scar. The stump did not seem to be talking about its own travail. It went downstream, turning and talking.

He felt the presence of the boy with disturbing intensity. That was flesh back there with all of its potential for good or evil...for both at once. Goodevil. Was there such a word?

Katsuk felt that he and the boy had fallen into a new relationship. Almost friendly. Was that Tskanay's doing? He felt no jealousy. Charles Hobuhet might have been jealous, but not Katsuk. Tskanay had given the boy a moment of life. He had lived; now he must die.

It was correct to feel friendship toward a victim. That subdued the enemy soul. But this new association went beyond such friendship.

How did we get into this new relationship?

It could change nothing, of course. The Innocent must ask for death and be killed.

Katsuk felt sadness twist in his breast. There could be no stopping this thing. There had been no stopping it from the beginning. It had come out of the ice. Bee's message had been cold. And Raven's. It must end with the Innocent slain.

The boy stood up, walked upstream off the grass, sat down with his back against the cathedral pillar of a rotten stump. He began searching for grubs in the rotten wood.

Katsuk refused to look at him.

Let Hoquat escape...if Raven would permit it.

The vine maple shadow lay black on the river. The water appeared calm on its surface, but Katsuk felt the wild power underneath. He felt himself being driven by such a power—Soul Catcher within. Soul Catcher moved like the water, deep and strong underneath.

Katsuk found one of the blankets beside him, wiped his eyes.

David cast an occasional sidelong glance at his captor. Why was Katsuk so changeable? The man hovered between friendliness and violence. One minute, he would explain a legend of his people. The next second, he could scream for silence. Katsuk had been very different since he had played the flute in the old mine shaft.

For the moment, the boy felt a strange happiness. He watched the river, the waning sun. He was aware of movements and patterns. For a time, he dozed. Katsuk would catch a fish soon and they would eat. Or Katsuk would find another poacher's cache, or make a bow and arrow and kill game. Katsuk had said he was thinking how to make a bow and arrow.

David's eyes snapped open. He felt no passage of time but knew he had slept. The sun had moved toward the horizon.

A long sandbar protruded into the current downstream. The river turned there in a wide arc against a thick stand of hemlocks. A matchstick pile of silver and gray logs lay stranded on the sand. The sun, about two log-widths above the hemlocks, colored the tops of the stranded logs yellow-orange.

The light and color reminded David of Carmel Valley and his home. He wondered what had brought that memory. He decided it was the heat waves dancing over the logs. This day had been so bone-cold when they had walked through the forest shadows, but the sun-warmed ground beneath him induced a comfortable drowsiness.

As they had come down from the high country, the land had grown increasingly wild and rugged. The steeper mountainsides and narrower canyons had given way to a broad valley thick with trees. Just before coming to this place, they had crossed a long, narrow benchland covered with stunted fir, pine, and spruce. An ancient storm had twisted the trees together, some fallen and dead, some leaning and still alive.

Katsuk continued to stare at the river.

David sighed, feeling hunger pangs. He searched for more grubs in the stump. They were juicy and sweet.

As he ate the grubs, he had a sudden vision of his mother delicately plucking hors d'oeuvres from a tray held by a maid. He imagined what his mother would say if she could see him now. She would be frantic and hysterical even when he told her about this. Her eyes would go wide. Gasps of shock would escape her. She would cry. David had no doubt these events would occur. Katsuk had promised: There would be no killing unless the victim asked for it.

David felt no special worry. It was a time for storing up memories. A wonderful curiosity drove him. This would end in time and he would have a glorious adventure to tell. He would be a hero to his friends— kidnapped by a wild Indian! Katsuk was wild, of course . . . and insane. But there were limits to his insanity.

The light on the stranded logs had become like sunshine on autumn grass. David watched Katsuk and the hypnotic flow of the river. He came to the decision this might be one of the happiest days of his life: Nothing was demanded of him; he had been cold, now he was warm; he had been hungry and had eaten. ...Soon, they would eat again.

A long orange-brown deerfly landed on his left wrist. He slapped it reflexively, wiped the dead insect from his hand on a clump of grass.

Katsuk began singing: low-voiced. It was a chant oddly in tune with the river and the golden sunlight. His voice rose and fell, full of clicks and coughing sounds.

The thought in Katsuk's mind was that he desperately needed a sign. He needed an omen to guide him from this place. Swaying, he chanted his prayer song, appealing to Bee and Raven, to Kwahoutze and Alkuntam. Soul Catcher stirred within him. Gusts of wind began to blow along the river—the wind that came before dark. Katsuk sensed a barrier, an obstruction to his prayer. Perhaps it was Hoquat blocking the way. Katsuk recalled Hoquat's dream. That was a powerful dream. The boy could have a wish—any wish. When he was ready. There was a powerful spirit waiting in that boy.

The wind chilled Katsuk's cheek.

A glacier filled the river source up there and the wind of evening blew down the valley toward the sea.

Katsuk sensed that he had left pursuit far behind in the upper reaches of the Wilderness Area. Not even a helicopter crossed the sky here, although earlier there had been a jet soundlessly drawing its white plume high over the peak that dominated the eastern skyline.

As he thought these things. Katsuk continued chanting. The memory of Hoquat's dream troubled him. It lay festering in his awareness. It was a thing which might defy Soul Catcher. How could the boy have dreamed a powerful spirit? He was a hoquat! But that was a warning dream, a thing to spread disquiet all around. And Hoquat appeared content. Had he wished the thing which would not be denied him?

Movement on the river stirred Katsuk from his reverie. A long, smooth limb, pearl gray, and glistening, drifted on the current. Katsuk's gaze followed the limb. It appeared to glide downstream independent of the current. It was headed with a sure inward direction toward the figure squatting beneath the vine maple. The limb pierced the vine maple's shadow like an arrow penetrating its target. The shadow moved along the length of the limb. Katsuk felt shadow darkness penetrating the wood.

He broke off his chant, breathed a long "Ahhhhhh."

The limb surged across a dark upswelling of current. It came directly at him. One end drove into the muddy embankment at Katsuk's feet. He knelt, lifted the limb from the water with a feeling of reverence. He sensed something powerful struggling in the wood.

Gently, he examined what the river had sent him. The wood felt smooth and vibrant beneath his fingers. Alive! Water dripped from it. One end had been burned, the other broken. The wood had not been long in the water. It was not soaked. Not a deformity or twisting of grain marked its smooth length—almost as long as he was tall. At its sthickest end, it was larger than his clenched fist. The tapering was almost indiscernible, less than a finger's width.

How supple and alive it felt!

Katsuk stood up, put one end on the ground, his hand in the center, and tried to flex it. He felt the wood fighting him. It quivered with hidden power. It was the wood of a god-bow!

The feeling of reverence strong in him, Katsuk lifted Hoquat's knife from its sheath to test the hardness of this wood. A large black bee darted across his line of vision—another, another.

He hesitated, the knife gripped tightly in his hand. Sweat broke out on his forehead.

Ahhhhhh, that had been close!

One touch of hoquat steel on this wood! Just one and the spirit power would leave it. His prayer had brought the wood of a god-bow and he had almost defiled it.

Katsuk's throat was dry from the nearness of that defilement. He returned the knife to its sheath, slipped the sheath from his waist, hurled the hated instrument into the river. Only when the blade had sunk beneath the current did he feel free from deadly peril.

How close that had been!

He glanced to where the boy sat, eyes closed, drowsing. The spirit had been strong in Hoquat, but not strong enough. That evil spirit with its subtle persuasions had almost tempted Katsuk into an act of defilement. Who knew where such an act could have led? It might even have given Hoquat the upper hand here. When two beings were bound together this way, captor and captive, the tie that bound them could be pulled in either direction.

Katsuk grasped the limb in both hands, held it high over his head. How beautiful it was! He sang the song of dedication. He dedicated it to Bee. Bee had sent this omen wood.

The whole course of what he must do came into his mind as he prayed. He must find obsidian and fashion a knife from it to work this omen wood into a bow. That was how it must be done: a bow fashioned in the ancient way, then an arrow tipped with the stone point from the ocean beach of his ancestors at Ozette. From ancient times to this time, it would all be connected.

Katsuk lowered the limb, relaxed.

He sensed his ancestors singing within him.

This is how the Innocent must die!

Carrying the omen wood reverently in his left hand, Katsuk went to where Hoquat lay asleep against the stump. The boy awoke when he felt Katsuk's shadow, stared up at his captor, smiled.

The smile heartened Katsuk. He returned it. Hoquat's dream spirit had been subdued.

The boy yawned, then: "What're you going to do with the stick? Are you going to fish?"

"This?" Katsuk lifted the limb. His whole arm throbbed with the power in the omen wood. "This was sent by my spirits. It will do a great thing."

❏

FROM A story in the Seattle *Post-Intelligencer:*

Sheriff Pallatt said he is concentrating his searchers in the virtually untracked Wilderness Area of the park (see map at right) and that he is instructing them to move with extreme caution. He said: "This is no ordinary kidnapping. This is a crime of revenge against the white race by an embittered young man who may be temporarily deranged. I am convinced Hobuhet knows what he is doing and is acting according to a plan. He's still in those mountains with that boy."

❏

KATSUK LAY stretched face down on a shale ledge, staring along his own arm immersed to the elbow in clear, cold river water. The omen wood for the bow was beside him. His hand in the water appeared wavery and distorted against the mossy rock. He could feel the pulse at his elbow. Intense awareness of the world around him permeated his being.

He saw two long gray logs high on the flood-scoured bar at the river bend across from him. Their shadows mingled in a staggering track across the bar, long, flat shadows in the low afternoon sun.

A scuffling sound behind him told Katsuk the boy had moved. Katsuk glanced back. Hoquat squatted beneath a big-leaf maple juggling his day-counting pebbles. There were eight pebbles now: eight days. A limb above the boy was strung with fuzzy moss, dirty green and straggling. It dangled above the blond head like wood on a sheep's belly. The boy was sucking on a grass stem.

Katsuk turned away, concentrated once more on his hand in the water.

The river was clear and deep here. He could see periwinkles on the bottom: irregular black marks against the varicolored rocks. For some time now, he had been observing the progress of a big fish as it worked its way along the mossy side of the ledge. It was a native whitefish—*kull t' kope*.

Katsuk mouthed its name under his breath, praying to the fish spirit and the water spirit.

Kull t'kope's tail wriggled spasmodically as it

186

concentrated on eating insects from the moss.

Katsuk felt the presence of the fish and the river all through him. The river was called Sour Water in his own tongue. A strange name, he thought. The water was sweet to the taste, clean, and with a musty edge of snow in it.

The chill water made his arm numb from the elbow down, but Katsuk remained motionless, waiting. He allowed his thoughts to contain only friendliness toward the fish. That was an old way, older than memory—from First Times. He had learned it as a boy from his Uncle Okhoots.

The fish encountered the barrier presence of Katsuk's arm, swam gently around it, nosed the moss beside it. Gently, slowly, Katsuk raised his hand. He stroked the fish along its belly. Motion set his hand tingling painfully and he felt the cold softness of the fish—stroking slowly, softly, gently. . . .

It was slow work . . . slow . . . slow. . . .

His opened fingers went under the flexing gills.

Now!

Grabbing and lifting in one motion, Katsuk leaped backward, hurled the fish over his shoulder, whirling to watch where it landed.

It was a big fish, almost as long as a man's arm, and it hit the boy full in the chest, sent him sprawling. Boy and fish went down in one big, writhing tangle on the riverbank—legs, arms, flopping tail.

Katsuk was on them in a scrambling, bounding dash. He pinned the fish with both hands over the back of its head, thumb and fingers of one hand in its gills.

The boy rolled away, sat up, demanding: "Did we get it? Did we get it?"

Katsuk lifted the still struggling fish, broke its neck.

The boy exhaled wordlessly, then: "Wow! It's a big one!"

Katsuk took the fish in one hand, helped the boy to his feet, leaving a smear of fish blood across the jacket.

The boy stared at the dead fish, eyes wide and fixed. His arms, hands, and the front of his jacket presented a splotched mess of fish slime, scales, sand, mud, and leaves from the mad scramble on the riverbank.

"You're a mess," Katsuk said. "Go splash that stuff off you while I clean the fish."

"Are we going to eat it right away?"

Katsuk thought: *Trust the hoquat to think only of his stomach, and not of the spirit in what we have killed.*

He said: "We will eat at the proper time. Go clean yourself."

"Okay."

Katsuk retrieved his omen wood. He searched among the beach rocks until he found a large one with a slim, jagged edge. He went to the shallows, sawed the head off the fish, pulled away the gills. He reached into the fish then, pulled the entrails out, cleaned the cavity in running water. A sharp stick through there and *kull t'kope* could be cooked over coals.

As he worked, Katsuk mouthed the prayer to Fish, asking pardon that this thing must be done. He heard the boy splashing below him.

The boy shouted: "Hey! This water's cold."

"Then wash faster."

Katsuk picked up fish and omen wood, started back to the ledge. The boy scrambled across the rocks, trotted beside him. He was dripping, shivering, and there was an odd look on his face.

"What are you thinking?" Katsuk asked.

"Did you mean for that fish to hit me?"

"No. I was just making sure we didn't lose it."

The boy grinned. "Did I look funny?"

Katsuk chuckled, felt oddly relieved. "You looked

funny. I couldn't tell which was fish and which was boy."

They came to the rim of the ledge where grass and moss began. Katsuk put the fish on moss, placed the omen wood gently beside it. He thought how it must have been for Hoquat—a big flash of silver as the fish tumbled through the air.

What a shock!

Katsuk began to chuckle.

The boy closed his eyes, remembering. Katsuk had said he was fishing, but it had looked stupid: just waiting there...waiting...waiting...Who could expect a fish to come from such inactivity? No pole, no line, no hook, no bait—just a hand in the water. Then: whap!

Katsuk was laughing now.

David opened his eyes. His stomach began to shake with laughter. He couldn't suppress it. The cold, flopping surprise of that sudden fish!

In a moment, boy and captor were facing each other, laughing like idiots. The noise brought a flock of gray jays, black-crowned camp robbers. They circled overhead, alighted in a stand of alders high up on the riverbank. Their querulous calls made a wild background for the laughter.

Katsuk doubled over with mirth. His mind held the entire compass of that scene: boy, legs, fish, the brown-green riverbank with its overhanging moss, that insane tangle of feet and fish. It was the funniest thing Katsuk could remember in all of his life.

He heard the boy laughing, trying to stop, then laughing more.

The boy gasped: "Oh...please! I...can't...stop ...laughing."

Katsuk tried to think of something to stop the laughter. *The pursuers!* He thought of searchers coming upon the pair of them at this moment. He thought of the puzzlement this scene would create. How ludicrous it was! He laughed all the harder. His sides ached from laughter. He struggled up the mossy bank, flopped on his back, sent great peals of laughter at the sky.

The boy scrambled up to sprawl beside him.

Man and boy—they lay there, spending themselves on laughter until fatigue overcame them, not daring to speak then lest it release new mirth.

Katsuk thought of the laughing game he had played as a boy, as the boy Charles Hobuhet. Make each other laugh, that was the game. Whoever could not control his laughter lost the game.

A spasmodic chuckle shook him.

The boy lay silent. Hoquat had won this game.

For a long while after the joy of that laughter had subsided, they lay on the warm ground, catching their breath.

Katsuk grew aware that the sky was darkening. Clouds covered the low sun. The clouds moved upriver on a cold, raw wind. Katsuk sat up, stared at the clouds. They hung above the trees, unsupported, mysterious gray turrets with the last glowing stripe of day beneath them.

He slapped the boy's arm. "Come. We must make a fire and dry you out."

The boy scrambled to his feet. "And cook the fish?"

"Yes—and cook the fish."

❏

FROM A scrap of note left at the Sam's River shelter:
When I am confused I listen with as much of my
being as I can allow. This was always what my people
did. We fell silent in confusion and waited to learn. The
whites do a strange thing when they are confused. They
run around making much noise. They only add to the
confusion and cannot even hear themselves.

❏

FOR A long while that night, Katsuk lay awake in their
shelter thinking. Hoquat, breathing beside him with
the even rhythm of sleep, remained a disturbing
presence. Even asleep, there was a spirit in the boy. It
was like the times when the hoquat first arrived and
some said they must be the descendants of Seagull,
who had owned the daylight. Grandfather Hobuhet
had recounted the tale often. The hoquat squawked
and ran around like Seagull; so the confusion was
understandable. This boy, though, no longer ran
around and squawked. He remained silent for long
periods. At such times, the spirit could be sensed
growing within him.
The spirit grew even now.
Katsuk sensed the spirit speaking to the boy. The

spirit stood there in the darkness in place of the man this youth would never become. It was a thing of excitement and peril.

The spirit of the boy spoke then to Katsuk: "You see this, Katsuk? In this flesh there are good eyes and a mind that has seen something you have not."

Katsuk felt that he must weep, must punish his senses for this recognition of Hoquat's spirit. But the revelation demanded that he deal with it.

"This is flesh that made something happen," the spirit said.

Katsuk fought to remain silent. He shuddered. If he answered this spirit, he knew it would gain power over him. It might pick him up and shake him. Katsuk would rattle in the Hobuhet flesh like a stick in a basket.

"What folly to think you can ignore me," the spirit said.

Katsuk clenched his teeth tightly. What a seductive spirit this was. It reminded him of the hoquat world.

"I give you back your own knowledge of what the world knows," the spirit said.

Katsuk groaned.

"I make you really know what you only thought you knew," the spirit said. "You think there is no place in you to receive this? Whether you say aye or nay, something is driven into your heart by the thing itself. This boy's hand and your eye have met. He has said something and part of you listened . . . without compromise. If you have as good an eye as his, you can look directly through his flesh and see the man he would become. He has shared this with you, do you understand?"

Katsuk rolled his head in the darkness, holding fast to his link with Soul Catcher.

"Where does such a thing begin?" the spirit asked.

"What made you believe you could master this matter? Do you not see the wonder of this youth? Bring your sight back to the surface and observe this being. How do you dignify yourself in this?"

Katsuk felt sweat drench his flesh. He was chilled inside and out. The temper of this hoquat spirit was emerging. It was looking far back into deeper things. It was primitive and tyrannous. Its concepts spanned all time. There was no greater tyranny. It struck through to the ultimate human. He felt vibrations of color in the night, sensed something wonderful and terrifying about these moments. The spirit had netted a piece of the universe and shaken it out for observation. The thing had been said without decision and without any concern for Katsuk's desire to hear. It was merely said. The spirit invited him to do nothing except listen. The message was brought to him as though painted on wood. In a time of madness, it said a simple thing:

"If you carry out your purpose, it must be done as a man to a man."

Trembling and awed, Katsuk remained awake in the darkness.

Hoquat rolled over, mumbled, then spoke quite clearly: "Katsuk?"

"I am here," Katsuk said.

But the boy was only talking in his sleep.

❏

FROM A paper by Charles Hobuhet for Philosophy 200:
The fallacies of Western philosophy fascinate me.

No "body English." Words-words-words, no feelings.
No flesh. You try to separate life and death. You try to
explain away a civilization which uses trickery, bad
faith, lies, and deceit to make its falsehoods prevail
over the flesh. The seriousness of your attack on
happiness and passion astounds the man in me. It
astounds my flesh. You are always running away from
your bodies. You hide yourselves in words of desperate
self-justification. You employ the most despotic
rhetoric to justify lives that do not fit you. They are
lives, in fact, not lived. You say belief is foolish, and
you believe this. You say love is futile and you pursue
it. Finding love, you place no confidence in it. Thus,
you try to love without confidence. You place your
highest verbal value on something called security. This
is a barricaded corner in which you cower, not realizing
that to keep from dying is not the same as "to live."

❏

"ABOUT THIRTY thousand years ago," Katsuk said, "a
lava flow pushed its way out of a vent in the middle
slope up there." He hooked a thumb over his shoulder.
"Some of it fell out in great lumps which you stupid
hoquat called Indian tears."

David peered up at the mountain, which he could
see shining in the morning sun beyond a stand of
hemlocks. The mountain was a series of rock pillars.
Cloud shapes drifted over it. There was an avalanche
scar on a slope to the south. A river ran somewhere
under that slope, but the sound of it lay hidden beneath
the wind soughing in the trees.

"What time is it?" David asked.

"By hoquat time?"

"Yes."

Katsuk glanced over his shoulder at the sun. "About ten o'clock. Why?"

"You know what I'd be doing at home right now?"

Katsuk glanced at Hoquat, sensing the boy's need to talk. Why not? If Hoquat talked here, that would keep his spirit silent. Katsuk nodded, asked: "What would you be doing?"

"Taking my tennis lesson."

"Tennis lesson," Katsuk said. He shook his head.

Katsuk squatted on the slope. He held a length of brown-black obsidian in his left hand. He steadied the obsidian on his thigh and chipped at it with a piece of flint. The sound of chipping rang sharply in the clear, high air. It produced a pungent smell which David sniffed.

"Tennis lesson," Katsuk repeated. He tried to imagine the boy as a grown man—rich and pampered, a romper man first class in the playboy army. No longer innocent. Black and white dress uniform for night. Black tie. A crew-cut, nightclub smoke-blower. Or whatever would pass for that in his time of maturity. It was a kindness to prevent that. It was a kindness to preserve Hoquat's innocence forever.

"Then I'd go swimming in our pool," David said.

Katsuk asked: "Do you want to swim in the river down there?"

"It's too cold. Our pool is heated."

Katsuk sighed, went on chipping. The obsidian was beginning to take shape. It would be a knife soon.

For some time now, David had been trying to plumb his captor's mood. There had been increasingly long silences between them while walking around the mountain slope. It had taken a full day. There were ten pebbles in David's pocket—ten days. Katsuk's few responses during the long hike had been more and more moody, snappish, and short. Katsuk was troubled by some new awareness. Was Katsuk losing his spirit powers?

David did not allow himself to think yet of escape. But if Katsuk's powers were weakening. . . .

A large chip flew off the obsidian. Katsuk held it up, turned it, examining the shape.

"What're you making?" David asked.

"A knife."

"But you've got . . . my knife." David glanced at Katsuk's waist. The Russell knife had been missing all during the walk around the mountain, but he had guessed it was in the deerhide pouch Katsuk wore.

Katsuk said: "I need a special kind of knife."

"Why?"

"To make my bow."

David accepted this, then: "Have you been here before?"

"Many times."

"Did you make knives here?"

"No. I guided hoquat in here to find pretty rocks."

"Did they make knives out of the rocks?"

"I don't think so."

"How do you know what kind of rock will make a knife?"

"My people made knives from these rocks for thousands of years. They used to come up here at least once a year—before you hoquat came with steel. You call this rock obsidian. We call it black fire—*klalepiah.*

David fell silent. Where was the Russell knife? Would Katsuk give it back?

Katsuk had caught a rabbit and two small quail in snares during the night. He had cleaned them with a sharp piece of the brown-black rock, cooked them in an earth oven heated by pitch balls. The pitch had made a hot fire with almost no smoke.

David found a remnant of rabbit leg, sat down, and chewed on it while he watched Katsuk work. The gray striking rock in Katsuk's right hand had one narrow end. Katsuk struck sharply and steadily at the obsidian, using the narrow end of the flint. Sparks flew. The sulfurous odor grew strong in the still air.

Presently, David summoned his courage, asked: "Where's my knife?"

Katsuk thought: *Ahhh, the sly, clever hoquat!* He said: "I must make my bow in the ancient way. Steel cannot touch this wood."

"Then where's my knife?"

"I threw it in the river."

Outraged, David hurled the gnawed rabbit bone to the ground, leaped to his feet. "That was my knife!"

"Be still," Katsuk said.

"My father gave me that knife," David said, his voice tight with fury. Angry tears began running down his cheeks.

Katsuk peered up at him, weighing the boy's passion. "Could your father not buy you another knife?"

"That one was for my birthday!" David shook tears off his cheeks. "Why'd you have to throw it away?"

Katsuk looked at the obsidian and flint in his hands. *A bithday gift, father to son: a man's gift to a man.* Katsuk experienced emptiness at the certainty that he would never have a son to receive the gift of manhood. The obsidian felt heavy in his hand. He knew he was experiencing self-pity and it angered him.

Why pity anyone? There could be no reprieve.

"Damn you!" David raged. "I hope your Cedar sickness kills you!"

Awareness blazed in Katsuk. There lay the source of the curse! The Innocent had found a spirit to work his curse. Where had Hoquat found this spirit? Had he received it from Tskanay? Then, where had she found it?

Katsuk said: "I was warned by Bee to throw away that steel knife."

"Stupid Bee!"

Katsuk jerked his chin up, glared at the boy. "Careful what you say about Bee. He might not let you live out this day!"

The glazed look of madness in Katsuk's eyes cooled David's anger. He felt only the loss now. The knife was gone, thrown into a river by this madman. David tried to take a deep breath, but his chest pained him. The knife would never be found again. He thought abruptly of the murdered hiker. That knife had killed a man. Was that why it had been thrown away?

Katsuk went back to his chipping.

David said: "Are you sure you didn't hide my knife in that pouch?"

Katsuk put down obsidian and flint, opened the pouch, exposed the interior to the boy.

David pointed: "What's that little package?"

"It's not your knife. You can see I do not have the knife."

"I see." Still angry. "What's that package?"

Katsuk sealed the pouch, went back to chipping his obsidian. "It is the down of sea ducks."

"Down?"

"The soft feathers."

"I know that. Why do you carry a stupid thing like that?"

Katsuk noted how anger spoke in the boy, thought: *The down is to sprinkle on your body when I have slain you.* He said: "It is part of my spirit medicine."

"Why'd your spirit tell you to throw away my knife?" David asked.

Katsuk thought: *He is learning to ask the right questions.*

"Why?" the boy demanded.

"To save me," Katsuk whispered.

"What?"

"To save me!"

"You told Cally nothing can save you."

"But Cally does not know me."

"She's your aunt."

"No. She had a nephew named Charles Hobuhet. I am Katsuk."

And Katsuk wondered: *Why do I explain myself to my victim? What is he doing that I must defend myself? Is it the knife I threw away? That was a link with his father, the father he had before he became Hoquat. Yes. I threw away his past. It is what those drunken loggers did to Janiktaht ... and to me.*

"I'll bet you've never even been in a heated pool," David said.

Katsuk smiled. Hoquat's anger darted here and there. It was like a creature in a cage. *Tennis lessons, a swimming pool.* Hoquat had lived a sheltered life, a life of preserved innocence in the fashion of his people. Despite Tskanay, he remained in that delicate transition place: part man-part boy. Innocent.

Sorrow permeated David. His mouth felt dry. His chest ached. He felt tired, frustrated, lonely. Why was crazy Katsuk making a stone knife? Why was he *really* making it? Had Katsuk lied?

David remembered reading that Aztecs had killed their sacrificial victims with stone knives. Aztecs were Indians. He shook his head. Katsuk had promised. *"Unless you tell me to do it, I will not kill you."* The stone knife had another purpose. Perhaps it was just to make the stupid bow.

Katsuk said: "You are no longer angry with me?"

"No." Still sullen.

"Good. Anger blocks the mind. Anger does not learn. There is much for you to learn."

Anger does not learn! David thought. He climbed deliberately close to Katsuk, went a short way up the slope, and sat down with his back against the bole of a hemlock. Bits of obsidian littered the ground around him. He picked up a handful, began throwing them past Katsuk at brush and trees down the slope.

The bits of obsidian made a clattering sound when they hit a tree. They went flick-flick in salal leaves on the forest floor. It was a curious counterpoint noise to Katsuk's chipping. David felt his anger pouring out in the exertion of throwing the rocks. He threw harder, harder.

Katsuk said: "If you wish to throw a rock at me, throw it. Do not play games with your feelings."

David leaped up, anger flaring. He held a sharp-edged piece of obsidian the size of a quail's egg in his hand. He gritted his teeth, hurled the rock at Katsuk with all of his strength. The rock struck a glancing blow on Katsuk's cheek, left a red slash from which blood oozed.

Terrified by what he had done, David stepped backward. Every muscle was in readiness to flee.

Katsuk put a finger to the wound, brought it away, examined the blood. Curious. The cut did not hurt. What could it mean that such a blow caused no pain? There had been a brief sensation of pressure, but no pain. Ahhh, Bee had blocked off the pain. Bee had interposed a magic to make the blow ineffective. It was a message from Bee. The Innocent's spirit would not prevail.

"I am Tamanawis speaking to you. . . ."

David said: "Katsuk? Katsuk, I'm sorry."

Katsuk looked up at him. Hoquat appeared ready

for flight, his eyes wide and bright with fear. Katsuk nodded, said: "Now, you know a *little* of how I felt when I took you from the hoquat camp. What a hate that must be to want to kill an innocent for it. Did you ever think of that?"

Kill an innocent! David thought. He said: "But you promised...."

"I will keep that promise. It is the way of my people. We do not tell hoquat lies. Do you know how it is?"

"What?"

"When we were whalers, whale had to demand the harpoon. Whale asked us to kill him."

"But I'd never...."

"Then you are safe."

Katsuk returned to his chipping.

David ventured a step closer to Katsuk. "Does it hurt?"

"Bee will not let it hurt. Be quiet. I must concentrate."

"But it's bleeding."

"The bleeding will stop."

"Shouldn't we put something on it?"

"It is a small wound. Your mouth is a bigger wound. Be quiet or I will put something in your mouth."

David gulped, wiped his mouth with the back of his hand. He found it difficult not to look at the dark scratch on Katsuk's cheek. The bleeding stopped, but coagulation formed a ragged lower edge to the wound.

Why didn't it hurt?

It outraged David that the wound did not hurt. He had wanted it to hurt. Cuts always hurt. But Katsuk had spirit protectors. Maybe it really didn't hurt.

David turned his attention to the obsidian knife taking shape under Katsuk's hands. The blade, about four inches long and sharply wedged, was held flat against Katsuk's thigh. With quick, glancing blows,

Katsuk broke tiny flakes from the edges.

The knife did not appear long or slim enough to stab anyone. The cutting edges were serrated. But it could cut an artery. He thought again of the hiker Katsuk had killed. That hiker had not asked to be killed. But Katsuk had murdered him anyway.

David found his mouth suddenly dry. He said: "That guy...you know, on the trail...the guy you...well, he didn't ask you to...."

"You hoquat always think mouth-talk is the only talk." Katsuk spoke without looking up from his work. "Why can't you learn body-talk? When Raven made you, did he leave that ability out of you?"

"What's body-talk?"

"It is what you do. A thing you do can say something about what you want."

"That's crazy talk about Raven."

"God made us, eh?"

"Yes!"

"It depends on what you're taught, I guess."

"Well, I don't believe that about body-talk and Raven."

"You don't believe Raven keeps you tied to me?"

David could not answer. Raven *did* do what Katsuk wanted. The birds went where Katsuk ordered them to go. To know where the birds would go—what a power that was.

Katsuk said: "You are quiet. Did Raven take your tongue? Raven can do that. Your stupid hoquat world does not prepare you to deal with Raven."

"You always say *stupid* when you talk about my people," David accused. "Isn't there anything good about our world?"

"Our world?" Katsuk asked. "*Your* world, Hoquat."

"But nothing good in it?"

"I see only death in it. The whole world dies of you."

"What about our doctors? We have better doctors than you ever had."

"Your doctors are tied to illness and death. They make as much illness and death as they cure. An exact balance. It's called a transactional relationship. But they are so blind, they do not see how they are tied to what they do."

"Transactional...relationship? What's that?"

"A transaction is where you trade one thing for another. When you buy something, that's a transaction."

"Ahh, that's just big words that don't mean anything."

"They are words from your world, Hoquat."

"But they don't mean anything."

"They mean doctors don't know they do it, but still they do it: They maintain a level of illness to justify their existence. Police do the same thing with crime. Lawyers keep up the legal confusions. Body-talk, Hoquat. No matter what they say they want, or how hard they work to overcome their defects, things work out in a way that keeps them busy and justifies their existence."

"That's crazy!"

"Yes, it is crazy, but it is real. It is what you see when you understand body-talk."

"But my world does lots of good things. People don't go hungry anymore."

"But they do, Hoquat. In Asia, they—"

"I mean people in this country."

"Aren't they *people* in the other countries?"

"Sure, but...."

"Even in this country—in the mountains of your East, in the South, in big cities, people are hungry. People die of hunger every year. Old people, young people. My people die that way, too, because they try to live like hoquat. And the world gets hungrier and hungrier...."

"What about our houses? We build better houses than you ever saw."

"And you destroy the earth to plunge your houses into it. You build where no house should be. You are insensitives. You live *against* the earth, not *with* it."

"We have cars!"

"And your cars are smothering you."

David quested in his mind for something Katsuk could not strike down. Music? He'd sneer the way adults always did. Education? He'd say it didn't prepare you to live out here. Science? He'd say it was killing the world with big bombs, big machines.

"Katsuk, what do you mean by body-talk?"

"What your actions say. You say with your mouth: 'That's too bad.' Then you laugh. That means you're really happy while you're saying you're sorry. You say: 'I love you.' Then you do something to hurt that person's feelings. Body-talk is what you *do*. If you say, 'I don't want that to happen,' and all the while you are making it happen, which thing are we to believe? Do we believe the words or do we believe the body?"

David thought about words. He thought about church and sermons, of all the words about "eternal life." Were the words true, or did the preacher's body say something different?

"Katsuk, do your people understand body-talk?"

"Some of them. The old ones did. Our language tells me this."

"How?"

"We say eat while eating, shit while shitting, fuck while fucking. The words and the body agree."

"That's just dirty talk."

"It is innocent talk, Hoquat. Innocent."

❏

FROM A note left by Katsuk in the abandoned park shelter at Sam's River:

My body is a pure expression of myself.

❏

KATSUK PUT down the chipping stone, examined his obsidian knife. It was done. He liked the way the smooth end fitted his hand. It made him feel close to the earth, part of everything around him.

The sun stood straight overhead, beating down on his shoulders. He heard Hoquat breaking twigs behind him.

Katsuk placed the omen wood from Bee across his knees, examined it once more for flaws. The wood appeared to have no irregularities. Every grain ran straight and clean. He took the smooth handle of his knife in his right hand, began scraping the wood. Long, curly shavings peeled back. He worked slowly at first, then faster, whispering to himself.

"A little bit here. More there. Some here. Ahhh, that's a good one...."

David came and squatted beside him. Presently, he said: "May I help?"

Katsuk hesitated, thought about the purpose of this

bow—to drive a consecrated arrow into the heart of the youth beside him. Was Hoquat asking now to be slain? No. But this showed Soul Catcher at work, preparing the boy for that final moment.

"You may help," Katsuk said. He handed the knife and the omen wood to the boy, indicated a bulge to be scraped. "Remove this high place. Work slowly, just a little bit at a time."

David held the limb as Katsuk had, resting it across his knees. "This place here?"

"Yes."

David put the knife to the wood, pulled. A curl of wood formed over the blade. Another. He scraped energetically, intent on the bulge. Perspiration ran down his forehead, into his eyes. Lengths of shaving curled away, dropped around his knees.

"No more," Katsuk said. "You have fixed that place." He took back the wood and knife, resumed his careful shaping of the bow.

"More here . . . and over here . . . that's right . . . now, in here. . . ."

David tired of watching the wood curl away from the bow. Chips and shavings were all around Katsuk. Light, reflected from the newly cut wood, played glowing patterns against Katsuk's skin.

Up the slope above them, a granite chimney climbed toward a sky of blue patches in bulging, fleecy clouds. David stood up, examined the slope, the outcropping of volcanic glass below the granite. He turned, looked down into the forest—dark down there: old-growth fir, hemlock, an occasional cedar. A game trail angled into the trees through heavy undergrowth of salal and wild huckleberries.

Katsuk's voice as he talked to himself carried a hypnotic quality. "Lovely wood . . . a bow of the old times. . . ."

Old times! David thought. *Katsuk certainly lives in a strange dream.*

David picked up an obsidian chip, hurled it into the trees. He thought: *If you go downstream, you come to people.*

The rock made a satisfying clatter which Katsuk ignored.

David hurled another rock, another. He worked his way down the slope to the game trail, picking up rocks, tossing them—a boy at play.

He threw my knife away! He killed a man.

Once, David paused to slash a mark in a tree trunk, peering back at Katsuk. The murmuring voice did not change pitch. Katsuk still paid no attention to his wandering captive.

He thinks his damned Raven is guarding me.

David searched the sky all around: no sign of the birds. He ventured about fifty feet down the game trail, pulling off salal leaves, sampling a sour berry. He could see Katsuk through the brush and trees. The sound of the obsidian knife on the bow remained clear: a slithering that noised its way oddly into the woods. Katsuk's murmurous conversation with himself remained audible.

"Ahhh, beautiful bow. Here's a beautiful bow for the message...."

"Crazy Indian," David whispered.

Katsuk hummed and chanted and mumbled at his work.

David broke off a huckleberry twig, studied his situation. No ravens. Katsuk distracted. An open trail, all downhill. But if Katsuk caught him trying to escape again.... David took a trembling breath, decided he wouldn't really try to escape, not yet. He'd just explore this trail for a ways.

Casually, he wandered down into the trees. The

neatly collected flight of a flicker dipping through the forest caught his attention. He heard deerflies singing. A dusty sunshaft spread quiet light on the brown floor of the woods, illuminating a delight of greenery. David saw it as an omen. He still felt anger at Katsuk. The anger might break the spirit spell.

David ventured farther down the trail. He crossed two fallen trees, went under a low passage of moss-draped limbs. The trail forked at the brink of a steep hill. One track plunged straight down. The other angled off to the left. He chose the steep way, went down through the trees to a long slope scarred by an avalanche. David studied the open area. A single cedar had survived the slide, sheltered by a prow of granite directly above it. Part of the tree had been shattered, though—one side half stripped away. Great shreds of wood had been left dangling.

Deer tracks led straight across the scarred area.

David stayed on the mossy, fern-patched forest floor, skirted the open area. Several times, he glanced around, searching out his back trail for signs of pursuit.

Katsuk was nowhere to be seen.

He listened, could not hear the scraping of the obsidian knife on the bow. There was only the wind in the trees.

The avalanche had lost itself in a small, gently rounded valley, leaving a tangle of trees and earth which damned a small stream. The stream already had cut a narrow way across the slide. Water tinkled over rocks below the scarred earth.

David broke his way through a salal thicket above the water, surprised a spotted fawn which splashed through the shallows.

For a moment, David stood trembling in the aftermath of the shock at the way the fawn had burst from the thicket. Then, he went down to the stream, pushed his face into cold water to still his trembling.

He thought: *Now, I'm escaping.*

❏

SHERIFF PALLATT:

There's a goddamned lot of horseshit around about who's going to get the credit in this case—us or the FBI. All I want is to save that kid—and the Indian, if I can. I'm tired of playing sheriff! Me'n Dan Gomper, my chief deputy, is gonna take our own crew in there and find that pair. A couple of old boar woodsmen like us can do it if anyone can. We're gonna camp cold so's the Indian don't see smoke and know we're trailing him. Gonna be outrageous hard work, but we'll do 'er.

❏

KATSUK LOOKED up from the completed bow. It was a lovely bow, just right for the walrus-gut string in his pouch. He felt the notches for the string.

His chest ached and there were sharp pains in his back from bending so long in one position. He coughed. Why was it cold now? He looked up. The sun stood low over the trees.

Katsuk got to his feet, sought his captive.

"Hoquat!" he called.

Forest silence mocked him.

Katsuk nodded to himself.

Hoquat thinks to escape.

Again, Katsuk studied the sky. No sign of Raven.

He thought: *Raven invites everyone to go with him and be his guest, but on the new day, Raven turns against his guests and wants to kill them. So the guests flee into the woods. Now, I am Raven. I have the bow; I need only the arrow.*

Again, Katsuk coughed. The spasm sent pain shooting through his chest.

It was clear where Hoquat had gone. Even from up on the slope, Katsuk saw the scar the boy had carved on the tree beside the game trail.

Is it a new test? Katsuk wondered. *Do my spirits test me now that the bow is completed? Why would they not wait for the arrow?*

He took the walrus-gut string from his pouch, fitted it to the bow, tried the pull. His grandfather had taught him to make such a bow and use it. He felt his grandfather beside him as he pulled the bow to its fullest arc.

It was a great bow, truly a god-bow.

Katsuk lowered the weapon, stared down into the forest. Sweat drenched his neck and waist. He felt suddenly weak. Had Hoquat cast a spell upon him?

He glanced over his shoulder at the snow peaks. He thought of the long night: Death lurked up there, calling to him with Soul Catcher's rattle. It was a spell, for sure.

Once more, Katsuk studied the forest where Hoquat had gone. The trail beckoned him. He measured the way of it in his memory: by shadows of trees and passages of moss. He sensed the way that trail would feel beneath his feet: thinly flowing dampness of springs, the roots, the rocks, the mud.

Janiktaht's moccasins were growing thin. He could feel the raw ground through them.

The trees—Hoquat had gone that way, trying to escape.

Katsuk spoke aloud to the trail: "I am Katsuk, he who buried Kuschtaliute, the land otter's tongue. My body will not decompose. Boughs of the great trees will not fall upon my grave. I will be born again into a house of my people. There will be many good things to eat all around me."

Deadly whirlwinds of thought poured through his mind, shutting off his voice. He knew he must go after Hoquat. He must plunge down that trail, but lethargy gripped him. It was a spell.

An image of Tskanay filled his mind.

Tskanay had cast this spell, not Hoquat! He knew it. He felt her eyes upon him. She had looked upon him and found him alien. She stood this moment amidst the perfume of burning cedar needles, reciting the ancient curse. Evergreens arose all around her, a green illusion of immortality.

"Raven, help me," he whispered. "Take this sickness from me." He looked down at the cinnamon leather of the moccasins Janiktaht had made for him. "Janiktaht, help me."

The vision of Tskanay left him.

He thought: *Has the curse been taken away?*

Far away, with inner ear and eye, he heard and saw a vaporous river speaking with its primitive tongues. He saw dead trees, wind-lashed, sparring with eternity. Amidst the dead, he saw one live tree, torn and scarred but still standing, a cedar, straight and tall, straight as an arrow shaft.

"Cedar has forgiven me," he whispered.

He stepped out onto the trail Hoquat had taken then, strode down it until he saw the tree standing alone on the scarred earth—exactly as his vision had shown it to him.

Cedar for my arrow, he thought. *And already consecrated.*

The hullabaloo of a raven caucus sounded over the forest. They came over the avalanche scar, settled into the cedar.

Katsuk smiled. *What more omen do I need?*

"Katlumdai!" he shouted.

And the sick spirit of the curse left him as he called it by name. He went down into the scarred earth then to make his arrow.

❏

CHARLES HOBUHET'S DREAM, as recounted by his aunt: When I was small I dreamed about Raven. It was the white Raven I dreamed about. I dreamed Raven helped me steal all of the fresh water and I hid it where only our people could find it. There was a cave and I filled it with the water. I dreamed there was a spirit in the cave who told me about creation. The spirit had created my cave. There were two entrances, a way to enter and a way to leave. There was a beach in the cave and waves on it. I heard drums there. My dream spirit told me there really is such a place. It is clean and good. I want to find that place.

❑

KATSUK SAT with his back against a tree, praying for
the earth to forgive him. The bow lay in his lap with the
arrow and it was dark all around him, a cold wind
blowing dampness onto his skin. The bow was not as
well made as those of the ancient people. He knew this,
but he knew also that the spirit in the wood of this bow
would compensate for the way he had hurried the
making of it. The arrow in his lap had been fitted with
the stone tip from the beach village where his people no
longer were permitted to live. The ancient times and
the present were tied together.

Clouds hid the stars. He felt the nearness of rain.
The cold wind made his flesh tremble. He knew he
should feel the chill of that wind, but his body
possessed no sensation except the loss of Hoquat.

Hoquat had run off. Where?

Katsuk's mind slipped into the spirit chase of which
his ancestors had spoken. He would search out Hoquat's spirit. That would lead him to the boy.

Katsuk stared into the darkness. There was a small
fire somewhere and he could not tell if he saw it with
the inward vision or outwardly. Flames from the fire
cast ruddy light on raw earth and a tangle of roots.
There was a figure at the edge of the firelight. It was a
small figure. Now, Katsuk knew he was having the
spirit vision.

Where was that fire?

Katsuk prayed for his spirit to guide him, but
nothing spoke to him from Soul Catcher's world. It
was another test then.

FRANK HERBERT

A small animal ran across Katsuk's outstretched legs, fled into the darkness. He felt the tree behind him growing, its bark searching upward. The damp earth and the cold wind moved all through him and he knew he would have to fight a spirit battle before he could reclaim Hoquat.

"Alkuntam, help me," he prayed. "This is Katsuk. Help me send my message. Lead me to the innocent one."

An owl called in the night and he sensed its tongue bringing rain. It would rain soon. He was being called to an ordeal within an ordeal.

Slowly, Katsuk got to his feet. He felt his body as a remote thing. He told himself: *I will begin walking. I will find Hoquat in the light of day.*

❏

FROM AN interview with Harriet Gladding Morgenstern in the San Francisco *Examiner:*

My grandson is a very brave lad. He was never afraid of the dark or any such nonsense as that, even as a small child. He was always thoughtful of his elders. We taught him to be respectful and considerate of those around him, no matter who they were. I'm sure these are the qualities which will bring him through his present trial.

❏

SHORTLY BEFORE nightfall, David found a sheltered place where a tree had been uprooted by a storm. The tree had fallen almost parallel to a small stream and its roots formed an overhang whose lip had been taken over by moss and grass.

David crouched in the shelter for a moment, wondering if he dared build a fire. Katsuk had made a fire bow and showed the captive how to use it as a diversion, but David wondered if smoke and fire might lead Katsuk here.

It was late, though. And there was a cold wind. He decided to risk it.

Bark had been ripped from the tree by its fall. David found long lengths of bark and leaned them in an overlapping row against his shelter to make a heat pocket. He collected a pitch deposit from beneath a rotten log as Katsuk had taught him. A dead cedar lay along the slope above him. David slipped on wet salal and bruised his forehead getting to the cedar, but found, as he had hoped, that the tree's fall had splintered it, leaving long dry sections underneath which could be torn off by hand. He assembled a store of the dry cedar under the roots, brought in dead limbs and more small pieces of bark, then went in search of a short green limb for a fire bow. It would have to be short to fit a shoestring.

"Preparation, patience, persistence," Katsuk had told him in explaining this way to make fire.

David had wanted to give up in his first attempt with Katsuk's fire bow, but the man had laughed at "hoquat impatience." Goaded by that laughter, David had persisted, running the bow back and forth across its driver stick until friction made a spark in the dry grass tinder. Now he knew the careful way of it.

With a slab of cedar notched by pounding with a stone, with a shoestring bow to drive the tinder stick, with pitch and cedar splinters ready at hand, he persisted until he had a coal, then gently blew the coal into flame which he fed with pitch and cedar. When it was going well, he thought: *Katsuk should see me now.*

The thought frightened him, and he peered out of his shelter at the forest. It would be dark soon. He wondered if he would be safer from Katsuk in the night. The man had strange powers. Hunger gripped his stomach. He looked down at the stream. There would be trout in that stream. He had seen Katsuk build a weir. But the night would be cold and he knew he would get wet trying to trap a trout. He decided to forego the trout. Tomorrow . . . tomorrow there might be hikers or the people he knew must be searching for him. They would have food.

It was a long night.

Twice, David went out to replenish his firewood, dragging back dead limbs, bark. It was raining lightly the second time and the wood sizzled when he put it on the fire. His shelter turned the rain and most of the wind, though, and it was warm by contrast with the night outside.

Several times he dozed, sitting up with his back against the earth which had been exposed by the upheaval of roots. Once, he dreamed.

In the dream, he was running away, but there was a long brown string trailing behind him. It was tied around his forehead the way Katsuk wore the braided cedar around *his* head. David sensed the string trailing him wherever he ran. The string went up the mountain to Katsuk and the man up there spoke along its length. Katsuk was calling for help. "Hoquat, help me. Help me. Hoquat, I need you. Help me."

David awoke to find dawn breaking and his fire almost out. He covered the coals with dirt to extinguish them and prevent telltale smoke. An attack of shivering overcame him when he went out into the misting dawn.

I'll keep following the stream down, he decided. *There have to be people downstream.*

As he thought this, he stared upstream, searching for any sign of pursuit. Where was Katsuk now? That had been a crazy dream about string. Was Katsuk really in trouble up there? He could have fallen in the night or broken a leg or something. Crazy Indian.

Still shivering, David set off down the watercourse.

◻

SHERIFF PALLATT:

Sure, some of these Indians can do strange things. Make your hair stand on end, some of them. I tell myself that if you live close to something like this wilderness you get a feeling for it that others don't have. I guess that's it. Maybe.

❑

IN LATE afternoon David worked his way through a
stand of big-leaf maples in a creek bottom. His little
stream had become a torrent more than ten feet across.
A thick carpet of moss covered the ground beneath the
maples. David thought how soft a bed the moss would
make. He had found a few berries to eat and he drank
water frequently, but hunger was a persistent ache
now. It had moved from his stomach to a tight band
around his head. David wondered if the ache in his head
could be real. Was it really that brown string he had
dreamed about? Was Katsuk up there somewhere
holding the other end of that string? He was tired and
the moss invited, but when he pressed his hand into it,
water ran up between his fingers.

He noted then that his feet were soaking wet.

The wind had turned to the southwest. That meant
rain. Patches of blue showed in the sky, but gunmetal
clouds were scudding toward the peaks behind him.

He paused beside a beaver-downed cottonwood,
studied his surroundings: trees, trees, trees ... the river,
a black pier of rocks buffeted by gray current ... a
squirrel running on a log. Was Katsuk out in that forest
nearby, silently watching? It was a thing he might do.
He could be there.

David put this fear out of his mind. That wouldn't
help. He plunged on, masking his passage wherever he
could in ways he had learned from watching Katsuk:
walking on rocks, on logs, avoiding muddy places.

For a time, he wondered if he had used sufficient
care in putting out his fire. If Katsuk found that

fire.... Would Katsuk know his escaping captive was
following the watercourse? David considered leaving
the stream, striking out over the hills. But the hills went
up. They might go right back to Katsuk.

A small stream entered the larger one he was
following. It came in from a ravine and barred his way
with a thick growth of salal and devil's club along the
watercourse. David worked his way up the small
stream, found a green hole through the barbed thicket,
a footlog scarred by the passage of many hooves. He
peered across the footlog at the water, saw fish flicker
in the current. They reminded him of his hunger, but he
knew he dared not take the time to try catching one.

He crossed the footlog, shirted a nettle patch. The
trail branched upstream and downstream. David went
downstream, avoided the upthrust and twisting roots
of a recently fallen tree. Brown dirt there to take his
footprints. He climbed the steep hillside above the tree
to conceal his passage.

David began to wonder at his escape. It didn't seem
possible, but he was daring to hope. He knew he was in
a place called the Wilderness Area. Katsuk had
described it in general terms. There were park trails at
the edge of the area. If he found park trails, there would
be signs to tell him he was going in the right direction.

There would be hikers.

There would be food.

He paused to drink from the stream before going
on.

There was the smell of mint along the stream and
many patches of nettles. The back of his left hand
burned from brushing the leaves. The game trail he was
following twisted away from the stream and back to it,
up the hill to avoid trees on the bank, back down to
mossy rocks in the water. He could see no farther than
fifty feet down the watercourse. Bright yellow skunk

cabbages glistened in shadows downstream. The water would be slower there.

David found himself preoccupied with the many things he could sense about his surroundings, things he had learned from being with Katsuk: where a stream would run slower and deeper, where to seek a footlog, how to avoid leaving signs of his passage.

Just beyond the skunk cabbages, he returned to the larger stream he had been following earlier. A muddy elk trail ran parallel to the stream, fresh tracks on it. Some of the tracks had not yet filled with water. A patch of elk droppings still steamed on the trail.

He studied the trail ahead, the hillside, looking for the yellow patches of elk rumps. No sign of them, except the trail with its tracks and droppings.

David stayed in the trees just off the trail, moved downstream, keeping the water in sight. Trees and undergrowth became thicker. He caught occasional glimpses of the opposite shore, strips of gray water. His feet were wet and cold. His toes ached.

How far have I come from Katsuk? he wondered.

David knew Katsuk must be seeking him by this time. The question was how? Was Katsuk tracking the fugitive? Was there another way to find him?

He stopped to rest beside a cottonwood whose base had been partly chewed out by beaver. Yellow chips covered the ground. They were at least a week old from the color of the wood. A thick spruce towered into the sky across the muddy elk trail from him. He looked down, saw the puddles in the trail reflecting the spruce's brown bark, the sky painted with branches, his own wet feet. The vision filled him with a sense of his own smallness in all of this immensity.

Where was Katsuk?

David wondered if he dared build another fire to dry his feet. They throbbed with the cold. There was plenty of dry cedar around, lots of dry wood under the fallen trees. The cottonwood chips would burn easily. But Katsuk might see the smoke. Others could see it, too— but who would arrive first?

He decided against a fire. It was too much of a gamble even for the sake of warm feet.

Movement helped him to stay warmer, he knew. David resumed his cautious passage through the trees. There was a blister forming on his left heel and he tried to ignore it.

Once, he heard a raven call. He cowered for five minutes under the sweeping limbs of a cedar before daring to go on. Even so, he kept a cautious outlook on the sky, wondering if those were Katsuk's ravens.

The elk trail turned, angled up a steep hill.

David chose to stay with the river and abandon the trail. He leaped across the trail to avoid leaving tracks, forced his way through underbrush along the river, worked his way around a thin rock ledge above a waterfall taller than himself. Logs left by the last high water lay in a red-brown tangle across from him, swept up onto a muddy beach beneath an alder copse.

Below the waterfall, the rock barrier forced him to cross the stream. He got wet to the waist doing it, almost lost his footing. He floundered through a pool, frightened a big trout from beneath a cutbank. The trout went arrowing downstream, half of its back exposed across a rocky shallows before it plunged into deeper water.

David followed the trout across the shallows, the river loud in his ears, climbed into the forest on the other side, and found a game trail there.

He estimated three hours to nightfall. The stream down which he moved now was a wide and roaring river, its edges lost in the shadows of steep banks. Hemlocks and cedars on both banks hid the upper ridges. Vine maples bowered the water in places.

For a time, he found relatively easy passage along a dry slough back from the stream. Bleached-white alders lined the slough, scrawling sharp lines against the evergreen background. He came on a logjam at the lower end of the slough. There were rough gray trunks of long-dead trees to cross, another maple bottom on the far side of the jam.

Fatigue and hunger forced him to a stop before crossing the logjam. He sat on a log. His chest heaved. Beneath his fear and fatigue, he felt the growth of elation. All during the night he had nurtured his hope as he nurtured the tiny fire. All through this day, he had lived in the shadow of signs and portents. But there had been no evidence of Katsuk except that brief flurry of ravens, and even they were gone. The sounds all around him were dominated by the river working its way under the edge of the logjam.

Katsuk had said once that this river sound was the voice of Water Baby, a monster who could take human form. The man's words had given a sense of reality to the monster which David had found it hard to discount. Water Baby trapped your soul by getting you to tell it your name. David shuddered at the memory, listened to the water. There were voices in the water, but no words.

David looked up at the sky. It was getting darker. The light had dropped markedly and the wind possessed a new chill. Rain began to fall—big drenching drops. David got up, looked for shelter. There was only the steep hill beyond the maples, the logs. He was soaked to the skin in a minute, shivering with cold.

As swiftly as it had come, the rain passed.

Blue patches could be seen in the scudding gray clouds.

Once more, David set off downstream. He longed for shelter, despaired of finding it. The river ran beside him, flowing noisily in its canyon. There were more patches of blue sky, but he felt no sunlight.

An osprey took off from a gray snag ahead of him. It climbed out over the watercourse, circled. David stared up at the bird, letting his mind fly high, but his feet still blundered through the rocks beside the river.

Osprey.

David recalled Katsuk describing a tribal chief of the old times: blanket of dog wool, raven's beak headdress, osprey feathers in his headband.

The river made a wide curve to the left, debauched from a spruce copse into a meadow full of blue camas.

David stopped within the tree shadows.

The river grew wider out there, moved slow and meandering through the meadow before it plunged into thick green darkness of brush and trees at the far side. A flood-scoured bar marked the nearest river bend. Milky wavelets clawed at sand there.

David let his gaze traverse the meadow's rim, right to left, gasped as he saw a sign. He saw the park trail then, off to the left. A small stream came down into the meadow there, reaching out to the river. A man-made footbridge crossed the small stream. Big letters on the sign beside the bridge read KILKELLY SHELTER 2 MI.

Shelter!

David felt his heart beating faster. He and Katsuk had stayed in shelters. One had been in a deep stand of cedar, water running down the trail beside it. There had been a wet smell of ashes, a fire pit under an overhanging porch. The shelter's lower logs had been rotten, chipped out at the bottom by hikers in search of dry fuel.

The arrow on the sign pointed to the right, downstream.

David thought: *There may be hikers!*

He stepped from the tree shadows, stopped in confusion at a great flapping of wings and bird cries overhead. A flock of ravens had leaped into the sky at sight of him, filling the air with their uproar. David stared up at them, terrified.

Ravens! Hundreds of them!

They darkened the sky, wheeling and calling.

As though the birds had summoned him, Katsuk emerged from the trees across the meadow on the far side of the river. He stood a moment beside a great spruce, his headband dull red, a black feather in the back. He came straight then toward the river, one arm brushing aside silken green leaves at the bank. He stopped only when he was thigh deep in the water. The river around him ran milky with snowmelt.

David stared at Katsuk, unable to move.

The ravens continued to wheel and call.

Katsuk waited in the water, holding his bow and arrow high, staring up at the birds.

Why is he waiting? David wondered.

At the river's near shore, David saw the silvery white of raindrops on reeds, then gray rocks, then the river, and Katsuk standing in the water like an animal startled into stillness, undecided which way to turn, waiting.

Why!

The ravens whirled out over the trees beyond the meadow, went away with diminishing noise, grew abruptly silent. They had settled down.

As the birds fell silent, Katsuk plunged into motion, crossed the river, climbed dripping into the meadow. He came straight on to where David stood, walking with slow, deliberate steps. The strung bow was carried in his left hand, a single arrow clutched to it with two fingers. He wore the obsidian knife in a loop of his rope belt near the pouch. His loincloth was stained with brown earth. Water ran from it down his legs.

Katsuk stopped a pace from David, stood staring into the boy's face.

David trembled, not knowing what to do or say. He knew he could not outrun Katsuk. And there was that bow with an arrow ready for it.

"Raven told me where you would be," Katsuk said. "I came straight here after I had made my arrow. You followed the river as Raven told me. That is the long way here."

David's teeth chattered with cold and fear. There was an oddly deliberate pacing to Katsuk's words.

Katsuk held up the bow and the arrow. "You see— they are finished." He nodded. "But I did not feel it when you lured me to that arrow tree. I thought the arrow wood was a gift and took it. I thanked Cedar. But you tricked me. It was a trick."

Katsuk coughed, deep and racking. When the spasm passed, he stood trembling. The skin of his jaws and cheeks was pale.

What's wrong with him? David wondered.

"You have put the Cedar sickness upon me," Katsuk said. "You and Tskanay."

David thought: *He really is sick.*

Katsuk said: "I am cold. We must find a place to be warm. Cedar takes the heat of my body and sends it to the sky."

David shook his head, tried to still the chattering of his teeth. Katsuk had been waiting here at the meadow with his birds. But he sounded so...strange. The sickness had changed him.

"Take this sickness from me," Katsuk said.

David bit his lip, seeking pain to help stop the chattering of his teeth. He pointed to the sign. "There's a shelter. We could—"

"No! We cannot go that way. People come." Katsuk peered at the spruce copse from which David had emerged. "There is a place . . . in there."

"I've just come that way," David said. "There's no—"

"There is a place," Katsuk said. "Come."

Walking with that odd, stiff-legged stride, Katsuk stepped past the boy, moved into the trees. David followed, feeling that he had moved into Katsuk's delirium.

Again, Katsuk coughed, deep and racking.

At the logjam where David had rested, Katsuk paused. He studied the water hurtling against the logs: dark, blue-gray river crossed by smoky driftwood. Yes, this was the place.

He stepped up onto the jam, crossed the river, jumping from log to log. David followed.

On the far shore, David saw what he had missed earlier: an abandoned park shelter, part of its roof caved in. The logs and shakes were mottled with moss and lichen. Katsuk entered the shelter. David heard him digging in there.

David hesitated on the riverbank, looked downstream.

People coming? Katsuk had said it.

The air was cold. He felt an added chill of madness. *Katsuk is sick. I could run back to the meadow. But he might catch me, or shoot me with that arrow.*

The sky was dark over the trees downstream. Rain walked on a black line up the river, that hard sky behind it, clouds crouched over the sunset, the wind floating the leaves, whipping night before it.

Katsuk called from the shelter. "Hurry up. It is going to rain."

Again, Katsuk coughed.

David entered the shelter, smelling raw earth, the damp fungus odors of rot.

Katsuk had a hole dug in one corner. He pulled a small metal drum from it. The lid popped with a rusty creaking. Katsuk extracted two blankets and a small, tightly wrapped package.

"Fire tinder," Katsuk said, tossing the package to the boy.

Katsuk turned, moved toward the shelter's entrance. David saw that the man was almost staggering.

"You thought to kill me with Cedar sickness," Katsuk said. "I will yet do what I must do. Raven will give me the power."

❏

CHIEF PARK Ranger William Redek:

It's cold in there for this time of year, been more snow and rain than usual. Snow line's lower than I can remember for years. I hear Indian fakirs have a trick for keeping warm without lots of clothes or fire, but this Hobuhet is a different kind of Indian. Doubt if he knows that trick. If he and that boy are in there, they have to be in shelter of some kind, and with fire. That, or they're dead. You lose enough body heat and that country kills you.

❑

KATSUK LAY on moss between two logs, his mind howling in a fevered nightmare. There was a wood path, an arrow. The arrow must balance just right. He had found the wood for the arrow in the avalanche scar of a tall cedar. It had been a trick, all a trick. He held the arrow and the arrow held him. He led a cortege up the wood path from the most ancient times to the present. His mind was drunk with all the lives it held.

A spirit shouted in his mind: "The earth does not know who owns it!"

Katsuk groaned.

Delirium moved his feet on the wood path. He sang the names of his dead, but each new name brought a change in the nightmare. When he sang Janiktaht's name, he saw Hoquat running, hair flying like a wind-whipped bush.

Another name: *Okhoots.*

He was in a field embroidered with yellow flowers, a bubbling spring beside the field. He drank at the spring, but the water failed to slake the dry burning of his throat.

Another name: *Grandfather Hobuhet.*

He was confronted by wave tops blown white in a gale, a sorrel weaving in green water. A dead whale rose out of the water, said: "You dare disturb me!"

Another name: *Tskuldik.*

Father . . . father . . . father!

He called a nameless name in a canyon, was back on the nightmare trail of his ordeal. He heard the woods' dirge, felt wet bracken at his waist. He was marching upcountry from the hoquat places. There was a dirty yellow logging rig parked beside the road, heavy green of second-growth fir behind it. Side roads poked out into the tree wall. Dead snags thrust up through the green.

There was an alder bottom, a stump ranch glimpsed through the bleached-white maze of trunks. He saw platform notches on old stumps, ragged bark dangling. There was a corrugated culvert with arsenic-yellow skunk cabbages on one side of a rutted road, water trickling out the other side. He saw the open scar of a logged-off hillside, a sign: WARNING: UNDERGROUND POWER AND TELEPHONE CABLES.

As he read the sign, Katsuk felt his mind plunge into a cold river. He saw moss-covered boughs vibrating in the water. He became one of the boughs.

He thought: *I have become a water spirit.*

In his delirium, he screamed for Raven to save him. Raven swam by him under the water, became a fish, *kull t'kope!*

Katsuk awoke, trembling with terror. Cramps contorted his body. He felt weak, drained. Dawnlight glared gray through the shelter's open entrance. Sweat bathed him. He shivered with chill. Blankets had been tucked around him, but he had thrown them off in his nightmare thrashing.

Painfully, his knees trembling with Cedar sickness, he managed to stand, forced himself to the entrance. He leaned against a log upright, shivered, half conscious of some ultimate necessity which he could not name.

Where was Hoquat?

A piece of wood broke with a clear snapping off to his right. The boy came around the shelter there, his arms loaded with firewood. He dumped the wood beside the gray ashes of the fire pit.

Katsuk stared at the boy, at the fire pit, trying to put the two together in his thoughts.

David saw the weakness in Katsuk, said: "I found a can of beans in that little barrel and heated them. I left most of them for you."

He used a split length of green wood to lift the can from the ashes and place it at Katsuk's feet. A flat piece of wood for a spoon protruded from the can.

Katsuk squatted, ate greedily, hungry for the warmth more than for the food. The beans tasted of ashes. They burned his tongue, but he gulped them, felt heat radiate from his stomach.

The boy, working to restore the fire, said: "You had a nightmare. You yelled and tossed around all night. I kept the fire going most of the night."

Flame began to climb through the wood the boy had placed in the coals beneath the ashes.

Katsuk nodded dumbly. He heard water dashing on stones only a few steps from the shelter but could not find the strength to go to it. A burning dryness filled his throat.

"Wa-ter," he croaked.

The boy stood up from the fire, took the empty bean can to the river.

The way the leaf-broken sunlight dappled the boy's hair made Katsuk think of a lion he had seen in a zoo: a lion draped in sunlight and shadows. The memory caged him. He thought: *Does Hoquat have a new spirit? Is it Lion? I do not know that spirit.*

David returned from the river with the can slopping icy water. He saw the glazed look in Katsuk's eyes. Katsuk clutched the can with both hands, drained it, said: "More."

The boy brought another can of water. Katsuk drank it.

A distant engine sound came into the valley, rising

above the noise of the river. It grew louder: a plane flying low over the ridge above them. The sound went away upcountry.

David stood, stared through the trees, hoping for a glimpse of the aircraft. He failed to see it.

Katsuk ignored the sound. He seemed to have lapsed back into his dream-sleep, squatting in the shelter's doorway, occasionally shuddering.

David put more wood on the fire, piled rocks around the flames to heat them. He said: "It's going to rain again."

Katsuk stared through slitted eyes at the boy. He thought: *The victim is here, but he must desire my arrow. The Innocent must ask for death.*

Low-voiced in the ancient tongue, Katsuk began chanting:

"Your body will accept the consecrated arrow. Pride will fill your soul at the touch of my sharp and biting point. Your soul will turn toward the sun and people will say to one another: 'How proudly he died!' Ravens will alight beside your body, but they will not touch your flesh. Your pride will send you outward from your body. You will become a great bird and fly from one end of the world to the other. This is how you will accept the arrow."

David listened until the low chanting stopped, said: "There are more beans in that barrel. Do you want some?"

"Why do you not run away?" Katsuk asked. "You have given me the Cedar sickness. I could not stop you."

The boy shrugged, said: "You're sick."

Katsuk felt at his waist for the obsidian knife. It was gone! He stared around him, wild-eyed. His pouch with the consecreted down to place on the sacrificed body—that, too, was gone. Katsuk lurched to his feet,

231

clutching at the boy, fell heavily beside the fire pit.

David jumped up, then hurried to kneel beside Katsuk.

"Knife," Katsuk whispered.

"Your knife? I was afraid you'd cut yourself tossing around on it. I hung the knife and your pouch in the corner back there where you put the bow and arrow." He gestured into the shelter.

Katsuk tried to turn his head, but his neck ached.

David put an arm under Katsuk's shoulders, said: "You should be in the bed. I'm heating rocks. Come on." He helped Katsuk back to the moss between the logs, pulled the blankets over him.

Katsuk allowed himself to be tucked into the blankets, asked: "Why do you help me? It was you who put the sickness on me."

"That's crazy."

"It is not! I know you did it. I saw you in my dream. You put it into these blankets."

"Those are *your* blankets! You took them out of that barrel!"

"You could have changed the blankets. You hoquat have used sickness blankets on us before. You gave us the smallpox with your blankets. You killed us with hoquat sickness. Why do you do this to me?"

"Do you want more beans or don't you?"

"Hoquat, I have had my death dream. I have dreamed the way it will be."

"That's crazy talk."

"No! I have dreamed it. I will go into the sea and become a fish. You hoquat will catch me."

The boy shook his head, went back to the fire. He put more wood on it, felt the outsides of the rocks around the flames.

It grew suddenly dark under the trees and began to rain. Cold wind blew up the river canyon. It drove big wet droplets before it, drummed rain into the trees and onto the mossy roof of the shelter. Water ran from the eaves and blew in across the fire. It hissed on the rocks.

Katsuk felt a nightmare take him. He tried to scream but could make no sound. *Water Baby has me!* he thought. *How did it learn my name?*

After what seemed only a few seconds, Katsuk awoke to find warm stones piled on the blankets around his feet. A smell of scorched wool drifted on the damp air. Rain still fell from a dark sky.

The boy came then, replaced a stone on the blankets. He used a bent green limb of alder to handle the stone. Katsuk felt the warmth.

"You've been asleep all day," the boy said. "Are you hungry? I heated more beans."

Katsuk's head felt light. His throat was a dry patch of sand. He could only nod and croak.

The boy brought him a can of water. Katsuk drank it greedily, then permitted himself to be fed. He opened his mouth like a bird for each bite.

"More water?"

"Yes."

The boy brought it. Katsuk drank, fell back.

"More?"

"No."

Katsuk felt himself returning to the middle of his own being, but it was all wrong. It was himself where he had come into this primitive world, but pieces had been snipped away, the lines changed. If he could see his own face in a mirror, he knew it would be unfamiliar. He might reject that face. The eyes would be those of a stranger. He longed for restful sleep but felt nightmares lurking. The spirits waited with their willy-nilly purpose, unreasonable and demanding. He tipped his head back, stretching his neck. His mind rang like a bell.

He thought: *I am being overwhelmed by the spirits!*

The boy came with a can of water. Katsuk lifted his head to drink. Part of the water spilled down his chin. He lay back. The drink weighed on him, made his body torpid.

Katsuk thought: *He has poisoned me!*

The rain beat on the roof over him, a drum sound, whispering at first, then louder. He thought he heard a flute with the drum: pitiful music but marvelous. His life danced on the flute song, a summer moth, about to die.

I have become the soul of this place, he thought. *Why has Soul Catcher brought me here?*

He awoke in darkness. The silence was resonant, the silence after a drum. The rain had stopped. Faint, unrhythmic drips came from the eaves. The fire had burned low. A shadow near the fire revealed itself as the boy asleep curled up beside the warm rocks. As Katsuk stirred, the boy sat up, stared into the shelter's darkness.

"Katsuk?"

"I am here."

"How do you feel?"

Katsuk felt the clarity in his head. Cedar sickness had left him. He sensed his weakness, but the dry juice of his fear had been squeezed into oblivion.

"The sickness has gone from me," Katsuk said.

"Are you thirsty?"

"Yes."

The boy brought a can of water. Katsuk drank it, his hand steady.

"More?"

"No."

Katsuk sensed the multiplicity of his universe, knew the spirits remained within him. He said: "You drove the sickness from my body, Hoquat. Why?"

"I couldn't just leave you. You were sick."

"I was sick, yes."

"May I come in there now and sleep under the blankets?"

"You are cold?"

"Yes."

"It is warm here." Katsuk opened the blankets.

The boy scrambled over the logs that contained the moss bed, crawled under the blankets. Katsuk felt the thin body trembling.

Presently, Katsuk said: "Nothing has changed, Hoquat."

"What?"

"I still must create a holy obscenity."

"Go to sleep, Katsuk." The boy sounded exhausted.

"We have been gone thirteen nights," Katsuk said.

The boy made no response. His trembling had stilled. Soft, even breathing betrayed sleep.

Katsuk thought: *Nothing has changed. I must produce for this world a nightmare they will dream while awake.*

❏

SHERIFF PALLATT:

They only give me thirty-five men and one helicopter to cover the whole goddamned Wilderness Area. It's a goddamned mess. My feet hurt. Look how swollen they are! But I'm gonna find that pair. They're in there and I'm gonna find 'em.

❑

DAVID OPENED his eyes into white darkness, a collision of sight. It was several heartbeats before he realized he was staring at the moon, another arc of it eaten away by Beaver. It was cold. A moon river glowed through the trees outside the shelter. The river whispered to him, reminding him of rain and silence. A mountain slowly revealed itself through the trees. It had been there all along, but now it showed itself to him: moon-drenched, awash with snow. A star mantle wound through the sky beyond the mountain.

With sudden shock, David realized Katsuk was not beside him.

"Katsuk?" he ventured, voice low.

No answer.

Katsuk had added more wood to the fire. Coals glowed brightly in the fire pit.

David pulled the blankets more tightly around himself. Smoke from the fire pit blurred the moon's pale witchery. The sky was full of stars! He recalled Katsuk saying the stars were holes in a black deerhide. Crazy Katsuk! Where was he?

Katsuk had prayed: *Net of stars, Deer and Bear in the sky—I take care for thee!*

"The moon is the eye of Kwahoutze!"

Again, David called: "Katsuk?"

But there was no answer to the call—only the wind in the trees, the voices of the river.

David peered into the darkness, searching. Where was Katsuk?

In the remembered green of the night, a shadow moved. Katsuk stood beside the fire pit, flung there by his own movement.

"I am here, Hoquat."

Katsuk stared into the shelter's blackness, seeing the boy there and not seeing him. It was as though he stared at the boy's dream and the spirit talking:

"You are not yet ready. When you are ready, I will come for you. Pray then, and a wish will be granted you."

Those were the spirit's words.

David asked: "Where have you been?" He said it accusingly, aware of a change in Katsuk's manner, but unable to identify that change.

Katsuk heard the question like a voice calling within his skull and wondered: *Should I tell him where I've been? Is that what the spirit demands of me now?*

The question disturbed Katsuk, setting up currents within him that left his mind in turmoil. He recalled how Raven had awakened him in the night, speaking from a dream that bridged the two worlds. Raven had ordered him to go downstream to the big meadow, warning him of danger there. Searchers were camped there now, a big party of them with tents and rifles and radios.

Katsuk recalled his stalking approach to the camp. He had crawled through the tall grass to within a few yards of the searchers, close enough to hear the men awakening in the dark and preparing for their day of hunting for human quarry. Their mouths full of sleep, the men had talked. Their words had revealed much. The smoke from the fire in the abandoned shelter on Sam's River had been seen by an aircraft searcher just before dark last night. Could Hoquat be blamed for building up that fire? Had it been a breach of innocence? Katsuk thought not. The boy had been concerned with his captor's illness and with the need for warmth.

With that fire as their goal, though, the men from the meadow would be here soon. Even now, they could be in the hills around the shelter, waiting for dawn before moving.

"Where were you?" the boy pressed.

"I've been walking in my forest."

David sensed evasion in the answer, asked: "Will it be dawn soon?"

"Yes."

"Why did you go walking, Katsuk?"

"Raven called me."

David heard the remoteness in Katsuk's voice, realized the man stood half in the spirit world, in the place of his dreams and his visions.

"Are we going to stay here today?" David asked.

"We are going to stay."

"Good. You should rest after your sickness."

And David thought: *Maybe if I just talk to him calmly he'll come out of it and be all right.*

Katsuk sensed then that the boy had also developed another self which must be reasoned with, influenced, and understood. The immobility in the surface of this youth was not to be mistaken for peace. Hoquat's spirit was no longer hiding. And Katsuk asked himself: *Why shouldn't this happen to Hoquat as it happened to me?*

Why else had Hoquat nursed his captor through the Cedar sickness? Logic said the boy should flee while Katsuk was weak, yet he stayed.

David felt the pressure of Katsuk's silence, asked: "Do you need anything? Shall I get up now?"

Katsuk hesitated, then: "There is no need for you to get up. We have a little time left us yet."

Katsuk thought then of the bow and its single arrow

hidden in a tree behind him. The past and the present were tied together, but the great circle had yet to be completed. He felt the pouch at his waist, the packet with the down from sea ducks in it to scatter on the slain victim as it had been done through all time. He knew his mind grazed above its old levels. He sensed Soul Catcher speaking to him and through him. The passionate simplicity of Bee had caught him up in full awareness of death and world-silence. The spirit power of his realization reached all through him. He felt death not as negation but as the assignment of his life. It was why he stood in this place. It was why he had made the bow, touching the wood only with a stone knife. It was why he had fitted the old arrowhead from the ocean beach into its new wooden pocket, preparing it for the death to come.

Spirits had energized him. They were spirits without shape or smell or sound—yet they moved this world. They moved it! They moved the men in the river meadow. They moved the aircraft and machines engaged in this primitive contest. They moved the Innocent who must die. They moved Katsuk, who had become more spirit than man.

Katsuk thought: *I must do this thing to the perfection which the old gods have ordered. It must have the unmistakable spirit pattern that all men may understand it: good and evil bound one to the other by unbreakable form, the circle completed. I must keep faith with my past. Goodevil! One thing. That is what I do.*

With inward vision, he sensed elk horn lances in the dark all around him. Their shafts were trimmed with tufted bear fur. They were held by people from the past. Those people came from the time when men had lived with the land and not against it. He dropped his gaze to his hand. The shape of it was there, but details were lost in shadow. Memory provided the image: Bee's slug-white accusation in his skin.

Katsuk thought: *Any man may emulate the bee. A man may sting the entire universe if he does it properly. He must only find the right nerve to receive his barb. It must be an evil thing I do, with the good visible only when they turn it over. The shape of hate must be revealed in it, and betrayal and anguish and the insanities we all share. Only later should they see the love.*

David sensed undercurrents in the silence. He found himself afraid *for* Katsuk and *of* him. The man had become once more that wild creature who had bound his captive's arms and half dragged him to the cave a night's march from Six Rivers Camp.

What's he thinking now? David wondered. And he said: "Katsuk, shouldn't you come back to bed?"

Katsuk heard two questions in the boy's words, one on the surface and one beneath. The second question asked: *"What can I do to help you?"*

"Do not worry about me, Hoquat," Katsuk said. "It is well with me."

David heard a softness in Katsuk's voice. Sleep lay at the edge of the boy's awareness like a gray cloud. Katsuk was concerned for his captive now. The boy readjusted the blankets around him, shifted closer to the coals in the fire pit. The night was cold.

Katsuk heard the movement as a demonstration of life. He thought in sudden fearful awareness of the thing he had to do in this world of flesh and time. Would people misinterpret his actions?

The spirits had summoned him to perform an artistic act. It would be a refinement of blood revenge, a supreme example to be appreciated by this entire world. His own people would understand this much of it. His own people had blood revenge locked into their history. They would be stirred in their innermost being. They would recognize why it had been done in the ancient way—a mark upon raw earth, an incantation, a bow untouched by steel, a death arrow with a stone head, the down of sea ducks sprinkled upon the victim. They would see the circle and this would lead them to the other meanings within this act.

What of the hoquat, though? Their primitive times lay farther back, although they were more violent. They had hidden their own violence from their surface awareness and might not recognize Katsuk's ritual. Realization would seep upward from the spirit side, though. The very nature of the Innocent's death could not be denied.

"I have in truth become Soul Catcher," Katsuk said, realizing he had spoken aloud only after the words were uttered.

"What'd you say?" The boy's voice was heavy with sleep.

"I am the creature of spirits."

"Are you sick again, Katsuk?" The boy was coming back from sleep, his tone worried.

"I no longer have the Cedar sickness, Hoquat."

His flesh gripped by anguish, Katsuk thought: *Only one thing remains. The Innocent must ask me for the arrow. He must show that he is ready. He must give me his spirit wish.*

Silently, Katsuk prayed: *"O, Life Giver, now that you have seen the way a part of your all-powerful being goes, put all of you that way. Bring the circle to completion."*

Somewhere down the river behind Katsuk, a man shouted. It was a hoarse sound, words unintelligible but full of menace.

David started from sleep. "What was that?"

Katsuk did not turn toward the sound. He thought: *It must be decided now*. He said: "The searchers have found us."

"People coming?"

"Your people are coming, Hoquat."

"Are you sure?"

"I am sure. That was where I went walking in my forest, Hoquat. I went down to the meadow. There was a camp in the meadow. The people from that camp will be here by daylight."

David heard the words with mounting panic. "What're we going to do?"

"We?"

"You've gotta run, Katsuk!" Even as he spoke, David felt the mixture of reason and unreason in his words. But the demand for flight was larger than any other consideration.

"Why must we run?" Katsuk asked. He sensed the spirit guiding the boy's reason through a maze of panic.

"You can't let them catch you!"

Katsuk spoke with the calming presence of his vision: "Where would I run? I am still weak from the Cedar sickness. I could not go far."

David dropped the blankets from his shoulders, jumped up. The man's serenity outraged him. "I'll help you!"

"Why would you help me?"

"Because... because they...."

"Because they will kill me?"

How could the man be so calm? David asked himself. And he blurted: "Katsuk! You've gotta run!"

"I cannot."

"You've just gotta!" The boy clutched up the blankets, thrust them across the glowing fire pit at Katsuk. "Here! Take the blankets and go hide on the

hill. There must be someplace to hide up there. I'll tell
'em you left yesterday."

"Why would you do such a thing?"

Katsuk's patience filled David with panic. He said:
"Because I don't want you caught . . . and put in jail."

"Hoquat, Hoquat," Katsuk reasoned, "until these
past few weeks I've lived all my life in cages."

The boy was frantic now. "They'll put you in jail!"

"No. They will kill me."

David immediately saw the logic of this. Katsuk had
murdered a man. David said: "I won't tell them about
that guy."

"What . . . guy?"

"You know! The hiker, the guy you . . . You know!"
How could Katsuk be this stupid?

"But they will kill me because I kidnapped you."

"I'll tell 'em I came of my own free will."

"Did you?"

"Yes!"

Katsuk thought: *Now, the spirits guide us both.* The
Innocent had not yet asked for the consecrated arrow.
He was not yet ready. But the circle was closing.
Katsuk said: "But what about my message?"

"What message?" *There he went, talking crazy
again!*

"The spirit message I must send to the whole world,"
Katsuk explained.

"I don't care about your message! Send it! Just don't
let them catch you!"

Katsuk nodded. Thus it went. He said: "Then it is
your wish—your *spirit* wish, that I send my message?"

"Yes! Only hurry. I can hear them coming."

Katsuk sensed the calmness of his vision sweep
upward through his body from the soles of his feet. He
spoke formally, as one did to the properly prepared

sacrificial victim. "Very well, Hoquat. I admire your courage, your beauty, and your innocence. You are admirable. Let no man doubt that. Let all men and all spirits. ..."

"Hurry, Katsuk," David whispered. "Hurry."

"Let all men and all spirits," Katsuk repeated, "learn of your qualities, Hoquat. Please sit down and wait here. I will go now."

With a sigh of relief, the boy sank to a sitting position on one of the bed logs beside the shelter's entrance. "Hurry," he whispered. "They're close. I can hear them."

Katsuk cocked his head to listen. Yes, there were voices shouting directions in the dark, a movement seen only by its noises. Still in the formal tone, he said: "Hoquat, your friend Katsuk bids you good-bye."

"Good-bye, Katsuk," the boy whispered.

Quickly now, because he could feel the predawn stillness in the air and see the flashlights of searchers coming through the trees across the river, Katsuk faded back in the shadows to the young spruce where he had secreted the bow and arrow. Murmuring his prayers, he set the bowstring, that hard line of walrus gut. The bow trembled in his hands, then steadied as he felt the power of it. Truly, it was a god-bow. He nocked the arrow against the bowstring. Now, his vision focused down to the infinity of this instant.

A bird whistled in the trees overhead.

Katsuk nodded his awareness. The animals of this forest knew the moment had come. He felt the spirit power surge all through his muscles. He turned toward the shelter, sensed the morning world begin to glow all around him, all platinum and gray movement. The boy could be seen behind the fire pit, sitting wrapped in a blanket, head bowed, a primordial figure lost to the world of flesh.

Although he heard no sound of it, Katsuk knew the boy was crying. Hoquat was shedding spirit tears for this world.

Steadily, Katsuk drew the bow taut, sighted as his grandfather had taught him. His thumb felt the fletching of the arrow. His fingers held the unpolished cedar of the arrow. All of his senses were concentrated upon this moment—river, wind, forest, boy, Katsuk ...all one. In the magic instant, feeling the bow become part of his own flesh, Katsuk released the arrow. He heard the *whang* of the walrus gut. The sound flew straight across the clearing with the arrow. Straight it went and into the boy's chest.

Hoquat jerked once against the log post at the shelter's entrance. The post held him upright. He did not move again.

For David, there was only the sharp and crashing instant of awareness: *He did it!* There was no pain greater than the betrayal. Hunting for a name that was not *Hoquat*, the boy sank into blackness.

Katsuk felt anguish invade his breast. He said: "Soul Catcher, it is done."

Carefully measuring out each step, Katsuk advanced upon the shelter. He stared at the arrow in Hoquat's breast. Now, the circle was complete. It had been a clean and shattering stroke, straight through the heart and probably into the spine. Death had come quickly to the Innocent.

Katsuk felt the ancient watchers of the spirit world departing then. He stood alone, immobile, fascinated by his own creation—this death.

In the growing daylight, the folds of the boy's clothing took on a semblance of the mossy post behind the body. Part of the body appeared ready to dissipate into the smoke winding upward from the fire pit. It created an illusion of transparency about Hoquat. The

245

boy was gone. The Innocent had left this place in company with the ancient watchers. That was as it should be.

Katsuk heard the searchers then. They were climbing onto the logs which crossed the river. They would be here within minutes. What did it matter now?

Tears coursed down Katsuk's cheeks. He dropped the bow, stumbled forward across the fire pit, fell to his knees, and gathered up the small body.

When Sheriff Pallatt and the search party entered the clearing at the shelter, Katsuk sat with Hoquat's body in his arms, cradling the dead boy like a child, swaying and chanting the death song one sang for a friend. The white down of the sea ducks floated in the damp air all around them.

About the Author

Frank Herbert has been (among other things) a professional photographer, TV cameraman, oysterdiver, and West Coast newspaperman.

Although he is best known for his epic science fiction novel DUNE, he is the author of some twenty other novels including CHILDREN OF DUNE, THE DOSADI EXPERIMENT, and DESTINATION: VOID. The DUNE trilogy developed in great detail the ecology and inhabitants of a desert-world. His timely and detailed description of an alien ecosystem won Hugo and Nebula awards in 1965.

In 1971 he retreated with his typewriter and family to a six-acre farm on Washington's Olympic Peninsula. One of his major projects is to turn the acreage into an 'ecological demonstration' with a five-year plan showing that a high quality of life can be maintained with minimal drain on the total energy system.